# MORE THAN A MASQUERADE

*Ladies of the Order - Book 2*

## ADELE CLEE

**More titles by Adele Clee**

**Lost Ladies of London**

The Mysterious Miss Flint

The Deceptive Lady Darby

The Scandalous Lady Sandford

The Daring Miss Darcy

**Avenging Lords**

At Last the Rogue Returns

A Wicked Wager

Valentine's Vow

A Gentleman's Curse

**Scandalous Sons**

And the Widow Wore Scarlet

The Mark of a Rogue

When Scandal Came to Town

The Mystery of Mr Daventry

**Gentlemen of the Order**

Dauntless

Raven

Valiant

Dark Angel

**Ladies of the Order**

The Devereaux Affair

More than a Masquerade

Mine at Midnight

***More than a Masquerade***
Copyright © 2021 Adele Clee
All rights reserved.
ISBN-13: 978-1-8383839-4-7

Cover by Dar Albert at Wicked Smart Designs

# CHAPTER 1

*Valentine Masquerade*
*Vauxhall Pleasure Gardens, London*

LOVE WAS akin to downing badly brewed arrack punch, Rachel Gambit decided. The crowd at Vauxhall's Valentine Masquerade were drunk with excitement, intoxicated by the prospect of finding a willing mate. Those dancing before the raised bandstand in the Grove had lost all semblance of sanity, all sense of decorum.

Rachel turned to Mr and Mrs D'Angelo, her chaperones for the evening. "A vicar tending his flock is no longer considered an epithet." She pointed to the gentleman in a cassock, fondling a shepherdess. "He's out to steal more than her crook."

Mrs D'Angelo laughed. "Their tomfoolery could amuse us all evening." She was an attractive woman with golden hair and an amiable spirit. "Making mischief appears to be the theme tonight."

"No doubt they're excited to have a night at Vauxhall." It was a gala event to raise funds before the gardens officially opened in May.

"It's a shame we're here for professional reasons."

Rachel's heart pounded as she recalled why she'd come to Vauxhall. She had not come hoping Cupid might fire his gold-tipped arrow in her direction. Heavens no! As an enquiry agent for the Order—a group who helped the victims of crimes seek justice—she had come to meet a potential new client.

"You'll struggle to find Hunter in the crush." Mr D'Angelo scanned the hordes of dissipated revellers. "Did he give you a clue to his identity?"

"No clue at all."

She had been told to wear a red gown, red slippers, don a red mask. Lord knows why. Mr Hunter would only hire her to help solve his problem if she passed a series of tests. Her first was to find him in a crowd of eight hundred people. An impossible feat, all things considered.

"Mr Hunter wishes to evaluate my deductive skills," Rachel added. "He needs to know I can arrive at logical conclusions and can think on my feet." The man's situation must be grave indeed to resort to such extreme measures.

"We've been instructed to remain with you until you locate Hunter." Mr D'Angelo pulled his watch from his pocket and noted the time. The formidable enquiry agent of Italian heritage was one of a handful of men who refused to parade in a costume tonight. "Hunter despises tardiness. It's half-past eight. That leaves you thirty minutes to find him in the throng."

Panic ensued. While festoons of twinkling lights hung from trees lining every walkway, a man might easily hide in the shadows. It was imperative she focused her mind and began eliminating certain gentlemen.

But where to start?

"You're acquainted with Mr Hunter." Rachel directed her comment to Mr D'Angelo. He'd mentioned Mr Hunter's preference for black meant he dressed as if in mourning. "Might you at least give me a clue as to his height and build?"

"You know I can't," he replied firmly. "The tests have some bearing on the reason he needs to hire you. As your safety is important, I need to know you can handle this case."

"We cannot help you, Rachel." Mrs D'Angelo cast a wary glance over her shoulder. "Mr Hunter will undoubtedly know if we do. Though I'm sure it's not breaking any rules if I remind you to use what you know of the man to make informed decisions."

She knew nothing but his name. That he was a hard taskmaster who always wore black. She turned to the couples dancing in the Grove, to the orchestra playing a lively country tune.

Would a man with a pressing dilemma dance and make merry?

No. Mr Hunter had come to Vauxhall to hire an agent, not to enjoy the festivities. He would be alone. She would wager he was a sedate gentleman who distrusted most people, one focused and regimental. Not one whose gaze wandered at the mere glimpse of a scantily clad shepherdess.

So, she was looking for one man dressed in black.

Ah, but wait. This was supposed to be a challenge. If Rachel didn't find him in the allotted time, she'd fail the test. Half the men wore black dominos, yet she suspected Mr Hunter was too sombre to prance around in a cape. There was such an air of mystery about him, she suspected he was notably unique.

"Where will you start?" Mrs D'Angelo said, her excitement palpable.

"I eat or sleep when my mind is in a quandary. I'll begin with the supper boxes, though I doubt I'm looking for a man in a costume." Serious men did not behave like buffoons.

Mr D'Angelo's expression remained unreadable. "The

supper boxes by the Chinese Temple, or those by the Gothic or Handel Piazzas?"

"The Chinese Temple."

Having been to Vauxhall once with her previous employer, Madame Dubarry, Rachel recalled the piazzas were a stone's throw from the orchestra. Mr Hunter would seek to avoid noisy places when conducting his evaluation.

"We'll follow you as far as the Grand Walk and linger there." Mr D'Angelo gestured for Rachel to lead the way. "I'll keep you in my sights until I'm assured you've found Hunter."

"Honestly, there is no need. I shall be perfectly safe." Madame Dubarry had left Rachel alone during their visit to Vauxhall. The modiste had disappeared down the Dark Walk with a gentleman friend and had not returned for two hours.

"I have my orders, Miss Gambit."

Mr Daventry—the master of the Order and a man one did not cross—was a little protective of his female enquiry agents. Which was rather ironic, considering he'd hired them to catch criminals.

"Very well." Rachel cut through the row of elm trees lining the Grove. She stopped by a lit brazier to warm her hands and gather her composure.

Needing to scour the crowd without looking obvious, she raised her hand-held mask. It narrowed her peripheral vision considerably. Hence why she didn't see the drunken fellow in a black domino approach from the flank.

"Come with me, pretty lady." The dandy grabbed her arm and tried to drag her back to the Grove. "Come and dance with Freddie."

Why did rolling drunks always speak in the third-person?

Having spent five years living with two wicked reprobates, Rachel wasn't the least bit startled. "Get your hands off me, Freddie. Go away, else I shall be forced to stamp on your feet and crush your toes."

"You've crushed my heart. Why not my toes?" The fellow

burped, assaulting her with his brandy breath. "Come on, lovely. Dance with Freddie."

For a fleeting second, Rachel wondered if this fop was Mr Hunter playing a prank, but a dangerous man wouldn't be so pathetic.

"Go away, Freddie." Rachel hit him on the head with her mask. She had to get rid of the sot before Mr D'Angelo charged in and broke the poor man's fingers. "My brother is two steps behind and will likely kill you." She gestured to Mr D'Angelo, who looked like he might rip out the man's throat with his bare hands. "He shot a man last week near Primrose Hill, straight between the brows. Blew his brains across—"

Freddie clasped his hand to his mouth and retched. Then he took to his heels to hurl into the nearest bush. Rachel cast the D'Angelos a confident grin before continuing her search for Mr Hunter.

Of the innumerable booths situated along the colonnade, all were crammed with patrons, bar one. A young man, no older than thirty, with dark brown hair and a handsome profile, sat alone. He stared absently at the wine in his glass while twirling the stem between long, elegant fingers. Like the hard taskmaster she'd expected, he possessed a powerful, athletic physique, though something about the way he gazed at the glass roused her pity.

The man was like an unnamed island in a vast sea—a lonely figure amongst an ebbing crowd. Was that why Mr Hunter wished to hire an agent? Did he long for a partner to share the burden?

She straightened, her pulse thumping a steady beat in her neck. If she approached the wrong man, she would fail her first task. Was Mr Hunter watching from the shadows? Or was he the gentleman in the booth, absorbed by the hue of his claret?

A waiter approached. The stranger gestured to the empty seat opposite before removing his pocket watch and inspecting the time. Then Rachel caught a flash of a red waistcoat, and every instinct said this solitary figure was her prospective client.

Her legs turned to jelly, but she raised her mask and approached the booth. If she made a mistake and lost her position with the Order, she could always return to the pawnbroker's shop or find work with another modiste.

She swallowed deeply. "I pray you've ordered for two, sir."

The gentleman faced her, and she almost gasped. There should be a law against men having eyes so blue they looked like the soul of the heavens. Eyes so uniquely blue, they hypnotised a woman into forgetting her own name.

Rachel caught herself and recalled what she had been instructed to say at their meeting. "The goddess Themis wears a blindfold to show justice should be impartial."

His intense gaze slipped slowly over her mask, cloak and gown. He moistened his lips before speaking. "We have a duty to crush the snakes underfoot."

Merciful Mary! Her heart skipped a beat. So this was Mr Hunter, the man who trusted no one, the man who played a hard game to test a woman's mettle.

He stood, straightening to a commanding height a little over six feet. Heavens. Rachel felt like throwing her hands in the air and asking the Lord what the hell he was playing at. Never, and she meant never, had a man made such an impact. Part of her hoped she failed the next test. How on earth was she to deal with this devil?

"Would you care to sit, Miss Gambit?"

Even his voice held the husky notes that made women swoon. And yet there was nothing warm about his manner or expression. Bronzed skin covered a face of steel. The planes were hard and rigid. Those mesmerising eyes turned frosty, so cold it chilled her blood.

"Are we to dine, sir?"

"We're not here to partake in pleasantries." His assessing

gaze moved to the flamboyant black feathers adorning her mask. "Though this will be the shortest interview ever conducted."

"Why?" Had she made a dreadful faux pas? "Do you have a problem with my feathers, sir?"

"You failed to follow instructions."

She had followed his instructions to the letter.

"I was told to wear a red mask. This is a red mask."

"It's brown with black trimmings." His sigh echoed his annoyance. "You might think me a pedant, Miss Gambit, but people have died deviating from the rules."

She thought him a pedant, and a miserable ogre to boot.

"The mask is russet-red, not brown. No rules were broken because you did not stipulate the colour of the trimmings." She offered a serene smile as she lowered her mask. "But rest assured, I shall rectify the problem immediately."

Rachel gripped the tip of a black feather and ripped it from its bindings, then removed all the feathers and let them blow away in the breeze.

"There. Now we have a red mask without feathers." Well, he wanted a woman who could make swift decisions. "Does that meet your strict criteria?"

But Mr Hunter wasn't interested in the mask or the errant feathers. Instead, he fixed her with his impenetrable gaze. "Are you always so impulsive, Miss Gambit?"

"This is my first assignment for the Order. It's imperative you hire me. I don't have time to dither."

Any other man would have smiled, not Mr Hunter. He looked as if he'd rather gouge out his eyes with a letter opener than hire an agent. He pointed to the ornate bench, a blunt instruction to sit.

Rachel slid into the booth and placed her reticule beside her. Mr Hunter sat opposite, though he cursed beneath his breath when their knees touched.

"I suppose I should be grateful for your honesty." He

sounded like the most ungrateful wretch alive. "I trust you'll not have a fit of hysterics when I afford you the same courtesy."

Rachel raised her chin. "Sir, I survived a shipwreck and spent ten hours clinging to the debris. It will take more than your blunt opinion to rattle my nerves."

A muscle in his cheek twitched, and his eyes narrowed in suspicion. "A shipwreck? When did this unfortunate event occur?" It was obvious he doubted her word.

"In the spring of 1817. I was aboard *The Canton,* journeying from Bombay. Unfortunately, we were caught in the mother of all storms and floundered on Chesil Beach off the Dorset coast. My name is on the list of survivors should you wish to check the records."

"You were sixteen?" He must have made a quick mental calculation.

"Yes." Mr Daventry had surely mentioned her age. "I turned four and twenty a few months ago. I assume that's acceptable."

"Acceptable, not ideal." He rang for the waiter. "Did your parents survive the shipwreck?"

Emotion bubbled in her chest at the mention of her parents. She missed them terribly. "They died together in an accident in Bombay. My father worked for the East India Company. The Company put me aboard *The Canton* with other families returning to England." It had been a long voyage marred with sickness and storms, omens for the tragedy that followed.

Mr Hunter remained silent for a few uncomfortable seconds. "You came to live with relatives in England?"

"I came to live with my godmother, Lady Hanaway."

It should have been a respite from her trauma. A safe haven. Instead, it was akin to entering the nether regions of hell. Like the gate in Dante's underworld, the entrance to

Lady Hanaway's home should have carried the same warning —abandon all hope, those who enter.

The waiter appeared with his receipt pad and silver tray.

"What will you drink, Miss Gambit?" Mr Hunter spoke as if it were another test. So much for not passing pleasantries.

"Thank you. I shall have fruit punch."

"No, you won't." He ordered a bottle of burgundy. "I need a woman who doesn't fall over herself after one glass of wine. I need a woman who can think even when her judgement is impaired."

"You wish to get me drunk, sir?"

Good grief. The man meant to test her to her limits. It was a pointless exercise. Rachel's mind had turned to mush the moment he said he needed a woman. The moment she imagined satisfying a hunter.

"Exactly the opposite. I need you to drink without losing all rationale."

"Sir, you'll have to look to the dockside taverns for such a woman."

"Should you pass the other tests, I shall train you to take your drink."

Train her? Would he host an intimate party for two? Would he smile and laugh while they rolled about the floor in a drunken stupor? Oddly, she was rather keen to find out.

The waiter returned. Mr Hunter sampled the wine, paid the bill, then dismissed the fellow. He poured the ruby-red liquid into her glass and pushed the vessel across the pristine white tablecloth.

"Is there a reason you asked me to wear red tonight?"

"Take a mouthful of wine, Miss Gambit. Feel the heat as it slips down your throat."

She brought the glass to her lips and sipped the wine. It tasted rich and earthy, carried the faint aroma of cherries, and warmed her all the way down to her toes.

"You didn't answer my question, sir. Why insist I wear

9

red?" Did he like playing the dominant master? Did he want her to know she was here purely to serve his needs?

"So I can find you in the dark."

Perhaps the wine had made her head fuzzy. Perhaps this man knew how to play havoc with her senses, and his sensual drawl was nothing more than a means to intimidate. She stole a glance at the lamps glittering in the trees, fearing what fate awaited her on this chilly night at Vauxhall.

"Tell me what you have in your reticule, Miss Gambit." His demand sent her mind careering completely off course.

"Is it a requisite to you hiring me?" Surely a lady was entitled to some privacy.

"Women are secretive by nature. Do you have something to hide? Are you carrying a laudanum tincture so you might take a nip when under pressure?"

"Not exactly."

"Then let me see what you're carrying."

Rachel fought to curb her temper. She snatched her reticule and dumped it on the table but then decided to play a little game of her own.

"What do you suppose is in there, Mr Hunter?" She took another courage-boosting sip of wine. "Let's see if your intuition serves you well."

He shifted in his seat. "I'm not the one on trial."

"If I'm to risk my life for a man, I wish to be assured of his mental agility."

"Rest assured, I possess the stamina and agility of a man in his prime."

Her pulse fluttered in her throat. From the hard angle of his jaw and the breadth of his chest, Mr Hunter was a perfect specimen of masculinity.

"And yet you seem so stiff and rigid, sir."

The inebriated Freddie might have offered a salacious reply, not Mr Hunter. The steel shutters closed, and he maintained his stern expression. Even so, Rachel felt a frisson of satisfaction when he tossed back his burgundy as if needing to soothe his agitated spirit.

"Can I use my hands?" he suddenly said.

"Your hands? For what purpose?" Heat rose to her cheeks as she imagined being at the mercy of those wide palms and elegant fingers, imagined the sheer strength of his grip.

"To examine your reticule."

"You don't need to fondle my purse to identify the contents. But I shall be impressed if you guess two out of the six items inside."

A spark of amusement flashed in his eyes before quickly dying. He looked at Rachel as if he possessed the power to see into her soul.

"You pose such a contradiction, Miss Gambit."

"How so?"

"You've a gentle manner, yet beneath the attractive facade lies a ruthless devil. You look like you should be strolling through the park on a gentleman's arm, yet you chase criminals for a living."

She stared at this impenetrable fortress of a man. "A lady cannot help but wonder what lies behind your barricade, sir."

He made no reply but continued to assess her to such a degree her heart thumped wildly. Eventually, he said, "You're not carrying a compact of rouge or a vinaigrette. The question is, what do you deem essential? My guess is a lady's pocket book and pencil."

A little annoyed he'd guessed correctly, Rachel reached for the reticule and opened the tasselled drawstrings. "How perceptive of you. They're the tools of an enquiry agent." She handed him the items. "You may open the book and read my notes."

His arched brow said he was more than keen to delve into her private affairs. He opened the small leather book, flicked to her expenses sheet, and examined the page beneath the candle lamp.

"You spent a shilling on lozenges, five shillings on wool stockings."

"It's been terribly cold, sir, and I never take risks with my health."

"Both sensible purchases, although you bought a shagreen etui from a pawnbroker for five shillings." There was a faint flash of triumph in his blue eyes. "I'll wager you have the etui in your reticule."

Rachel removed the small shagreen case and placed it on the table. "It contains scissors, pins, and two perfume vials. One is filled with lemon juice. I find it particularly effective in blinding an attacker. The other contains a strong tincture of opium made for me by a chemist who frequented the pawnbroker's shop where I worked. Five drops in a beverage are enough to subdue a man of your size."

Mr Hunter gave an appreciative nod. "You came prepared."

"Indeed." She removed two more items from her purse. "I always carry an almanack and a coin pouch with enough money for a hackney and a night's stay in a coaching inn."

Mostly because Lady Hanaway's sons had made her life a misery. In the dead of night, they'd dragged her kicking and screaming from their carriage and dumped her on the roadside.

Mr Hunter took the tiny almanack and removed the book from the beaded slipcase. "Do you always carry this?"

A flush of embarrassment rose to her cheeks. "It's foolish, I know, but I like to keep abreast of the moon cycles and tide tables." When left to walk along a dark lane alone, it also helped to know when the sun would rise.

With a rare glimmer of compassion in his eyes, Mr Hunter placed the book back in the slipcase and handed it to her. "It's not foolish. Having encountered difficult situations, we'd do anything to avoid suffering again."

"Yes," was all she said because their fingers brushed as she accepted the book, and a shiver of awareness raced down to her toes.

He snatched back his hand, filled his wine glass, and downed a mouthful of burgundy. "So, I've one item left to guess."

"I doubt you will."

"It's a weapon," he said confidently.

"It's a Skean Dhu, Mr Hunter." When he stared blankly, she took immense pleasure pulling the six-inch object from her purse and slapping it down on the table.

"It's a child's blade," he teased.

She arched a brow. "It's a blade sharp enough to gut a fish. A blade I had pressed to a man's throat when Mr Daventry hired me. A blade I'm not afraid to use."

# CHAPTER 2

FOR THE LOVE OF GOD, Eli was going to murder Lucius
Daventry with his bare hands. The man had promised to send
a woman who could fight her way out of a skirmish. One who
could talk her way out of volatile situations.

Miss Gambit was a damn siren.

A dangerous creature who could charm the devil.

There wasn't a chance in hell of him hiring her. The
woman would push him to the brink of insanity. She was
funny, charming, utterly unpredictable. Precisely the type of
female he avoided. But he needed to appease Lucius
Daventry and so had no option but to put Miss Gambit to
the test.

"The knife is so small, I can strap it to my thigh." She
gripped the ornate handle and drew the Scottish blade from
its sheath. "It slips easily into my boot."

Blood rushed to Eli's cock for the second time this
evening. The impudent devil first raised his head when she
accused him of being stiff. Stiff? He was as solid as a black-
smith's forearm. Hence the reason he needed to get rid of her.
Quickly.

"Put the blade away before someone calls a constable," he

urged between gritted teeth. "Has Daventry taught you nothing? An enquiry agent should avoid drawing undue attention."

She laughed in the light way that stirred something inside him. "People are far too drunk to notice. Despite the light of a thousand lamps, it's still rather dim tonight. And you were the one who insisted on snooping in my reticule."

The woman had an answer for everything. "If Daventry thinks you have the skill to assist me, why send you with chaperones?" Perhaps he could rile her enough she'd refuse to work for him.

Miss Gambit glanced at Dante D'Angelo, sitting with his wife in a booth on the opposite side of the colonnade. "Mr Daventry takes his responsibility to his agents seriously. As a gentleman, he would never expect a lady to come to Vauxhall alone."

Eli felt a sharp stab to his conscience. "Unlike me."

"Unlike you," she agreed.

Damn, he admired her honesty, too.

The siren set about putting her odd collection of objects into her reticule and then took another sip of wine. Teaching her to drink quantities of alcohol would only end in trouble. When in her cups, she was likely the tactile sort who stroked a man's arm as if it were his shaft, who brushed an errant lock from his brow and whispered sweet nothings. The sort who tangled a man in her web and left him paralysed with passion.

Eli pinched the bridge of his nose to ease the tension.

The minx noticed the crack in his defences. "Too much wine, Mr Hunter?"

"Not enough, madam."

She snatched the bottle and refilled his glass. "As your assistant—"

"Apprentice." Curse the saints! He had no intention of hiring her.

"As your apprentice, it's my job to perform the mundane tasks."

The tasks he wished she'd perform were anything but mundane. Hence the reason he needed to tell her she'd failed his stupid test. Daventry could send another agent, preferably one with greying hair and whiskers sprouting from her chin.

"I need an expert, Miss Gambit, not someone who stumbles about like a newborn foal."

"An expert in what exactly?" Her smile faded. "You haven't mentioned why you need an agent." The visible signs of insecurity left him wanting to play the affable gentleman, not the cold-hearted bastard.

"I need to recover a stolen artefact." And punish the traitor in their midst, though there was a damn sight more to the problem than that. "Which is why one of your tasks is to steal the ruby stick pin from my waistcoat. You have until the evening's end to complete your assignment."

"Steal the pin?" The lady narrowed her gaze. "How can I steal what I cannot see?"

Eli touched the ruby hidden in the red collar of his waistcoat.

"Heavens, it's so small." Miss Gambit leant over the table and peered at the tiny jewel. The edges of her cloak parted, drawing his attention to the lush curve of her breasts. "I'll have to grope around for five minutes to find it."

Eli inwardly groaned. Miss Gambit was like a gift that kept on giving. He made a mental note to visit Lucius Daventry and whip him with a birch.

"Fail to steal the pin, and you fail the task," he said in the blunt tone he used with most people. He poured a splash of wine into her glass. "You'll need to perform while slightly sotted. I can down a flagon of wine and not feel the effects."

"So you wore red tonight to conceal the pin." She spoke as if she knew all his secrets. "I thought you wished to complement my outfit, thought you'd worn red as a sign of solidarity."

He snorted. "Everything I do has a purpose. I'm not

prone to flights of fancy or bouts of emotion." Indeed, he'd not entertained a woman in his bed for years. The mere thought roused the bitter feelings he fought to keep buried. "I'm never swayed by sentiment."

He was not a slave to his wants and desires.

But Miss Gambit was the first woman in a long time to test his reserve.

Was that why Lucius Daventry sent her?

"You've been hurt," the mystic blurted in the carefree manner of someone ordering from the menu. "Quite deeply." She gave a nonchalant wave towards his person. "That's why you're so stiff, so reserved. That's why people say you're a man without feeling. You're running away from something, Mr Hunter, running from—"

"Enough!" Eli shot to his feet.

All conversation in the adjacent supper boxes died.

D'Angelo fixed them with his impenetrable gaze.

"It's time for your next test." Eli tossed back his burgundy before stepping out of the booth. His anger was a palpable beast clawing at his shoulders. "Keep hold of your silk purse, for you may need a weapon. I pray you're not afraid of the dark."

Her eyes widened, but she quickly hid her fears. It was not his intention to scare her, but if Miss Gambit insisted on dicing with danger, he needed to know she could protect herself.

"I'm ready to prove I have the qualities you need, sir."

Merciful Lord! Was there no respite from this torment?

"Follow me." Eli might have offered his arm, might have played the courteous gentleman, but work was a serious business. He'd not come to Vauxhall to promenade or dote on a woman he found attractive.

"Where are we going?" Miss Gambit hurried to keep his quick pace.

"To the end of this tree-lined avenue." Eli checked over

his shoulder to ensure D'Angelo wasn't following. "You're to cover the length of the Dark Walk unaccompanied."

She failed to smother a gasp.

Doubts surfaced. The need to play protector did, too. Damn. Every instinct said he should keep her in his sights. The logical voice in his head demanded he take her back to the supper box and find another way to test her mettle.

"Rest assured, sir, I shall pass your test. Should I encounter fools, know I can break a man's nose if necessary."

Eli might have laughed, but he found nothing amusing about the threat of danger. Miss Gambit must be prone to exaggeration. A woman with such dainty hands would struggle to hurt a boy, let alone a man.

"Daventry said you worked for Madame Dubarry. Rogues rarely frequent modiste shops, so where did you learn to fight?"

"You'd be surprised. Madame Dubarry had a certain allure that drew scoundrels in droves. Indeed, she eloped with the youngest son of a baron, and I was left to deal with her creditors."

Eli glanced at her. "With shocking frequency, you seem to find yourself in distressing situations. Rather than improve your needlework skills at Madame Dubarry's, did you learn to hit a man hard enough to break bones?"

"No, sir. I learnt to fight when living with Lady Hanaway."

Confusion clouded his already addled mind. "A lady of gentle persuasion permitted you to spar with the servants?" Now he knew she was spinning a yarn.

"Of course not. Lady Hanaway would have been mortified to know her sons treated me with such disrespect. The blighters made my life a living hell. It's partly why I never leave home without a weapon."

Her confident tone said she spoke in earnest, yet it all seemed so far-fetched. "You should know something else about me, Miss Gambit. I do not suffer fools or liars. There is nothing I detest more than dishonesty."

"Then it seems we were destined to work together, sir. I am of the same mind. The truth may sting, but lies leave a lasting wound."

He felt a small prick to his conscience. Was it wrong of him to put her through an ordeal when he had no intention of hiring her? Should he just hit her with honesty and advise she find a safer profession? One where she was in no danger of tempting the most hard-hearted men.

Eli came to an abrupt halt. "Let me speak plainly." Surely a woman who valued honesty could handle the truth. "I'll not hire you to help solve my dilemma. I suspect you're stubborn and too headstrong."

"I prefer tenacious. It sounds much more appealing."

"You'll be more of a hindrance than a help."

Miss Gambit's striking blue eyes widened in anger, not shock. "Mr Hunter." She folded her arms across her chest. "I have done everything you've asked. I have donned a ridiculous dress and played your silly game. I have—"

"There's nothing ridiculous about that dress." On the contrary, the red silk showed the curve of her breasts to perfection. The only regrettable thing was his need to voice his opinion.

Two lines formed between her brows. "You're somewhat of an enigma, sir. One minute I'm a thorn in your side. Next, you're admiring my clothes. Are you unwell? Perhaps it's the wine."

"It's not the wine."

"We could have met in the Order's office in Hart Street, yet you forced me to come to Vauxhall. I passed your first test easily. Did you congratulate me? No. You looked remarkably unimpressed."

"Only weak people need praise."

"And you're a man who makes assumptions." She hurled

the accusation like a powerful punch. "Let me complete both tests. If I fail to reach the end of the Dark Walk or fail to steal your ruby stick pin, then dismiss me." She arched a brow before playing her ace card. "Mr Daventry will accept your decision if you've treated me fairly."

And that was the crux of the problem.

Eli worked with Lucius Daventry, too. Though no one knew the identity of the men who toiled behind the scenes to see justice served. He was not an enquiry agent but a man who fixed problems. He did not work for the Order, per se, but for Daventry's secret organisation, the Order of Themis. And he'd have to give Daventry a bloody good reason for not hiring this woman.

"Then let's proceed to the Dark Walk, Miss Gambit."

They strolled the last two hundred yards in silence. Perhaps she would take one glimpse down the shadowy avenue and admit defeat. Perhaps she would approach the task with a confidence that belied her years.

"The Dark Walk is home to degenerates," Eli warned as they came to a halt at the entrance. The Walk was a verdant tunnel in the height of summer, a wild wilderness of bare boughs and lonely evergreens come winter. He didn't mention he would be following her every move. Though this was more a test of logic than bravery.

"People use the walk to conceal all sorts of nefarious deeds," she agreed before stepping into the dusky avenue and peering left and right. "But couples come here, too. Is there anything greater in this world than an expression of love?"

Miss Gambit stood beneath nature's canopy like an angel of light in the darkness. She made love sound so simple, so pure and sincere. But Eli knew the sort of love conjured by the devil. A twisted love full of bitterness and betrayal.

"Don't tell me," she said before he could answer. "You don't give praise, and you don't believe in love. Your heart lives in an impenetrable fortress, and you've thrown away the key."

She was rather astute, truth be told.

"And I thought I was unreadable. Perhaps it's time for a new mask."

"Pick one that allows you to smile on occasion." She glanced left. "I shall walk the longest path. It's not totally dark. I see hanging lanterns dotted along the route."

Soon she would realise that the strange sounds were more frightening than the lack of light. The grunts, the groans, the sinister chuckles were enough to make a man bolt, let alone a golden-haired nymph.

"Take the shortest path. Walk to the end and back again."

Miss Gambit bit down on her bottom lip and nodded.

The urge to comfort her came from nowhere. He hated how the foreign sensation took command of his senses and so blurted, "Be quick. I shall wait here."

Without another word, she took to walking the devil's road, a place where sinners with bestial appetites lurked, degenerates out to violate their fellow man. Eli stood at the junction and focused on the red silhouette moving amidst the indigo shadows.

When her head whipped left and right, he suspected she'd stumbled upon a couple fornicating. She quickened her pace, but didn't run, didn't swoon or suffer a fit of the vapours.

Eli's heart pounded. No, he could not hire Miss Gambit. He'd be a nervous wreck fit for Bedlam. Logic said it was a mistake to hire a woman, yet he knew it would cause uproar in the Sanctum.

Then his worst nightmare formed before his eyes.

Two prominent figures stepped out from the blackness to block Miss Gambit's path. Two boisterous devils who thought it amusing to snatch her mask and throw it into the shrubbery, to tug on the ribbons of her cloak.

"Turn around," Eli whispered. "For the love of God, run."

A sensible woman knew when to retreat. But the stubborn minx became embroiled in a verbal altercation. She tried to barge through the scoundrels, tried pushing them aside, but one grabbed her hood and yanked her backwards.

Anger reared.

An unholy rage had Eli sprinting along the avenue. He might have warned the bastards, demanded they keep their filthy hands to themselves. Might have tried to reason or bargain. But he was a man of action. A man who never gave miscreants a second chance.

Eli launched himself into the air, slammed his fist into one brute's face and knocked the bastard out cold.

"Simmons!" the man's accomplice cried.

"Release the lady." Eli gestured to the unconscious dandy sprawled across the path. "Else, you'll join your friend in the dirt."

Miss Gambit took matters into her own hands. She stamped on the man's foot and punched him on the nose. The devil clasped his hands to his face and dropped to his knees, howling in pain.

Struggling to control his temper, Eli kicked the rogue back onto his arse. "Should I see you here again, I'll not be so forgiving." Then he swept Miss Gambit into his arms and strode off towards the Hermits Walk.

"Put me down, sir!"

The nymph threaded her arms around his neck and fixed him with her piercing gaze. She was too close for comfort. The piquant scent of orange blossom teased his nostrils, a light fragrance that roused images of citrus groves in the height of summer. She was so soft, so supple. God, it had been so long since he'd craved a woman's touch.

"Put me down, Mr Hunter," she repeated, yet held him like she needed the heat of his body. "There's no chance of the degenerates following."

"Madam, I'll not put you down until I find Dante D'Angelo and hand you over to his care. You're a hellion who thrives on making mischief." A harridan who pushed him to the brink of insanity.

She wriggled in his arms, and he tightened his grip.

"Let me down, sir, else I shall punch *you* on the nose."

Strange. For a man who avoided intimacy, he found he could not let her go. "Punch me if you dare, but I'm not releasing you until I find D'Angelo."

"Oh! I knew you were an obnoxious oaf the moment our eyes met."

Yet he'd felt an odd stirring that had immediately set him on edge.

"People are staring," she complained.

"I wouldn't know. I'm so damn angry I can only see red."

"You said we shouldn't draw undue attention."

"Sometimes, I'm forced to break my own rules." Eli kept his gaze focused firmly ahead. He didn't want to notice the white flecks in her blue eyes or the way her long lashes fluttered against her porcelain cheeks. He didn't want to imagine setting his lips to hers and tasting heaven's sweetness.

But the lady knew how to get under his skin.

"Carry me if you must." Her hand slipped from his neck to cup his face. "Even your jaw is hard and rigid. What do you do to relax, Mr Hunter? What is your pleasure?"

In another lifetime, she would be his pleasure.

In this one, he was too damaged to succumb to temptation. If he wore his inner scars for all to see, he'd be a freak show at the fair. And she was an enquiry agent, a woman seeking independence. One with a mind clever enough to distract him while she attempted to steal his ruby stick pin.

Eli released her but set a steadying hand to her trim waist. "My pleasure is catching thieves in action, madam. You'll need to take a less obvious approach if you mean to best me."

Miss Gambit's frustration radiated. She marched alongside him until they reached the supper boxes. Dante D'Angelo was busy feeding his wife grapes in a way that seemed highly erotic.

Eli grabbed hold of Miss Gambit's wrist and stormed over to Daventry's lackey. "Miss Gambit failed the test. If you see Daventry before I do, tell him I'll not work with any of his agents and will source my own partner."

"What? But that's totally unfair." Miss Gambit sounded more than displeased. "You cannot blame me for being accosted on the Walk. If you'd left me to deal with the matter, I would have prevailed."

Eli swung around to face her. "A sensible woman would have retreated the moment the men blocked her path. You, madam, are illogical and a veritable shrew. You may take risks with your own life, but you'll not take risks with mine."

D'Angelo slipped out of the booth and squared his shoulders, ready for a confrontation. "Miss Gambit has the skill to assist you in your endeavour. Daventry will demand you reconsider."

"I might have overlooked her recent error had she managed to steal my stick pin. As she failed both tasks, that's the end of the matter."

Miss Gambit braced her hands on her hips and her cloak gaped open. Eli's traitorous gaze dipped to her breasts. Merciful Lord. No doubt she would ride roughshod over his dreams tonight.

Eli bowed and resisted bolting to the exit. "Good night, Miss Gambit. I'm sure you'll be the perfect agent for some other sorry fellow." Jealousy reared its head at the thought of her entertaining another man. Jealousy! Good Lord. This was worse than he feared. Four years without a woman in his bed was taking its toll.

"You'll not find another agent with Miss Gambit's skill," D'Angelo pressed. "Might you give her one last test?"

"No one gets a second chance." Not a cheating fiancé nor a backstabbing brother. Eli stole a glance at the woman who'd shaken his world in the space of an hour. "Might I suggest you find a safer means to earn a living?"

Then he turned on his heel and strode towards the Grand Walk.

As Eli left Vauxhall and made his way to the coach park, he convinced himself he would forget about Miss Gambit's pleasing countenance, forget she excited him as no woman had done before.

What the hell was Daventry thinking, hiring her to catch criminals? The woman was a menace. Only a man three pence short of a shilling would contemplate forging a partnership.

So why did he feel a pang of regret? Why did every instinct demand he hire her to assist with his dilemma? He couldn't answer either question. But as he climbed into his conveyance and settled into the black leather seat, his inner voice made a startling premonition.

Eli would encounter the confounding woman again.

He feared fate had decreed it.

# CHAPTER 3

THE DEVIL CAME in many forms. Tonight, he'd taken command of Mr Hunter's handsome countenance to steal Rachel's heart and destroy her spirit. The man had used witchcraft to worm his way under her skin. He must have added a potion to her wine, a tincture that affected her senses, that made her admire a man she hardly knew, made her believe this could be the start of a lasting friendship.

Mr Hunter had discerned her character from one silly test.

He had accused her of being stubborn and illogical. Both were true. He'd called her a shrew. Yes, her temper got the better of her, but only when provoked. If he had bothered to question why she'd learnt to fight, he would know of her struggle to survive while living in Lady Hanaway's home.

Rachel's throat tightened at the memory of those horrid boys. Those horrid boys had grown into cruel men. Cruel men who'd sought to punish her for being their mother's favourite.

She stole a glance at the people crammed into the supper boxes. It was only a matter of time before the Hanaway brothers found her and sought to test her sanity. It was partly why she'd joined the Order. Her colleagues would stand shoulder to shoulder with her should the brothers declare war.

"Daventry will want to know what happened." Mr D'Angelo's frustrated voice drew her from her reverie. "He anticipated some difficulties. Hunter is used to working alone."

Oddly, Rachel wasn't angry at Mr Hunter. It was hard to live in armour. The weight of the protective shell took its toll. And someone had hurt him in the past. Why else would a man confess to being heartless?

"Mr Hunter wished to test my courage. He asked me to navigate the Dark Walk alone. I'd barely covered a hundred yards when I encountered a problem."

Mrs D'Angelo frowned. "Would he have asked a man to do such a ridiculous thing? No! Dante wouldn't wander along the avenue at night, and he's a skilled pugilist."

"You would have passed the test had you refused." Mr D'Angelo spoke with the wisdom of an oracle. "You should have told him only a fool risks their life without a justifiable reason."

Rachel sighed. Mr D'Angelo was right. "To make matters worse, two rogues blocked my path. One grabbed me, and Mr Hunter charged to the rescue."

An independent woman might be annoyed at his interference. But the sheer power in his movements, the ruthless aggression in the set of his jaw, had left her breathless.

Mr D'Angelo shook his head. "A good agent knows when to retreat. A good agent rises above the need to make a point."

"Mr Hunter must have thought me a liability because he swept me into his arms and carried me the length of the Hermits Walk."

No man had ever held her so close. No man had ever teased every nerve to life with the warmth of his body and the potent scent of his skin. She'd struggled to identify the notes of his cologne. Bergamot or mandarin gave a fresh aroma that mirrored the man's confidence. Sandalwood or cedarwood echoed the dark sensuality he kept hidden behind his mask.

"He only released me because I tried to steal his ruby stick pin." Touching him had proved another unique experience. His jaw was as rigid as his resolve, his shoulders as hard as his heart.

Mrs D'Angelo glanced at her husband. "It's a shame Rachel didn't steal the pin. Had she succeeded, Mr Hunter may have overlooked the error in the Dark Walk."

"He knew I had no chance of stealing it." Had Mr Hunter been pressured to meet her? He'd come expecting her to fail. "He wanted an excuse to reject me."

The thought roused her ire.

She did not suffer rejection lightly, would not be so easily dismissed.

An idea popped into her head. A ridiculous idea that would probably end in embarrassment, her arrest, or the loss of her position with the Order. Sheer determination and strength of will helped her survive the shipwreck. She needed to call on those reserves again.

She looked at Mr D'Angelo. "Do you happen to know the time, sir?"

The gentleman inspected his pocket watch. "Half-past nine."

A flutter of excitement had Rachel grinning. "And would you happen to know Mr Hunter's direction? Is he likely to return home, do you suppose?" Or was he out hunting for the next victim to slay?

Mr Hunter was a bachelor and didn't seem the sort to visit a brothel or keep a mistress. Rachel imagined him lounging beside a roaring fire, drinking brandy and reading Voltaire.

"He owns a house on the Uxbridge Road, past the Oxford Street turnpike."

"Is he a gambler or a member of a gentlemen's club?"

Mr D'Angelo laughed. "No, Miss Gambit. Hunter prefers his own company. He believes gambling is a weak man's pursuit. He's an investor and managed to turn a reasonable inheritance into a property empire."

Admiration filled her chest. Perhaps because she sensed Mr Hunter had spent his life fighting for his position.

"Mr Hunter gave me until the end of the evening to steal his ruby stick pin. That means I have a little over two hours to sneak into his house and locate the object."

"Sneak into his house? I must advise against such a bold course of action," Mr D'Angelo cautioned. "Hunter will make no allowances for the fact you're a woman."

What's the worst he could do? Call a constable? Ravish her to teach her a lesson? Based on his brooding temperament, she doubted he could raise the enthusiasm.

Mrs D'Angelo ignored her husband's warning and clapped her hands with glee. "If you can enter Mr Hunter's house without his knowledge, he's sure to hire you."

"Hunter is as ruthless as he's cunning." Mr D'Angelo clearly doubted her chances of success. "Ultimately, the decision is yours, but be warned. He takes no prisoners."

Rachel felt compelled to act. Yes, Mr Hunter would likely whisk her into his strong arms and deposit her on the doorstep. But it would be worth the risk just to see the look on his face when she stole the stick pin.

"Then let us leave Vauxhall. We'll discuss a plan of action en route."

Mrs D'Angelo smiled. "You've the courage of an Amazonian, Rachel."

"I'll need more than courage. I'll need my wits if I'm to snare a hunter."

One could tell a lot about a man from his home.

Mr Hunter's mansion house embodied everything Rachel had learnt about the gentleman. It was set back from the road, quite a distance from the other houses in the vicinity. A dark, lonely place that proved wholly unwelcoming. The tall sash windows and dutch gables were pleasing to the eye. Though what lay beyond seemed empty, lifeless. The solid brick wall and mounted iron railings said the house was as guarded as Mr Hunter's heart.

"You'll not climb those railings in long skirts." Mr D'Angelo peered through the carriage window. They had parked twenty yards from the entrance and could only observe the house from the light of the carriage lamp. "The boundary wall stands eight feet high."

"There'll be a rear entrance through a door in the wall." Rachel delved into the leather satchel beside her, one she was rarely without, and removed the ring of skeleton keys. "I can pick the lock."

It was an invaluable skill when one found themselves trapped in cupboards and cellars. While living with Lady Hanaway, she'd taken to strapping numerous keys to her thigh and hiding them in all enclosed spaces.

Mr D'Angelo turned to her. "You must ask yourself if it's worth the effort, Miss Gambit. Hunter is not a man one crosses. Why not accept you failed the tests and wait for Daventry to assign you another case?"

She had not failed. Not yet.

She had until the stroke of midnight to complete the task.

Conceding wasn't an option. Mr Daventry was so protective of his female agents, it would be weeks before he found her another assignment. Besides, curiosity had her itching to take a glimpse inside Mr Hunter's domain. And she needed to understand why she felt an inner tug at the mere mention of his name.

"I shall scout the perimeter." Rachel opened the carriage door and jumped to the ground before Mr D'Angelo could protest. "Wait here. If I've not returned in ten minutes, it means I've found a way into the property."

"Good luck," Mrs D'Angelo whispered.

Nerves fluttered to Rachel's throat as she crossed the deserted thoroughfare. Darkness swamped everything, obscuring her vision like a widow's veil. But fortune favoured the bold, and so she clung to the eight-foot wall and navigated the blackness until she came to a door in the boundary wall.

She froze upon finding the door unlocked.

Was Mr Hunter lurking in the shadows, eyeing his prey?

Had he anticipated her next move?

Perhaps people were so terrified of the hunter, they wouldn't dare cross his threshold. Perhaps the man knew how to entice a daring lady into a trap.

The desire to prove herself worthy saw her enter the garden and creep past the path leading to the stable yard. Suspicion gripped her firmly when she left the herb garden and found the door to the house unlocked, too. Still, she entered Lucifer's lair, knowing she would likely get burnt.

Rachel tiptoed along the corridor.

Voices echoed from a room to her left, a servants' dining area next to the kitchen. She kept her breathing even, waited until the footman finished his bawdy tale and burst into fits of laughter. Then she slipped quietly past and made her way to the entrance hall.

Candlelight spilled from beneath the door of one room. Either Mr Hunter was taking a nip of port to chase away the chill, or the household staff were anticipating the master's arrival. A skilled agent would have checked for a carriage in the stable yard, would have known for sure.

The sudden tinkle of the servants' bell forced her to slip inside a dark room across the hall—Mr Hunter's study. Despite the lack of light, she noted the black brocade chairs, the imposing desk as solid as the man's thighs. The room carried his potent scent. A deeply sensual smell that roused a range of forbidden emotions.

She placed her ring of keys gently on the floor, kept the door slightly ajar and peered into the dim hall.

With the usual aplomb, the butler entered the room opposite. That's when Rachel heard the throaty voice that turned her insides molten. The voice that sent her heart leaping to her throat.

"I'll need a tray in my chamber at six. I plan to leave for St Albans at seven. As usual, I'll be away for two days."

What was in St Albans? Family? A lover?

"Very good, sir. Do you require anything else this evening?"

"No, Jacobs, you can extinguish the lamps." Mr Hunter paused. "Be alert. Tell Mrs Dowling to refuse any parcels or packages. No one is to enter the house. And leave all correspondence in the box outside for me to inspect upon my return."

"Of course, sir."

Mr Hunter spoke as if expecting an imminent attack from a penny boy. Why tell the staff to be alert then leave the doors open to intruders? The man was cautious, meticulous in his methods. Which was why she knew he'd left them open purposely, anticipating her arrival.

Mr Hunter appeared at the drawing room door in his shirtsleeves and the embroidered red waistcoat bearing the damned pin. He carried a glass of port, went to take a sip before mounting the stairs, but froze with the vessel a mere inch from his lips.

Had he sensed her presence?

Could he smell her perfume?

Panicked, Rachel clasped her hand to her mouth and tried to calm her breathing. Perhaps Mr D'Angelo had the measure of the situation. Was it not better to leave Mr Hunter to his brooding and wait for another case?

As luck would have it, Mr Hunter swallowed a mouthful of port and continued his ascent. From the creak of the boards beneath his feet, he'd turned right on the landing. She tried to count his booted steps, was certain he'd walked to the end of the corridor.

The butler extinguished the lamps in the drawing room. He closed the door gently behind him and then glided gracefully through the hall to the servants' quarters.

Rachel waited until the long case clock struck eleven before creeping upstairs. It wasn't hard to find Mr Hunter's bedchamber. She followed the fragrance that posed such an intriguing contradiction.

Pressing her palm to the door, she could almost feel the man's energy thrumming against her fingers. All was quiet, yet every instinct said he was looming, waiting to pounce. She gripped the iron doorknob and turned it slowly, took a deep breath and entered the room.

Mr Hunter's sanctum was as dark as the depths of Lady Hanaway's cellar. Still, one could not mistake the huge tester bed with solid black spears for posts and gothic arches for panels. The thick black hangings were closed. If she tore them open, would she find Mr Hunter's naked form sprawled across the counterpane?

Through narrowed eyes, Rachel scanned the room. She saw the red waistcoat draped over a chair, next to his white shirt and cravat. An enquiry agent should remain focused, emotionally detached, yet she couldn't resist the urge to snatch the shirt and inhale Mr Hunter's scent.

Divine! So divine it should be criminal.

Perhaps stealing the pin was a mistake. Mr Hunter's allure was as powerful as gravity's pull. Only a fool would have romantic notions for a man who admitted he was as cold as a year-old corpse.

"You've had a wasted journey, Miss Gambit." Mr Hunter's husky notes filtered through the darkness. "You're too late. The ruby pin is locked in the safe, and I'm the only one with the key."

Rachel's heart skipped a beat. "You've been expecting me, Mr Hunter." She scoured the blackness, searching for the man who slept in Satan's bed.

"I noticed D'Angelo's carriage parked outside. I had Jacobs open the doors to save you scrambling over the wall and smashing a windowpane."

Where on earth was he hiding?

His voice seemed to be everywhere at once.

"A hunter has keen eyes and sharp perception. I underestimated you." She quickly knelt down and lifted the counterpane. Nothing. "I'll not make the same mistake again."

"What makes you think you'll get a second chance? What makes you think I'll let you leave this room?"

The thought of spending endless nights bantering with Mr Hunter had distinct appeal. She had only ever known weak men, spiteful men, men who made the contents of her stomach curdle. She had never met a man whose voice warmed every cold extremity. He was a closed book she longed to read. A puzzle she had to solve.

"You cannot keep me prisoner."

"This is my house. I can do what I please."

"Mr D'Angelo will come if I fail to return."

A mocking snort echoed from somewhere near the bed. "I'm not afraid of Dante D'Angelo. I'm not afraid of any man."

"Then be afraid of a woman, for I'll have no choice but to draw my Skean Dhu." She crept closer to the bed and parted the hangings only to find the space empty. "You favour black in all things." Even his bedsheets were as dark as the devil's heart.

"Black suits my mood."

"Do you live in a permanent state of melancholy?"

Silence.

"Are you mourning the loss of someone you loved?"

Silence.

His failure to offer a retort said she'd hit a nerve. It had to be the reason for his serious disposition. Had his mother died tragically? Was he orphaned young? Had he lost the love of his life? Was that why he hid behind a mask?

She glanced at the red waistcoat draped over the chair. Mr Hunter always wore black. Did he not have an onyx stick pin? But then she recalled that red was supposed to make them both more visible at night.

"I should have refused to venture down the Dark Walk. You tricked me into believing I had to follow your commands. It was a novice mistake."

"It takes a strong woman to admit her failures."

Ah, she noticed a pattern. When she challenged him, he fought back. When she showed any sign of weakness, he came to her aid. Mr Hunter was a gentleman beneath his arrogant facade. How interesting.

"It takes an honest woman to admit she's wrong," Rachel agreed. "You let me believe you spoke in earnest. Next time, I'll not trust everything you say."

Indeed, had he lied about removing the stick pin from the waistcoat? Was this another test to see if she'd learnt anything from the exercise earlier?

Rachel crossed the room and snatched the waistcoat from the chair.

Mr Hunter made a swift appearance, somersaulting through the air from the solid canopy of Lucifer's bed. He landed on his feet with such ease and grace, Rachel couldn't help but gawp. Gawp at his skill and mastery. At the fact the man was naked but for a pair of loose black trousers. Gawp at his muscular torso, at the jagged scar following the teasing trail of dark hair down below the waistband.

"Give me the waistcoat, Miss Gambit." He prowled towards her like a wildcat on the hunt. "You failed the tasks. Admit defeat."

"By my calculation, I have forty minutes until this game is at an end." Rachel hid the garment behind her back while running her fingers over the material, searching for the tiny gem. "You said I had until the end of the evening to complete the task."

A sinful smirk played on his lips. "As a man who always keeps his word, I'll let you have your forty minutes." He closed the gap between them and gripped the ribbons securing her cloak. "Let's see how you fare when your mind is distracted. When you have to choose between keeping your clothes or relinquishing the waistcoat."

A delicious shiver of anticipation rippled through her body. "You wouldn't dare."

He tugged the ribbons slowly. "I need a woman who is focused, who can maintain her disguise when the odds are stacked against her."

"I'm the woman you need." Rachel continued fiddling with the waistcoat while Mr Hunter parted her cloak and set his ravenous gaze to her breasts. Mother Mary! "I witnessed the flicker of recognition in your eyes when we met at Vauxhall. Admit it. You want to work with me."

He ignored her provoking comments. "I asked you to wear a red gown but made no mention of hiding it beneath a red cloak. As such, I'm eager to assess the quality of your purchase."

He pushed the cloak off her shoulders. The heavy garment slipped down her back, forcing her to drop the waistcoat.

In a panic, Rachel swung around and scrambled through

the pool of red material. Mr Hunter did not make a mad dash to retrieve his waistcoat. No, for some reason, he wanted to play this game.

Then she saw the ruby shining in the darkness. Victory was but an arm's length away. She gripped the jewel and yanked hard.

Feeling a sudden rush of euphoria, she turned to face the man who would have to hire her now.

But Mr Hunter stared at her beneath hooded lids. He moved in sleek steps, forcing her to shuffle backwards until her heels hit the bedchamber door.

Rachel held up the ruby pin as if it were a cross to ward off sinners.

"I have your pin, sir." She tried to ignore the earthy scent of his skin, the hard muscles in his abdomen, the small stiff nipples her fingers itched to touch.

"I let you take it." His blue eyes turned predatory as he scanned the neckline of her gown. In a move that proved shocking, he stroked a finger seductively over her collarbone, leaving a blazing trail in its wake. "I could steal it back before you take your next breath. I could distract you to such a degree, you'd forget all about the tests."

"You would assault a lady in a rakish fashion just to prove a point?"

"In entering a man's bedchamber, you sacrificed yourself to get ahead."

Rachel raised her chin in a gesture of defiance. "You left me no choice. Had your test been fair, had you waited for me to beat the rogues and return to you unharmed, I wouldn't be in this predicament."

"You failed the test in the Dark Walk."

"It was a stupid test. Give me another."

"I'd rather give someone a first chance than you a second." So why was he staring at her as if she were a rare museum find?

"We both know that's a lie. You need a woman who can think on her feet. You'll find no one more qualified than me."

"Perhaps not." He stepped back, his assessing gaze taking in every inch of her form while he rubbed his firm jaw and contemplated the dilemma. "If you worked for anyone else but Lucius Daventry, I'd show you the door."

"Does that mean you'll give me another test?"

"I'm giving the matter my close consideration."

That meant yes. "What do you want me to do?"

He moistened his lips. "Persuade me to hire you."

# CHAPTER 4

THERE WERE many ways Miss Gambit might persuade him to hire her. She could strip out of that sumptuous gown, devour his mouth until they were breathless. She could massage his tense shoulders, stroke his throbbing cock.

Eli wanted her. He wanted to lift her off her feet, slam her back against the door, and drive long and hard into her warm body.

Should she offer any of those tempting things, Eli would whip her over his shoulder and dump her in Dante D'Angelo's carriage.

"Be careful," he warned. "Remember what I want, what I need." He spoke in a teasing voice that was so unlike him. Part of him hoped she'd pass the test because time was of the essence, and he needed to catch a cunning bastard. Part of him, a part he'd long since buried, hoped she would ravish him senseless.

"You said you needed a woman. I'm every inch a woman."

"As I'm most acutely aware, Miss Gambit." He braced himself, anticipating the touch of her hand against his bare chest. While he'd developed a sudden craving for an illicit affair, it was the last thing he needed.

"Most women are afraid of their own shadow. I'm not." She sounded confident, nothing like a temptress out to snare him in her trap. "It took courage to enter your house tonight, courage I have aplenty."

A man could measure his courage by the way he took his brandy. One mouthful and he could lead an army. One bottle would have him stumbling onto the battlefield without waiting for reinforcements.

"I'll not deny your bravery is something to be admired. But it's not cowardly to walk away from an untenable situation."

"If you're referring to the Dark Walk, then I've already admitted to acting in error. Surely you'd prefer to work with a woman who owns up to her mistakes. An honesty exists between us, Mr Hunter, one you'll struggle to find with anyone else."

Yes, she spoke her mind. He liked that.

And she could follow orders. The exercise in the Dark Walk hadn't been a complete failure. But how would he deal with this damnable attraction?

"I've an excellent memory, better than most," she added.

"You've told me of your strengths, madam. Now tell me your greatest weakness." Focusing on her faults would quieten the newly awakened beast.

She pursed her lips. "Impatience. Impatience and a quick temper. When I lived with Lady Hanaway—"

"I'm not interested in your past." The less he knew about her, the better. "I need someone who can play a role, who can act without letting the mask fall. I need someone who isn't intimidated by powerful men, someone with a backbone of steel."

"I can be anything you want me to be, sir." As quick as a wink, her expression changed from amiable to arrogant. The pads of her fingers settled on his chest, not to explore or caress but to push him away. "I came tonight to prove I'm determined, but I am finished playing games. If you will excuse me, I shall bid you good night. Should you decide I have the qualities you desire in a partner, speak to Mr Daventry, and he will arrange a meeting."

She turned and gripped the knob.

Eli braced his hand against the door to prevent her from leaving. "You're hired, Miss Gambit. You start immediately." He ignored his doubts, ignored his fears, ignored the warning voice that urged him to keep his distance. "You've half an hour to gather some clothes. We're leaving London."

She swung around, her topaz eyes twinkling in the darkness. "Leaving for St Albans? I heard you speaking to your butler."

"We'll visit a coaching inn north of London, then proceed to St Albans."

"What clothes will I need?" Excitement radiated from every aspect of her being. "What is it you want me to do?"

Eli hesitated. He would have to tell her about the Order of Themis, about the traitor secretly working to destroy his brethren. But should he trust this stranger? Daventry had every faith in her, and he was rarely wrong.

"Sit down, Miss Gambit." Eli crossed the room, snatched his shirt and gestured to the chair. "What I tell you tonight is confidential. You'll not repeat it to your friends or to Daventry's enquiry agents. Is that understood?"

Miss Gambit came to sit in the chair. She kept her hands clasped in her lap, sat with such poise and grace one would never suspect she carried a weapon in her reticule.

"Perfectly. I'm here to help you, Mr Hunter, not cause problems."

She watched him beneath lowered lids as he dragged the shirt over his head and covered his naked torso. His state of undress would have unnerved most ladies. Not Miss Gambit. The exercise had told him a little more about her character, made him wonder if she had ever taken a man to her bed.

"Do you know why Lucius Daventry became the master of a group of enquiry agents?" He moved to the nightstand and lit the charcloth in the tinderbox.

"Because the justice system favours the powerful and wealthy, and he sought to even the odds. The gentlemen of the Order are wealthy. They believe in the cause and give their services for free. The ladies accept a fee because Mr Daventry intends to use the funds to help the destitute."

Eli lit various candles dotted about the room. "That's not all. Lucius Daventry rescues boys from the streets and puts them through school. He finds intelligent men without funds and pays for them to train as barristers and doctors."

"His benevolence is inspiring."

"Truly inspiring. But he is the master of another Order. A secret council of men who seek to uncover lies. Men who have worked for him long before he hired enquiry agents. Men who infiltrate society and gather information."

Miss Gambit frowned. "Information? Information about what?"

Eli heard the question, but candlelight caught the golden tones of her hair, leaving him momentarily entranced. He tried not to notice her plump pillow-like lips or the soft swell of her breasts rising and falling with each excited breath.

"Mr Hunter?" she prompted.

"Yes, they compile lists of corrupt men. They uncover conspiracies."

"A secret council of which you're a member."

"Indeed."

"Has someone discovered their identity?"

Her instincts were as sharp as a winter's breeze.

"Not yet. A traitor lives amongst them. A man who has switched allegiances. A man who has turned his back on his friends and sold his soul to the devil. We need to discover who the man is before it's too late."

Miss Gambit swallowed. "Too late?"

Eli leant back against the bedpost. "Before men die, Miss Gambit. We must use clever means to trap him. Daventry will explain more when we arrive at The Wild Hare."

"At the coaching inn north of London," she clarified.

"Yes. Let's hope you're able to function without sleep."

She fell silent, her gaze coming to rest on his bare feet. Oddly, he felt more exposed than when he'd stood in nothing but his trousers.

"Why do you need to hire a woman?" Her tone rang with suspicion. "I sell my intelligence and my insight, Mr Hunter. I do not sell my body regardless of the cause."

"I would never ask you to demean yourself in such a manner." He was offended she thought so little of him, but then she knew nothing about him, not even his given name. "We need to unsettle the Council. We need to lure the serpent out of his basket. Goad him and bait him until he strikes."

Miss Gambit straightened. "If I'm not the snake charmer, where do I fit into this scheme?"

Eli observed her for a moment, prayed to God she was as strong as she proclaimed. "Congratulations, Miss Gambit. You've been promoted. You're the new mistress of the Order of Themis."

●

The Wild Hare stood eight miles from London on the Great North Road. The proud plaque above the door revealed the inn had served tired travellers since the sixteenth century. Eli had visited the place on numerous occasions. Never to take a fresh horse, quench his thirst or rest his weary head.

"Mr Daventry's office is in Hart Street." Miss Gambit scanned the deserted road, glanced up at the spangle of stars in the night sky. "Why would he meet us here at this late hour?"

"Daventry keeps his work for Themis separate from his work in Hart Street." Eli escorted the lady into the dimly lit taproom. The place carried the pungent smell of mould-ridden furnishings, stale smoke and baked herring. "We'll send word, and he'll arrive shortly."

Miss Gambit looked up at the rows of empty flagons hanging from hooks in the beamed ceiling. "Are you sure it's safe to wait here?"

"No one has died from a falling flagon." The corners of his mouth twitched, but he suppressed a smile. "Though I warn you, the beef stew is often rancid. And I have known the innkeeper scratch his sweaty crotch before accepting a man's coin."

"Then I'm thankful I'm a woman. And I make it a rule never to eat anything swimming in gravy."

Eli took the handbell from the crude oak counter and rang it twice. "Gravy hides a multitude of sins."

"Jacob Hanaway once hid maggots in my stew. I saw one crawling on my spoon." While she sounded amused, her eyes bore the harrowing reflection of a woman who'd suffered. "To show he couldn't scare me, I swallowed the thing whole. For days, I imagined it wriggling in my stomach."

"I'm sure they have some nutritional benefit." He rang the bell again. The sudden urge to find Jacob Hanaway and fill his mouth with maggots was the reason Eli swiftly changed the subject. "The wine here is tolerable. Find the cleanest seat, and I'll order while we wait for Lucius Daventry."

She nodded but didn't scour the taproom as he suggested. Instead, she chose the seat by the window with a view of the road. She lowered the hood on her blue travelling cloak but did not remove the garment. The fire in the taproom had burned to nought but glowing embers, and the air held the frosty nip common in mid-February.

Bill Stubbs, a man of average height and build, though his stomach protruded to such a degree it looked like he carried a barrel beneath his shirt, came stomping through a door behind the counter.

Upon recognising Eli, Stubbs didn't need to ask what he wanted. "I'll have Watkins ride to Bronygarth. Can I get ye anything while ye wait?"

Bronygarth was Lucius Daventry's country estate, where he lived with his wife and young sons. Few people knew the exact location, and Daventry paid Stubbs handsomely to ensure it stayed that way.

"Just a flagon of wine and two mugs." Eli slapped four shillings onto the counter. "Let Daventry know I've a woman keeping me company."

Stubbs craned his neck and glanced over Eli's shoulder. "And a mighty fine lookin' piece she is, too. I'll send Watkins on his way and then bring yer flagon."

Eli inwardly groaned. Miss Gambit's comely countenance would capture any man's attention. Still, her steely determination and unwavering honesty were qualities he found attractive. Working alongside her would test the limits of his resolve.

"Mr Daventry's residence must be within easy riding distance," Miss Gambit said when Eli dropped into the seat next to her. "Clearly he's used to being woken at such an ungodly hour."

"He should be here shortly," was all Eli said.

"Perhaps we should use the time to get to know each other better. Let me try to determine what lies behind your grim facade."

His grim facade was a means to ward off female attention.

"We should use the time to discuss the Order of Themis." Avoiding intimacy was his life's mission. "You must convince the Council that you're qualified to lead them. They will demand proof of your skills. What will we tell them?"

She shrugged. "I have an exceptional memory."

"How exceptional?" Was there anything unremarkable about this woman? "Perhaps I should put you to the test."

"Had you asked me to recite passages from the Old Testament instead of navigating the Dark Walk, you could have saved me the inconvenience of stealing into your house."

"Most of us can recite passages from the Bible," he said, sounding unimpressed. "That's hardly a demonstration of your skill."

"Start by naming a book in the Old Testament, and I'll tell you what precedes it." She looked so self-assured he knew he'd spoken prematurely. "Pick one at random."

"Ezekiel."

"Lamentations," she said with nary a pause.

"Esther." He'd tried to pick something less obvious.

"Nehemiah." She grinned. "Ask for a quote."

Eli glanced out of the window at the dusky yard. "Give me a quote from Deuteronomy containing the word night."

"*And thy life shall hang in doubt before thee; and thou shalt fear day and night, and shalt have no assurance of thy life.*" She arched a brow. "Chapter twenty-eight."

"And the verse?"

"Sixty-six."

"Impressive. No doubt if I asked you to recite the first word of Numbers, chapter ten, verse twenty, you would say ..."

"And." A light laugh breezed from her lips. "The odds were in my favour. At least half the verses begin with that word. I spent five torturous months aboard ship with nothing but a Bible for company. Sadly, I never got as far as the New Testament."

Eli found himself smiling. Well, the corners of his mouth curled upwards for the first time in years. "We must decide why Daventry needs someone with your skill to act as the temporary custodian of his organisation."

"We'll tell them there's a traitor in their midst. That Mr

Daventry wants me to memorise every document before destroying them."

Eli was pondering the suggestion when Stubbs returned and deposited a flagon of wine and two mugs on the table. "Watkins left five minutes ago, sir."

"Thank you, Stubbs. That will be all." Eli waited until the innkeeper was out of earshot. "No, we'll tell them Daventry is on his deathbed and appointed you to stand in his stead." He poured wine into their mugs. "Themis was a woman. We'll say Daventry sought to trust the deity because he could no longer trust the men."

"I'm not a goddess, Mr Hunter."

He begged to differ. She possessed Aphrodite's power to stun a man and leave him speechless. She could transform herself into air, for he could almost taste her essence with every breath.

"To the Council, you may as well be a creature of myth. They'll not accept you unless you prove yourself supreme." In that battle, he had to appear impartial. As a council member, he would be forced to challenge her, too.

"As long as you're aware, my experience is minimal. My training amounts to having overpowered two cruel dandies, fighting off the attentions of Madame Dubarry's numerous lovers. Still, men don't frighten me, sir."

Despite her faltering confidence, she refused to accept defeat.

"You conquered the sea, Miss Gambit. You survived against the odds. That sets you apart from us mere mortals."

Her eyes widened. "You surprise me, Mr Hunter." She stared at him with an unnerving air of wonder. "You never give praise. Or was that just a means to intimidate me?"

"I doubt the devil could intimidate you, Miss Gambit." No, he had the distinct impression she hid behind a fortress as great as his own.

She smiled in a light, carefree way that made him long to

break free from his shackles. "Tell me more about the Order of Themis."

Eli was grateful for the distraction and spent half an hour explaining that the Order was formed after the Norman Conquest. Over the years, the men had thwarted plots to assassinate heads of state and dignitaries from abroad. Had uncovered conspiracies to undermine the government.

"You would be the first woman ever to take the helm."

Miss Gambit gripped her mug and gulped the wine until the vessel was empty. "You recall this is my first case?" Wine trickled from the corner of her mouth, and she mopped it up with her tongue.

Eli took a calming breath and refilled her mug. "Madam, you have me struggling to anticipate your next move. The Council will have a battle to keep up with you."

"That sounds much like another compliment, Mr Hunter. You can be rather charming when the mood takes you."

"Such moments are rare." Extremely rare.

She made a quick scan of his attire. "Because people are too scared to speak to a stern man in black?"

"Because I rarely meet people worthy of admiration."

God's teeth! The mischievous twinkle in her eye said he'd spoken in error.

"So, you admire me, sir." She managed to grin while sipping her wine—another exceptional feat.

"I respect the fact you have a keen mind and the courage to confront those who dare pose a challenge."

"Unless I've taken to strolling along the Dark Walk. Then, I'm illogical and a veritable shrew." She clinked her mug against his to show she'd scored a point.

Damnation! The woman had his mind spinning in circles. "What do you want me to say? That seeing you being manhandled by two scoundrels roused my ire to such an extent I spoke out of turn?" He'd wanted to throttle them with his bare hands.

"Only if it's true."

"It's true." He expected her to punch the air in triumph.

She fell silent. Seconds passed before she spoke. "You mentioned creatures of myth. I always believed good, honest men were fictional beings, the stuff of legends. It's reassuring to know I was wrong."

The last woman to speak so intimately listed his faults, his failures, berated him for a catalogue of errors. "Don't make the mistake of thinking you know me. I have a reputation for being a heartless devil, a dangerous man few dare cross." It was a chain of armour he wore with pride. A chain of armour no one could penetrate.

"Regardless, good men champion the truth." Miss Gambit reached across the table and patted his hand. "Now, you must learn to speak from the heart."

Eli's throat tightened in response.

It was best to keep the emotions buried.

Thank God Lucius Daventry chose that moment to thunder into the coach yard on his black stallion. He dismounted and tied the reins to the hitching post before marching into the taproom.

Eli stood, noting the man's impeccable attire. "I see we didn't drag you from your bed."

"You insisted on vetting Miss Gambit the night before the Council meeting. I've been expecting you." Daventry brushed his hand through his coal-black hair. There wasn't a single strand of grey despite him being thirty and dealing with problems that would put most men in Bedlam. "I see you passed Hunter's rigorous tests, Miss Gambit."

The lady shook her head. "I failed miserably. He is the hard taskmaster you warned of, sir. Thankfully, I found a loophole that allowed me to prove my worth."

"Miss Gambit possesses remarkable determination," Eli admitted, keeping any hint of admiration from his tone. "I believe she has the qualities needed to help find the traitor."

Daventry gestured for Eli to sit. He strode behind the counter and found a mug, then joined them at the table and helped himself to wine.

"I trust you have a plan, Hunter."

A plan of sorts. "We'll tell the Council you're ill, that you've nominated Miss Gambit to stand in your stead. She'll confront them with our suspicions. They'll seek to prove their innocence. In doing so, the traitor is sure to reveal himself."

Daventry pursed his lips and glanced at Miss Gambit. "That's the reason you insisted on hiring a woman? Not to play the role of maid and rummage through our brethren's bedchambers? Not to move covertly through Trēowith without drawing attention?"

Eli cleared his throat. Daventry had a way of making the most hardened men nervous. "That was my initial plan. But we've been watching the Council for weeks and have no new leads. Men's lives are at stake. It strikes me that Miss Gambit has the temerity to draw the devil out."

Daventry sipped his wine while studying Miss Gambit over the rim of his mug. "It's too dangerous. She'll need round-the-clock protection. At Trēowith, you'll be without support."

"I can protect myself, sir," Miss Gambit snapped. "Need I remind you what occurred the day you hired me."

Daventry smiled. "Miss Gambit chased a thief from the pawnbroker's shop. She cornered him in an alley, pressed her blade to his throat and forced him to empty his pockets."

"My only regret is that he emptied his bladder," she added.

Eli found himself in the unusual position of being amused and horrified at the same time. He wondered when he might meet the vulnerable woman hiding behind the mask. The woman who hid behind the bravado as a means of survival.

"We'll be at Trēowith for one night, maybe two." Eli

feared they would be long, taxing nights where a man had to recite the Lord's Prayer to stave off temptation. "I can guard Miss Gambit until we return to London."

"Peter Hanaway held my head in the water trough until I was seconds away from drowning. I'm sure I can deal with scheming council members."

Daventry ignored the harrowing revelation. "If I'm on my deathbed, you'll protect her until we've caught the traitor."

Eli's gut twisted. "Can one of your agents not play nursemaid?"

"I don't need coddling," Miss Gambit complained.

"No, you don't," Daventry replied. "You've a sharp mind and a man's determination, but I wish to take all necessary precautions. Besides, Hunter won't be protecting you. You'll be protecting each other."

"What the devil?" Eli was about to shoot out of the chair, but Daventry raised a staying hand. Panic flared. To keep Miss Gambit safe, he would need to watch her night and day. "You're asking me to move her into my house?"

Daventry offered a half shrug. "It seems the logical solution. No doubt, Miss Gambit will find it an inconvenience, but one must push personal feelings aside when men's lives are at risk."

Miss Gambit would find it an inconvenience?

Hellfire! The bothersome woman would drive him to distraction.

"So, that's settled." Daventry shot Eli a look that told him not to argue. "Miss Gambit will visit Trēowith in my place. Lord DeVille wishes to hire an agent and has invited me to his clifftop estate in Whitstable. Upon my return, I'll remain at Bronygarth until you've caught the devil. I'll inform Ashwood of our plans should you need support."

Noah Ashwood was the overseer at the Order's offices in Hart Street. He was an excellent agent and a man his colleagues admired.

Daventry tugged his seal ring from his finger and handed it to Miss Gambit. "Guard this with your life. Present it to the Council. It's the only one of its kind. They'll know I gave it to you."

"They might think I've stolen it," she said.

"While they're concerned with the whys and wherefores, they will leave themselves open to scrutiny." He glanced at Eli. "Are we all in agreement?"

Eli reluctantly nodded, as did Miss Gambit.

"Excellent. Now let's devise a plan."

# CHAPTER 5

"MISS GAMBIT." The whispered words drifted into Rachel's mind. "Miss Gambit!" The next were as sharp as a stab to the ribs. "Wake up. We've almost reached our destination." A hot hand came to rest on her knee and shook her twice.

Rachel opened her eyes and met Mr Hunter's intense stare. It was so dark in the confines of his conveyance one might believe it was the dead of night. He sat like the master of the underworld, dressed in black, exuding a raw masculinity that would make the bravest men cower.

Mr Hunter raised the blind. "We've reached St Albans."

The sky was the deep Aegean blue one saw before sunrise, the horizon a glowing hem of orange, a prelude to the dawn of a new day. The carriage wasn't clattering along narrow town streets but thundering through open countryside.

"We'll take a room at the next inn, wash and change our clothes before continuing to Trēowith." His stern tone said he was still annoyed at Lucius Daventry. Mr Hunter preferred to live alone, eat alone, sleep alone. He did not want to share his house or life with anyone, least of all a stubborn shrew.

"What time is it, sir?" Her voice was thick from sleep.

"A little after six. And you'll need to call me Hunter, not sir."

Six! Heavens. Had he spent the last two hours watching her doze?

"I pray you weren't party to my incessant mumbling, Hunter." Strange, she had spoken his name many times, but it sounded so intimate without the prefixed title.

"You fidget. You nibble your lip. You don't mumble."

"And you've started talking in clipped sentences. Don't be angry. If spending time with me bothers you, perhaps you should hire someone else to take my place."

He dragged his gaze from the window. "It's not you, Miss Gambit. I like solitude, value privacy. I share nothing, least of all my time."

Lord, the man was as blunt as a butter knife.

"Well, it seems we have the makings of an excellent partnership." If she could just break down his barriers. "Honesty is the foundation of any strong relationship."

"And yet so many are based on lies and deceit."

The comment wasn't an opening for her to pry into his affairs. Still, she would not forgo an opportunity to know him better.

"You speak from experience, Mr Hunter."

"We all speak from experience, Miss Gambit, not always our own."

"As a man who solves problems, you must have seen the worst of people." From the age of sixteen, she'd seen cruelty that beggared belief.

"I've seen levels of depravity that would make the devil appear saintly." He took a silver flask from his coat pocket, unscrewed the cap, removed the plug and swigged the contents. "But to me, nothing is worse than betrayal."

"Do you speak of the traitor?"

Mr Hunter leant forward and handed her the flask. "Take a nip of brandy. It will stave off the cold." He meant it would keep her quiet and stop her asking personal questions.

She noted the engraving on the flask. "*Facta, non verba.* Acts, not words." It was the motto of a man who'd once believed someone's lies.

"You can tell a lot about a person from how they behave. Words are meaningless when one's actions are in discord."

Rachel sipped the brandy. "You must have loved her deeply."

"Who?"

"The woman who betrayed you."

Tension loomed. "Evidently, not deeply enough."

His confession spoke of progress. Indeed, Rachel resisted the urge to fly across the carriage and hug him for his bravery. She swallowed another nip of liquor, coughed to cool the burn, and handed him the flask.

He set his lips to the vessel without wiping it, pinned her to the seat with his gaze while he took a drink. The brandy must be potent enough to meddle with a lady's mind, for she imagined a sensual scene where he drank from her mouth, not the flask.

"I knew a man who collected secrets," she said as the carriage pulled into the Old Crown coaching inn and rumbled to a halt. "Family secrets, work secrets, financial secrets. They lived inside him, gorging on despair, growing until his heart could no longer take the strain."

Mr Hunter opened the door, dropped the steps and alighted. "I have the unnerving suspicion there's a point to your ramblings, Miss Gambit."

"A man needs someone to talk to at night. Someone to help share the burden." Rachel gripped his hand and descended. Her knees buckled the second her feet hit the ground.

Mr Hunter's strong arm snaked around her waist to keep her upright. "Perhaps you should spend time concentrating on where to place your feet and less about constructing interesting metaphors." He released her promptly and brushed imagined dust from his coat sleeve.

"Forgive me. Three hours sitting in a carriage has given me cramp." She curled her toes in her boot to ease the ache. "And it wasn't a construct. My father bore everyone's burdens until the stress killed him. I wish I could have recognised it sooner."

Mr Hunter had the decency to incline his head by way of an apology. "It's human nature to look to the past and contemplate what we could have done differently. But it's the worst sort of torment." He reached into the carriage, took her satchel and handed it to her. "I shall use false names when hiring a room. I trust you have no objection."

"A room? In the singular?"

"I've sworn an oath to Lucius Daventry. I have a duty to protect you, Miss Gambit. Consequently, we may be forced to bear uncomfortable situations."

"We're to protect each other," she corrected.

Those had been Mr Daventry's orders. Odd that he felt a man as dangerous as Mr Hunter should require assistance from a female agent.

Mr Hunter dismissed her comment. "We'll be expected to stay the night at Trēowith, so I doubt we'll return to the inn. You'll stay in Daventry's room. Mine is across the landing."

"Trēowith is a house, not a place?"

"It's a country estate owned by the Order of Themis where the brethren meet monthly. We'll sit with the Council this afternoon."

"Trēow is an old English word, I believe." Lady Hanaway had been a lover of history and an excellent tutor. She had devoted so much time to Rachel's studies it had fed her sons' jealousy.

"It stands for loyalty and truth. Trēowith is where we remember the noble men who've served this country since the Norman Conquest. We must do everything in our power to stop the traitor before he tramples over their memory."

It was a mammoth task, made colossal by a distinct lack of information. "It might help if you told me what evidence you have. We should make a list of suspects. Examine possible motives. I need to know more if I'm to be of assistance."

Or, like her father, did he intend to keep everyone in the dark?

"Madam, it's six o'clock on a bitter February morning. If we're not meeting the Council until this afternoon, why do you think we've come so early?"

Rachel raised her chin. "Why didn't you say so?"

"Because you spent most of the journey snoring."

"I do not snore."

Mr Hunter smiled. Good Lord! It was a magnificent sight to behold.

"You do when your chin touches your chest."

Rachel felt a blush of mortification. "I'd wager you grunt in your sleep."

"Come this evening, you're sure to find out."

Mr Hunter gathered their valises and closed the carriage door. He informed his coachman they'd be leaving for Trēowith at noon, then escorted her into the inn.

It came as some surprise at such an early hour to find two men seated around a table in the taproom, eating a hearty meal of ham and eggs. Mr Hunter observed the men through suspicious eyes and then proceeded to where the innkeeper's wife stood cleaning tankards behind the counter.

Mr Hunter gave their names as Mr and Mrs Monroe.

Rachel used the opportunity to test her acting skills. She hugged Mr Hunter's arm and gave an affectionate squeeze. "It's our first trip to St Albans. Our first trip anywhere since we married. My husband plans to show me the sights and buy me a new bonnet."

The buxom woman with red hair took one look at Mr Hunter's pleasing countenance and gave an envious sigh. "There's a quaint little tea shop near the cathedral that's not to be missed." She took payment and handed him an iron key. "You've room nine." She leant forward, flopping her bosom onto the counter, and whispered, "It's the only room where the bed don't creak. A keeper's got to think of her other guests."

Mr Hunter had no option but to return the teasing woman's grin.

He led Rachel upstairs to a room with oak furnishings and shabby blue curtains. The sterile smell of soap lingered in the air, along with a waft of cooked ham. The tempting aroma had her stomach grumbling as loud as rolling thunder.

Being a man who noticed everything, Mr Hunter headed for the door. "I'll order a simple bill of fare to break our fast."

"And a bottle of burgundy to wash it all down?"

"You know me so well, Miss Gambit."

"Mrs Monroe," she corrected. "We should maintain our cover story. Hurry back, my love."

"My heart aches every second we're parted," he countered drily.

He left her to stare at the narrow tester bed, half the width of Mr Hunter's imposing bed at home. The man disliked physical contact, so it was just as well they had separate rooms at Trēowith.

He returned promptly and locked the door. "The keeper's wife is excited we're taking a tray in our bedchamber. Don't be surprised if she folds our napkins into kissing swans."

Rachel laughed. "I doubt many men order wine in the morning. She must think you're out to seduce me, Mr Monroe."

"In bed, I prefer a woman to have full command of her faculties."

58

The odd fluttering in her stomach started again. "Two drunkards would hardly make for a memorable coupling."

Mr Hunter studied her. "Do you speak from experience, Mrs Monroe?"

"Not at all." Heat crept up her neck to warm her cheeks. "I've never known a man's touch, though I've seen Madame Dubarry falling over herself from a heady concoction of gin and lust. She collapsed on the stairs, comatose, while her lover tried to haul her to bed."

"Daventry said you lived with the modiste for two years."

"Yes. I suffered cramp on the stage from Shoreham to London. Madame Dubarry had just met her lover in the yard of the Lion and Crown. She saw me tumble down the carriage steps and rushed to my aid."

"For you, cramp seems to be a constant blight."

"And restless legs. That's why I fidget in my sleep."

A glint of amusement flashed in his eyes. "It seems you suffer from a restless spirit, too."

"That's a result of living on a knife-edge for five years."

"The five years you spent with Lady Hanaway?"

"Indeed."

Mr Hunter opened his mouth to speak but thought better of it. He crossed the room, searched inside his valise and returned to hand Rachel a small blue book. Embossed in gold leaf on the cover board was the same symbol carved into the carnelian stone in Mr Daventry's ring.

"The scales of justice." She traced her finger over the gilding.

"It's what the Order of Themis stands for."

It was a noble cause, but there would never be true justice in the world. Not while hardworking people starved, and the Hanaway brothers ran amok.

Rachel opened the book and flipped through the pages. "It's nought but a set of rules."

"Rules handed down over centuries. Rules we've sworn to

obey." He gestured to the new book. "Daventry had these copies made from the original manuscript. You must memorise the edict on page twenty. You'll need to recite it when we address the Council."

A quick scan of the page explained his reasoning. "It's a rule relating to the temporary absence of the master. Mr Daventry can choose a replacement, and only one member of the Council need agree."

Mr Hunter nodded. "I'll have the deciding vote. Nowhere does it mention the replacement must be a man. It will be the basis of your argument should the Council contest your appointment."

Nerves gnawed away inside. When dealing with these men, she would need to apply the same defiant arrogance she'd used with Jacob and Peter Hanaway.

"How long will it take you to commit it to memory?"

Rachel cast him an assured grin. "Thirty minutes. I sing the words in my head. Finding a rhythm helps me to remember."

"Do you need me to leave the room?"

"No, but I concentrate better in enclosed spaces." It stemmed from time spent locked in dank cellars and hiding in the hold of *The Canton*. Rachel pointed to the folded dressing screen next to the washstand. "I'll position a chair behind the screen. That should suffice."

A knock on the door brought the keeper's wife. The woman carried the tray while the girl scuttling behind lugged the trestle table.

"That 'ere's the best bottle of burgundy you'll find for miles around," the buxom woman boasted when Mr Hunter snatched the bottle and examined the label. She glanced at the bed and gave another coy wink. Then she set down the tray, shooed the girl out of the room and promptly closed the door behind them.

"I doubt she'll be satisfied until she hears bumps and moans."

Mr Hunter arched a brow. "A bad case of cramp will have you howling and hopping on the boards. That should appease her." He scrutinised the food on the tray with an unnerving level of intensity. Then inhaled the aromas as if expecting to catch a whiff of arsenic.

"You fear the traitor is seeking ways to get rid of the Council?"

"Poison is the weapon of a coward. In one fell swoop, it can kill a horde of men. It's why I ordered a corked bottle of wine, not a flagon." He motioned to the plate of ham and eggs. "I'll sample the food first." Fork to the ready, Mr Hunter tucked into the scrambled eggs.

Rachel watched his mouth move, watched his Adam's apple bob as he swallowed. Lord knows why she found him so fascinating. "Too much salt, not enough butter, but otherwise safe to eat."

Jacob would have grabbed his own throat and pretended to choke, but Mr Hunter did not joke about serious matters.

They spent the next hour eating their meal and discussing the Order of Themis. Rachel hid behind the screen to memorise the edict, which took forty minutes because Mr Hunter took the opportunity to wash and change clothes. She'd imagined water trickling down his chin and neck, rivulets running down his naked torso. Had he stripped off his breeches? Did he wear linen drawers or was he strolling about naked?

"You've not told me why you suspect there's a traitor," she called.

"My suspicions were first roused almost a month ago when someone stole the sacred seal from the wall plaque in the Sanctum."

"The sacred seal?"

"It's made of walrus ivory and pre-dates the Norman

Conquest. It was made for the first men of Themis. The emblem unites all those brethren who came before us." He suddenly pulled back the screen. "Stealing it is like inciting war."

Mr Hunter had changed out of black clothes into black clothes.

"Who had access to the Sanctum?"

"Only the men on the Council. Daventry, Truscott, Cantrell, Young and Swanson."

Mr Hunter was a council member, too, but made no mention of himself. Was hiring an agent a matter of subterfuge? Was Mr Hunter so angry with the world, he was on a mission of destruction?

"Please tell me you have more evidence than that. Valuable artefacts are stolen all the time."

"You'll understand when you see the Sanctum." He went to his valise and returned with a letter. "Crocker is the custodian at Trēowith. He chased a cloaked intruder who dropped this while making his escape."

Rachel took the letter and peeled back the folds. She scanned the shapes and letters and runes and the odd little arrows dotted about the page.

"It's written in code. Are you able to decipher it?"

Mr Hunter snorted. "Sadly, I've not the patience for such things. I hoped you might make sense of the symbols."

She was touched he thought her intelligent enough to crack the code. "These things take time. Weeks, months, maybe years." On *The Canton*, she'd had nothing better to do than memorise passages in books.

"The sands are running out, Miss Gambit. This letter is the only clue we have to the Council member who wore a disguise and entered the tunnels."

"The tunnels?" The mention of enclosed spaces brought a flutter of panic.

"The Sanctum is underground. Two keys are needed to access the passageways and the inner chamber. All six council members have a key. Swanson reported his key stolen from his room at a coaching inn."

Heavens! The case grew more complicated by the minute. But it explained why Mr Daventry had left them at The Wild Hare and returned with an intricate brass key he'd given to Mr Hunter.

"And the intruder stole the seal," she clarified.

"The seal and the portfolio containing details of the current cases."

Rachel sighed. "The current cases!" Themis helped thwart plots against the government. Helped save poor boys from the noose. She would lay odds someone had blackmailed a council member into destroying evidence of their nefarious deeds. "Why let me sleep on the journey when we could have spent the time examining motives?"

"Because you'll need your wits when we confront the Council." He nodded to the blue book resting in her lap. "Have you memorised the text?"

Rachel handed him the book and stood. "I can recite it verbatim."

"Excellent."

"May I keep the letter? Perhaps I might find the pattern that's the clue to deciphering the symbols."

Mr Hunter appeared conflicted.

"You can trust me, sir. I shall keep it close to my heart."

"I'd rather keep it on my person."

"Why when you haven't the patience to sit and stare at it for hours?" She didn't have the patience either, not anymore, but she had to solve this case if she hoped to keep her position with the Order.

With some reluctance, Mr Hunter nodded. "Very well." He scanned her plain blue dress. "What will you wear when you present yourself to the Council?"

Having had little time to pack, she'd had to make a quick decision. A woman in frills and flounces gave the impression she could handle nothing more taxing than choosing an ice at Gunter's.

Miss Trimble, the lady paid to manage the house in Howland Street, the home of the ladies of the Order, had come up with a sensible suggestion.

Rachel tapped Mr Hunter affectionately on the arm. "I thought I'd take a leaf out of your book, sir. Indeed, is there anything more intimidating than a person dressed in black?"

# CHAPTER 6

Miss Gambit had her pretty nose pressed to the carriage window as Eli's conveyance lumbered up the steep drive to Trēowith. Her eyes widened in wonder upon seeing the battlements of the old hilltop fort.

"You didn't say Trēowith was a castle." Despite being dressed soberly in black, she exuded a brilliance that proved blinding. A radiance that could melt the ice around any man's heart. "The Order of Themis owns this, you say?"

"Yes, the master oversees the upkeep, though Daventry used his own funds to renovate the property when he accepted the role."

As the illegitimate son of a duke, who had inherited much of his father's wealth, Daventry was a man of many resources.

Miss Gambit kept her gaze trained on the fortress that had stood for three centuries. "I cannot help but admire him all the more. He could live in pleasant idleness for the rest of his days, yet he works tirelessly to save the innocent."

A tinge of jealousy unsettled Eli. He wanted to tell her about his benevolent acts, wanted to hear her speak of him with heartfelt admiration.

"Daventry has his reasons. He might have been a dissipated rogue had his father-in-law not saved him from reckless pursuits."

"How interesting. Now he's the saviour." Miss Gambit sat back in the seat and asked the one question Eli had been dreading. "Are your parents alive, Mr Hunter?"

His stomach twisted into knots. Family was a topic he avoided. "My father died four years ago. My mother lives in Chichester."

"Do you have any siblings? I'm an only child myself."

"A brother." A conniving brother he would stab through the heart if their paths crossed again. A brother who would steal the breath from Eli's lungs given half a chance.

"Why do I get the sense he's unlike you in every regard?"

An image of Dominic crashed into Eli's mind. Tall, dark and with an irresistible charm, it was easy to see why women adored him. Some men captivated all those in the room. Some men preferred to linger quietly in the shadows.

"Do you have the ring Daventry gave you?"

"It's safe, Mr Hunter. Have no fear." Miss Gambit clasped her hand to her chest and cast a knowing smile. "But then you knew that and merely sought to change the subject. I'd rather you tell me to mind my own business than ignore me completely."

How could he ignore someone so vivacious? How could he ignore the fact the precious item lay nestled between her breasts?

"I've not spoken to my brother in years and have no desire to revisit the past."

"And yet the past informs everything you do." As they trundled through the barbican, she leant forward to stare at the raised portcullis. "You don't strike me as a man who plans for the future."

Eli didn't bother to tell her she was right, for it would only lead to endless questions, and Leonard Truscott had marched into the small courtyard to greet them. Daventry was always the first to arrive at Trēowith. No doubt the master's absence unsettled Truscott.

"The game is about to begin, Miss Gambit. Truscott has sat on the Council for thirty years and will greet us the moment we alight. He set his sights on becoming master of Themis, but the predecessor awarded Daventry the role."

Miss Gambit sat back and inhaled a calming breath. "Good Lord. My heart is racing so fast I can hardly breathe."

Eli's heart was racing, too. Not because her inexperience might cost him the chance of catching a cunning devil, but because he was crippled with the need to quell her fears.

"You'll need to think quickly when Truscott bombards you with questions."

Her face turned ashen. "As we're partners, I don't mind admitting I'm terrified. Terrified I'll disappoint you. Terrified I'll fail."

"We've sat idle for almost a month waiting for the black-guard to act. If anyone should be afraid, it's me. There's every chance you'll make me look like an incompetent fool."

"Not likely. You're the most astute man I've ever met."

Pride swelled in Eli's chest. "Besides Lucius Daventry."

"Well, one must question if he's mortal."

A sudden rap on the window made Miss Gambit jump.

Eli gritted his teeth. Truscott was annoying at the best of times. The fact Eli distrusted the devil made matters a damn sight worse.

"Be prepared to meet the most arrogant man in England."

"Arrogant? Are all members of Themis not altruists?"

"To some people, good deeds are a means to inflate their egos." Eli opened the carriage door and greeted the grey-haired gentleman.

"Is Daventry with you?" Truscott thrust his head inside the carriage. His eyeballs bulged upon meeting Miss Gambit's curious stare. "No guests allowed, Hunter. You know the rules."

Yes, Truscott was a stickler for regulations.

Miss Gambit flicked her hand at the fellow. "Move away from the door, Mr Truscott, so I may alight."

"Who? What?" The fact she'd used his name confused the man all the more. He fixed Eli to the seat with his irate glare. "Great Father Almighty, where is Daventry? Crocker said there was an intruder. He said someone has stolen the sacred seal."

Miss Gambit shuffled to the edge of the seat. "Settle yourself, Mr Truscott. All will be revealed once we're gathered in the Sanctum. I'll not tolerate council business being discussed in such a slapdash manner. Now step aside."

Truscott practically stumbled back in shock. Eli jumped to the ground, lowered the steps and assisted Miss Gambit's descent into the courtyard.

The lady brushed the creases from her skirt. "Lead the way, Mr Hunter." When Truscott opened his mouth to protest, Miss Gambit raised a staying hand. "Not until we're inside, Mr Truscott."

Eli suppressed a grin.

At this rate, she'd have the Council on their knees.

After offering a disgruntled mumble, Truscott followed behind like a sullen child. He shuffled impatiently while Eli introduced Miss Gambit to Mrs Gale, the forty-year-old housekeeper whose unruly red hair made her seem like a woman with wicked intentions. Mrs Gale had worked at Trēowith for ten years, since the previous master saved her from the hangman's noose.

"And you require a room, Miss Gambit?" Mrs Gale seemed puzzled. In all her years of service, she had never welcomed a woman at Trēowith.

"That's correct, Mrs Gale. I shall stay in Mr Daventry's room." She beckoned Truscott forward. "I would have preferred to discuss the matter in the privacy of the Sanctum.

But you should both know, Mr Daventry has taken ill and appointed me to act in his absence."

"You!" Truscott's cheeks ballooned. "But that's preposterous! No! This is outrageous!" He stamped his foot, never thought to ask after Daventry's health. "Good God, Hunter. Tell me you disagree with this nonsense."

"Daventry summoned me to his bedside so I might bear witness to Miss Gambit's appointment and support the motion. She carries the ring, has a signed letter from Lucius Daventry stating his intention."

Upon hearing the commotion, Swanson, Young and Cantrell came striding out of the drawing room. One look at Miss Gambit brought them all to a crashing halt. They might have gawped less if they'd seen a ghost.

"What the devil's going on, Hunter? And what's happened to the seal?" Giles Cantrell wore a stern expression. A distinguished man of middling years with hair as dark as night, he had the profile of a ruthless Roman emperor. "Where's Daventry?"

"*She's* taken his place." Truscott thrust a finger at Miss Gambit. "Have you ever heard anything so absurd? A woman has never sat on the Council and never will! By Jove, this is sheer lunacy."

Guy Young was the calm voice of reason. "I think it only fair we hear what the lady has to say." He brushed his hand through his golden-brown hair and smiled at Miss Gambit. "Perhaps there's been a misunderstanding."

Miss Gambit straightened. "There is no misunderstanding, Mr Young." Clever. She had remembered Eli's detailed descriptions of the men and sought to use it to her advantage. "Once we've gathered in the Sanctum, you shall all be party to the facts."

Truscott threw his hands in the air. "The Sanctum is a sacred—"

"Silence!" Miss Gambit spoke with Daventry's

commanding tone. "You will follow me to the Sanctum, Mr Truscott, or you will leave Trēowith and forfeit your position on the Council."

Ambrose Swanson cleared his throat. "All council members must vote to remove a colleague, madam. It's written in Themis' constitution."

Miss Gambit grinned like a confident Boudicea staring down the enemy. "Do you have a copy of the constitution to hand, Mr Swanson?"

"No, madam."

Desperate to prove his case, Truscott hurried to the drawing room and returned with his copy of the blue book. "Here we are, madam." He waved it in Miss Gambit's face.

Eli's temper flared. He snatched the book, shot the man a menacing glare before handing it to Miss Gambit.

"Thank you, Mr Hunter." She flicked through the pages and then offered Swanson the open book. "Article twenty states, should a member use forceful means to overthrow the master, he will be immediately discharged from his position. I consider Mr Truscott's manner aggressive, don't you?"

Swanson studied the relevant article. "Yes, you're correct, madam. But being concerned is not being aggressive."

"You can't be the master," Truscott countered. "You're a woman."

Miss Gambit ignored him. "And if you skip three pages, Mr Swanson, you will see the rule explaining that, in extreme circumstances, the master may appoint someone to act in his stead. Only one member need agree. That member is Mr Hunter."

Eli had held his tongue for long enough. If it wasn't for Miss Gambit's need to prove her worth, he'd have ripped these men to shreds minutes ago.

"You will support Miss Gambit in her temporary role, or there'll be hell to pay. There's a reason Daventry appointed her, so I suggest we move to the Sanctum and discuss the matter there."

"Nowhere in the constitution does it state the replacement must be a man," Miss Gambit pressed. "Indeed, Mr Daventry asked me to draw your attention to one of Themis' journals from 1654. Mrs Sowerby sat on the Council for two weeks while her husband was incapacitated."

It was a blatant lie, but no one argued. Not even Truscott. Having proved she understood every article in the constitution, no one dared challenge Miss Gambit's word.

And so it was the ever graceful Young who inclined his head and said, "Then let us proceed to the tunnels. No doubt we're all eager to hear the reason behind this unconventional appointment."

Eli waited until the men charged ahead before addressing Miss Gambit. "You were superb." He placed a light hand on her back, a gesture of camaraderie. "Don't be fooled by Young's charming manner. Any one of them could be the traitor."

"Knowing I had your support made the task considerably easier." Miss Gambit leant closer. "They say charming men often have something to hide. I prefer the brooding type myself."

The minx was teasing him.

What would she make of his brother Dominic?

Would she see disloyalty hiding in his charming smile?

"Expect a host of objections when they discover why you're here."

Miss Gambit's hand fluttered to her throat. "If you sense I'm faltering, find an excuse to end the meeting swiftly."

"Of course, but I believe you'll manage perfectly well."

He led her through the entrance hall. With its dark oak stairs, gothic fireplace and array of weapons displayed on the wall, the room was reminiscent of a scene from the Dark Ages.

The tunnels were accessed through a wrought-iron gate at the rear of the property. The men had unlocked the door and disappeared down the flight of stone steps.

Eli was set to follow, but Miss Gambit froze at the threshold.

"The tunnels are so narrow, so dark." She peered into the passage, clutched her throat and gasped for breath. "Must we go down there? Can we not hold the meeting in the drawing room?"

"Daventry insists on holding the meetings in the Sanctum. We don't want to make matters worse by challenging the status quo."

In a panic, she gripped his arm. "Mr Hunter, I'm likely to suffer a fit of hysteria if I venture below ground. It's not the dark, you understand. Jacob Hanaway drugged me with laudanum and left me in a homemade coffin in the cellar."

A vision burst into Eli's mind—a young girl tormented by two cowardly bullies. When the case was over, Eli would hunt them down and deliver a fitting punishment.

"You've done remarkably well so far." He cupped her cheek—a gentle caress to calm her volatile spirit—but the need to protect her raged inside. "You must conquer your fears. We cannot turn back now. Trust me. I'll keep a firm hold of your hand until we're near the Sanctum."

"Promise you won't let go."

"You have my word."

She closed her eyes briefly and released a sigh. "Very well."

Eli gripped her hand. "Crocker will have lit the wall sconces. There'll be no scrambling around in the dark. No lingering. The men will have used their keys to access the Sanctum."

He led her down the stone steps into the spooky subterranean passageways, where insects and spiders skittered across the limestone walls. Eli had no fear of enclosed spaces, but the mere touch of her hand had his blood pumping rapidly through his veins.

"Is it far?" Miss Gambit clutched him tightly. She kept one hand on his shoulder as she shuffled tentatively behind.

"We take a left turn at the end of this corridor. The Sanctum is along the next passage."

"Hurry," she whispered, her breathing ragged.

Eli quickened his pace. Had the tunnels been wider, he would have hauled her into his arms and carried her to the Sanctum.

Crocker stood guard outside the Sanctum door. At a towering six feet four and with shoulders twice the width of an average man, he cut a menacing figure. He gave no indication he was shocked to see a woman in the tunnels.

One question entered Eli's mind as he released Miss Gambit's hand and introduced her to the custodian. Had Crocker chased an intruder, or had he lied and was an accomplice in the theft?

"Daventry's taken ill. He's appointed Miss Gambit to act as master in his absence. It's unconventional, I know, but she has the skills required to assist us with our dilemma."

Crocker inclined his head respectfully. "I serve the master, Miss Gambit, and am at your disposal."

"That's good to hear, Mr Crocker." Miss Gambit smiled at the rugged hulk of a man whose bald head shone in the candlelight. "I wish to discuss the theft of the seal at your earliest convenience."

Crocker held a stone-like expression. "I seek to serve whenever called upon, ma'am."

Miss Gambit nodded. "Then might you show me how members access the Sanctum, Mr Crocker?"

The man stepped aside to reveal a small metal panel in the wall. He gestured to the two keyholes. "Two members must insert their keys and turn them simultaneously. You'll find another panel on the gate leading to the tunnels."

"Or one member in possession of two keys may undertake the procedure," she suggested. "I believe someone has recently stolen Mr Swanson's key."

"Yes, ma'am."

"Has he received a replacement?"

"The keys are unique, ma'am, and cannot be copied. Two new mechanisms are being made, and all members will receive keys. In the meantime, I patrol the tunnels every half hour."

"And what happens when you sleep?"

"Mrs Gale checks the outside gate is locked."

"I see." Miss Gambit gestured to the open door leading to the underground room. "Shall we see what Mr Swanson has to say about his stolen key, Mr Hunter? Let's hope he has a convincing explanation."

She bit down on her bottom lip—the same telltale sign of nerves he'd seen when she took to the Dark Walk at Vauxhall. While he admired her strength in the face of adversity, these rare glimpses of vulnerability drew him like a moth to a flame.

One thing was certain.

The closer he got, the more likely he'd get burnt.

# CHAPTER 7

THE SANCTUM WAS A CRYPT, an underground chamber with a vaulted ceiling and more than enough space for Rachel to breathe. Bookcases filled with leather-bound volumes lined the walls between the arched limestone pillars. Burning braziers and standing candelabra gave the room light, as did the candles in the wrought-iron chandelier. All the men of the Council, bar Mr Hunter, stood behind red velvet chairs positioned around a circular oak table.

"They cannot sit until the master takes her seat." Mr Hunter spoke loud enough for the men to hear. He turned to them. "We must welcome Miss Gambit into the fold. Treat her as we would Lucius Daventry. We must teach her our traditions while she holds this temporary position."

Mr Truscott took to grumbling again until Mr Swanson shot him a warning glare. Still, he couldn't keep his moaning mouth shut. "You say you have Daventry's ring and a letter of recommendation, yet you fail to present both."

"Mr Daventry does not recommend me for the position," Miss Gambit countered. "He demands I stand in his stead. As for proof, you will have it once we're seated."

Mr Hunter stepped forward and drew out the porter chair. "This is your seat, Miss Gambit."

He kept an impassive expression, but his eyes told a different story. Like inviting blue pools in the height of summer, they swam with compassion, perhaps admiration, too. It was a look that warmed her insides. A tender look she'd witnessed when he'd cupped her cheek and assured her she could place her faith in his character.

"Thank you, Mr Hunter."

The men waited for her to sit and then followed suit.

"You ask for proof of Mr Daventry's intention—"

Mr Hunter coughed into his fist to stall her. "Forgive me. But we must perform the pledge before we begin."

"Pledge?" Rachel frowned. Was it an initiation? Was she expected to draw a blade across her palm and share her brethren's blood? "There was no mention of it in the constitution."

Mr Young spoke up. "It was introduced in the seventeenth century. It's a simple practice of sharing wine before we delve into serious matters. A means to cement the bonds of brotherhood."

Was this why Mr Hunter needed a woman who could think while slightly sotted? Surely she need only sip the wine.

"As I sit in Mr Daventry's stead, you must consider me a brother."

Mr Truscott was like a snake rising from a basket, ready to lunge at its prey. "You can't take the oath."

"If she's taking Daventry's seat, she must repeat the pledge." Mr Young stared through compassionate eyes. The man's face held a childlike innocence so opposed to his muscular frame.

"I agree," Mr Cantrell said, though it was clear he thought it an opportunity to prove her weak. "If she sits in the master's seat, she must follow tradition."

Mr Hunter jumped to her defence. "Gentlemen, Miss

Gambit is here because she has the skills to assist us, not because she knows how to take her wine. She has my full support. Daventry would expect those loyal to the cause to respect his decision."

Mr Hunter's earnest plea brought a lump to Rachel's throat. It left her wondering about the woman who had hurt him. A woman who placed no value on a man so loyal and steadfast. Whoever she was, she had no sense of his worth.

"I shall take the wine and repeat the pledge," she insisted. "Afterwards, I shall hear no more about my suitability for the position."

Mr Crocker entered and took a silver tray laden with six silver goblets from a stone bench near the door. He circled the table, placing a goblet at each setting. His expression changed when he reached Mr Swanson. Indifference became a shadow of mistrust. He left the room, returned with a crystal decanter full of wine, and proceeded to pour.

"It's customary for the master to recite the oath." With his brows knitted in a permanent frown, Mr Swanson appeared constantly annoyed. "But as we've already broken with tradition, I suppose I can perform the task."

"The pledge is a Bible quote from Amos. Also introduced in the seventeenth century." Mr Hunter met her gaze and gave a covert quirk of his brow. "A quote about justice and human decency."

Rachel smiled. There was no man she'd rather have as her ally. "Then I believe I know the pledge. Do we raise our glasses?"

"You repeat the pledge, then we drain our wine goblets."

Rachel gripped the stem and pulled the goblet closer, hoping to note just a mouthful of wine, not see it swimming close to the rim.

All the men stood, prompting Rachel to follow. She raised her goblet and recited what she hoped was the right verse.

"Let justice roll on like a river, righteousness like a never-failing stream."

Mr Truscott gritted his teeth in displeasure, then downed his wine as if plagued by an uncontrollable thirst. The other men followed suit, then waited for Rachel to comply.

She drained the goblet. Heat coated her throat and windpipe, the fruity aroma doing little to temper its potency.

"There we have it, gentlemen." She pasted a confident smile. "The pledge is made, and so let us move promptly to the reason I'm here." She paused for dramatic effect. "Someone at this table broke into this room and stole the sacred seal."

Tension thrummed in the air like the prelude to a storm.

Beneath the table, Mr Hunter tapped her foot and drew her attention to the ornate wooden plaque on the far wall. The centrepiece was missing.

Rachel told the men to sit. She walked over to the plaque and pointed to the empty space. "The seal stands for all those men who've gone before you. Men who sacrificed their lives for the welfare of this country. The theft is tantamount to treason. Treason against your brethren. Treason against Themis."

Distrustful gazes crept towards Mr Swanson.

The man raised his hands in mock surrender. "My ancestors have served Themis for two hundred years. The villain drugged my wine, I tell you! He entered my bedchamber and stole my key. Not a pouch of coins nor my silver card case, but a useless key, useless to anyone other than the men here today." He thumped his fist on the table. "For the love of God, I'm innocent."

Rachel thought he protested too much. "There are two possibilities." There were likely more than two, but they were her focus until they uncovered more information. "One of you stole the seal, or two of you stole it. Either way, the guilty person is currently looking me in the eye."

"And what do you propose to do about it?" Mr Truscott snapped.

"Rest assured, Mr Truscott. I believe Mr Swanson's story. Someone entered his bedchamber." It was a complete fabrication, but she wished to unsettle them further. "A witness came forward to confirm his claim."

Mr Swanson raised a brow in surprise. "They did? Thank the Lord."

"You're not off the hook, Mr Swanson. You may have planned it that way. Currently, all members of the Council are suspects."

Mr Hunter drew his brows together. "Including Lucius Daventry?"

"Indeed. We cannot rule out the possibility that Mr Daventry is involved." She ignored the incredulous gasps emanating from those seated around the table. Mr Daventry expected her to solve the case and would understand why she'd named him. "Perhaps he appointed me as temporary master because he knew you'd be unhelpful. I don't believe it, but if I'm to determine the truth, I must remain impartial."

A heavy silence descended.

It was then the effects of the wine took hold. Her head felt a little fuzzy, and the room swayed back and forth like a sapling in the breeze. Rachel returned to her seat, hoping the sensations would pass.

She reached for her satchel. "Here's the proof you requested, confirmation of my appointment." She handed the letter to Mr Hunter. Concern lingered in his vibrant eyes as he scanned her face. "If you will excuse me, gentlemen, I need privacy if I'm to retrieve the ring."

Rachel gripped the gilt arm of the chair and stood. The room whirled, but she gathered her composure and reluctantly retreated to the stifling tunnel.

Mr Crocker stood statue-like outside the door.

"Might you turn your back, Mr Crocker? Just for a moment."

The man instantly obeyed.

Eager to escape the tunnel, she slipped her hand down into the bodice, delved into her loosely tied stays, and removed Mr Daventry's ring. She'd often seen the ring on his finger and presumed the scales of justice engraved into the carnelian stone represented his work in Hart Street.

"You may turn back now, Mr Crocker."

The man obliged without comment. Would Mr Crocker follow her every command? Or was his loyalty to the Order of Themis the reason for his unwavering compliance? Was the man open to bribery? That was the question uppermost in her mind.

The Council members were speaking amongst themselves when she entered, except for Mr Hunter, who sat silently observing his colleagues.

The sight of him alone on the outskirts of this tight-knit group brought a lump to her throat. The need to draw him to her bosom and soothe his woes, to make him smile and laugh and chase away the loneliness proved more compelling than her need to solve this case.

Rachel strode over to Mr Truscott and handed him Lucius Daventry's ring. "The accompanying letter proves I've not stolen the ring, nor have I murdered your master."

"We have no choice but to accept Daventry's request," Mr Cantrell said.

The men took a minute to observe the ring before handing it back. Rachel slid it onto her thumb for safe-keeping.

"Mr Hunter said you gather information, prevent uprisings and assassinations. You work with poor people who've been charged with crimes. You seek to prove their innocence and save them from the hangman's noose."

Mr Young smiled. "We see justice served, Miss Gambit, in

whatever form it takes. These monthly meetings help us determine which cases to take and the level of our involvement. We decide which members in the field will be called upon for their services."

It would be impossible to investigate all the men who served Themis. And so, the obvious place to start was with a list of the most recent cases.

"The theft of the sacred seal takes precedence today," Rachel stated. "We will assemble again tomorrow to discuss prospective new cases. Agreed?"

With obvious annoyance, the men nodded.

"Mr Truscott, tell me about the current cases, those with trials outstanding. Those where you're still gathering information."

Singling out the man would achieve two goals. It would play to his vanity and give her a chance to study him closely.

"You'll need pen and ink, Miss Gambit."

"I have an amazing memory which I'm sure you'll put to the test."

Mr Truscott's arrogant grin said he hoped she'd fall short. "The case for Mary Harcourt is pending. She was a maid in Lord Meyer's household, caught with his wife's stolen jewels under the boards in her attic bedchamber."

"She is awaiting trial in Newgate," Mr Hunter added.

"Can they prove she stole the jewels? Did she not share the room with another maid?" That was usual in most wealthy households.

"Miss Harcourt acted as lady's maid to Lady Meyer and had her own attic room," Mr Truscott informed.

"And what is Mary's plea?"

"She claims she was paid to give birth to Lord Meyer's child. That someone planted the jewels to get rid of her and cast doubt on her word."

Mr Hunter turned to her. "There's no proof there was a child. The servants support the Meyers' version that Miss

81

Harcourt is grasping at any means to prove her innocence. Unless we find evidence to support her claim, she'll hang."

Rachel inwardly seethed. She had been mentally and physically abused by men who would see her in Bedlam before she inherited a penny of their mother's wealth. There'd been no one to turn to for help. This case would allow her to help someone in a similar position.

"I require all documentation relating to the case." Rachel rubbed her temple. Despite the sudden rush of confidence, her head felt woozy. "Have it delivered to my chamber this afternoon."

Mr Hunter stood. "The intruder stole more than the sacred seal. He stole the current case files. Daventry only stores completed files in his underground vault at Bronygarth."

Panic erupted. The men bombarded Mr Hunter with questions. Through the din, Rachel felt the potency of the wine take effect. It didn't help that Mr Crocker stormed into the room, rang a handbell, and then refilled everyone's goblet.

The room quietened.

"At Lucius Daventry's behest, Mr Crocker is charged with keeping proceedings under control." Mr Hunter looked at her through narrowed eyes. "It can get rather hot down here, Miss Gambit. Perhaps we should adjourn the meeting until later this afternoon."

Mr Truscott sneered. "If Miss Gambit is not up to the task, perhaps someone else should take her place. Naturally, as the senior member, I offer my services."

"Perhaps you should focus on which one of your colleagues wishes to bring Themis to its knees, sir, and not your lofty ambitions."

Truscott's cheeks flamed.

Mr Young called for calm and insisted they repeat the pledge. The men scooped up their goblets and looked to her to recite the passage from Amos.

Rachel repeated the oath and was forced to drink more wine.

"You must empty the goblet, Miss Gambit." Mr Truscott grinned as if he'd moved his bishop into checkmate. "Hurry. We'll not wait for you."

Rather than be beaten by an arrogant toad, she drained the contents. By her estimation, she had ten minutes until she turned into a bumbling wreck.

"I'll hear of one more case, and then I shall retire to my room to consider the facts. This evening, I wish to interview you all separately, including Mr Crocker and Mrs Gale." She glanced at Mr Hunter. "I shall leave you to make the arrangements."

He nodded. "Of course."

"I'm overseeing a case of treason." Mr Cantrell had the bearing of a war hero. He looked strong, capable, intelligent, a man resistant to displays of emotion. "Our fellow working in the Home Office believes someone is passing government information to the French."

"Do you have any suspects?"

"Not as yet." Mr Cantrell moved the conversation to the other men in the room. "Young and Swanson are working together. A youth is charged with murdering his stepfather inside Belton's Emporium though the boy claims the owner killed the man by driving a longsword into his chest. The owner then locked the boy in the pantry."

Young and Swanson. Two men working together on one case.

Two men needed to open the Sanctum.

Was it a coincidence?

Mr Young sat forward. "Has the thief stolen our files, too?"

"I'm afraid so." Mr Hunter's face was like a slab of granite, all rigid angles and strong lines. If he believed Mr Young was guilty of conspiracy, he gave no indication. "I suggest you spend a few hours noting all you can remember of the case, and we'll confer later this afternoon."

A sudden burst of energy had Rachel pushing out of her seat before she engaged her brain. The wine's potency had taken command of her senses. The urge to laugh at these men and make fun of their stern faces meant it was time to bring the meeting to an end.

"I shall take some time to contemplate what I've learnt so far." Her tongue felt thick in her mouth. Soon she would start slurring. "Then I shall meet with you all individually." She turned to the indomitable Mr Hunter and ignored the childish impulse to run her hands over his broad chest, tickle him and make him laugh. "Is there a parting ceremony?"

"We drink and repeat the oath."

Merciful Mother! She wished she'd not asked.

On cue, Mr Crocker entered and set about filling the goblets. The men looked unimpressed that the meeting had ended so abruptly. But she couldn't worry about that now. In a matter of minutes, she'd become a bumbling fool. They would oust her from her position on the Council and demand Daventry choose someone suitable.

Rachel recited the oath, downed the wine, and waited for the men to leave.

Mr Hunter was at her side in seconds. "You've drunk far too much." He kept his voice low. "You'll need a few hours rest to recuperate."

The room spun.

Rachel swayed.

She slung her satchel across her body, placed a steadying hand on Mr Hunter's firm shoulder. "I've never tasted wine so strong." A laugh escaped her. "Forgive me if I say anything untoward. I fear I am losing all grip on reality."

Muttering a curse, he clasped her elbow. "Damnation. We can't let them see you like this."

Too much wine seduced the senses. Perhaps that's why

she reached up and brushed her hand through Mr Hunter's thick hair. Perhaps that's why she gave a coy smile, why her voice turned husky.

"There's only one solution, Mr Hunter."

"Thrust your head into the horse trough?"

The comment brought a frightful image of Jacob Hanaway to mind.

"No. You'll have to take me to bed."

# CHAPTER 8

*TAKE ME TO BED.*

The words replayed in Eli's mind as he escorted Miss Gambit along the dimly lit tunnels. This time she didn't walk behind, gripping his shoulder, maintaining some distance. He might have coped with that. No. The woman wound her arms around his waist and snuggled into him as he helped her navigate the subterranean passageways.

"You smell divine, Mr Hunter." Miss Gambit spoke in the arousing voice of a woman in her cups. She pressed her nose to his neck and inhaled deeply. "It strokes the senses like a lover's sweet caress."

*Dear God!*

Eli cleared his throat. "It's just cologne. Let's concentrate on getting you upstairs without Truscott pointing the finger and calling you a drunkard."

"Hmm. You smell good enough to eat."

*Lord almighty!*

"The drink is taking effect, Miss Gambit. Might I suggest you concentrate on placing one foot in front of the other and resist the temptation to spout nonsense?" He should have insisted Crocker pour her half measures, but it would have drawn attention to her weaknesses.

"It's not nonsense." The lady brought them to an abrupt halt. "Even after downing three goblets of wine, I speak the truth." She swayed as she glanced up at the low ceiling, remembered they were in a confined space and panicked. "Oh, I need air!"

She gathered her skirts and took to her heels before Eli had time to react. He chased after her, watched her trip up the stone steps and scramble on her hands and knees into the rear courtyard.

Clasping her elbow firmly, he hauled her to her feet.

Her fear turned to frustration. "Oh, if there's justice in the world, Jacob Hanaway would spend the rest of his days on a prison hulk. Perhaps I could drug him with laudanum and bundle him into a crate bound for India."

"Vengeance is a fool's game. It won't bring peace." They were Daventry's words, not Eli's. Every night, in those quiet moments before sleep, he prayed fate served his brother a hearty dish of comeuppance.

"What would bring you peace, sir?" Possessed by a sudden playful manner, the lady gripped him by the upper arms, her dainty hands wrapping around his biceps. "Tell me, and I shall do everything in my power to fulfil your desires."

*God's teeth!*

"Let's have this conversation when you're sober, madam. In the meantime, I shall rest easy once you're safe in your room."

"Yes, you're supposed to be taking me to bed." She grabbed his hand and pulled him towards the house as if she might ravish him once she had him alone upstairs.

Blood raced to Eli's loins. Still, he managed to bundle her up the servants' stairs and usher her into the bedchamber. Relieved they'd avoided an altercation with Truscott, he scanned the corridor, promptly closed the door and turned the key in the lock.

He faced the only woman who unnerved him, expecting to find her comatose, sprawled on the red counterpane like a sumptuous feast, tempting him to gorge on every morsel. Her discarded satchel lay on the bed, but Miss Gambit had taken to dancing about the room, humming a waltz.

"This chamber is fit for a queen." Her wide eyes took in the vast tapestries hanging on the red papered walls. "Do you dance, Mr Hunter?"

"No." He'd not danced in years and had no intention of doing so now. Still, that didn't stop him devouring the scene before him. "Serious men solve problems. They drink to numb emotions. They do not prance about like popinjays because it's the only way they'll ever hold a woman."

Eli had not taken a woman in his arms since that fateful night three years ago. Had not even considered it until now.

"People say dancing is a prelude to seduction."

Like the temptress Delilah, Miss Gambit was determined to steal his strength. She pulled pins from her hair, scattering them on the floor as she twirled about the room. The sight stirred something deep inside. A longing to escape the ropes of restraint. A craving to break free. But the need to protect his heart, to ensure he never again felt the bitter taste of betrayal, was the reason he retreated to his inner sanctum.

"You're an agent of the Order, Miss Gambit. I suggest you start acting like one." The words sounded sharper than he'd intended.

Had she been in full command of her faculties, she would have offered a witty retort, the sort of set down that made her so appealing. But the lady swept towards him and captured his hands.

"Come dance with me, Mr Hunter. You owe me a waltz after the terrible way you treated me at Vauxhall."

"Madam, I rescued you from the clutches of scoundrels,

near broke my back carrying you the length of the Hermits Walk." He tugged his hands free, though the devil on his shoulder begged him to pull her closer. "I would hardly call that unfair treatment."

Dizzy and drunk, Miss Gambit stumbled.

Eli caught her, his arm snaking around her back before his mind engaged.

The lady laughed as she shook her golden locks free, transforming into an enticing vision that would leave any man wanting.

She wrapped her arms around his neck, pressed her luscious body to his and moved as if an arousing melody breezed through the room.

"So you do dance, sir. Very well, I might add."

He rocked against her like a man intoxicated. Intoxicated by the seductive sway of her hips. Intoxicated by the playful glint in her eyes.

He pictured Lucius Daventry watching from the shadows. Perhaps he'd stolen the damn seal just to prove there was a woman in the world who could tempt Eli. And by God, Miss Gambit would tempt the Lord to sin.

"I'm not dancing, madam. I'm preventing you from falling."

"Always the gentleman, Mr Hunter." She reached up and brushed an errant lock of hair from his brow. "Will you assist me while I cast up my accounts? Will you carry me to bed and tuck me in, sir?"

"My only focus is catching the traitor," he lied. At the present moment, he could think about nothing but how glorious it felt to hold her in his arms. "I need you sober. I'll do whatever it takes to accomplish the task."

"You were supposed to teach me to take my drink." She fixed him with a brilliant blue stare as if it were the only way to stop the room spinning.

"I hadn't planned on bringing you here so soon."

"What changed?"

"You seemed competent enough to start immediately." He couldn't tell her that an inner force had taken command of his senses. That for some illogical reason, he'd wanted to keep her locked in his bedchamber, keep her close. "This is a minor setback, but you should recover in a few hours."

A playful laugh escaped her. "Dancing will get the blood flowing and speed up the process. Let me teach you to waltz."

It was drunken bravado. She could barely move her feet without falling.

"I can dance, Miss Gambit. I simply choose to refrain."

"You're dancing now." She looked down at their feet, lost her balance, and collapsed into him.

It was time to bring an end to this nonsense—his restraint was hanging by the thinnest thread—and so he scooped her into his arms. "Time to rest your muddled head. You'll sleep off the effects for an hour or two."

She didn't object when he carried her to the mahogany four-poster. Yet she kept her arms linked around his neck as he lowered her down onto the mattress. Eli waited for her to release him, but she pulled him closer.

Golden locks spilled over the pillow. Her cheeks were rosy, her eyes glazed, her lips the purest pink. The lady looked like a Renaissance painting, a breathtaking symbol of hope and rebirth.

"You're very kind to me, Mr Hunter," she drawled. "You behave just like a man should. Noble. Dignified."

There was nothing noble about the tightening in his abdomen.

There was nothing dignified about his lascivious thoughts.

"I swore to keep you safe. Gave Daventry my word." He reached for her hands, but they were locked tightly around his neck.

"I like you, Mr Hunter." Her warm breath caressed his cheek. "Shush. Don't tell anyone, but I made an oath, too."

"To protect me, I know."

She chuckled. "No, to free you from your prison."

"I don't need rescuing. I'm happy behind bars." He was happiest when keeping everyone out. "I don't want you to like me. I don't need anyone to like me."

"Then what a terrible inconvenience. I like you immensely."

"Rest now." Their gazes locked. Lust shot through him like a bolt from the heavens. He had to get out of the room, slow his heart, catch his breath.

"Wake me in an hour."

Without warning, she reached up and pressed her lips to his. He should have pulled away—he was not the sort to take advantage of any woman, let alone one in her cups—but every traitorous muscle in his body held him rigid.

The gentle brush of their lips became one slow, open-mouthed kiss. A tantalising melding that only intensified the inner ache. Then she released him, flopped back onto the pillow, and drifted into a peaceful slumber.

Eli stood fighting the violent rage of emotions, beating them back behind the barricade. Damn Lucius Daventry. He'd sent the devil's disciple, not an enquiry agent. Sent a woman who made him want and desire, left him ravaged with need.

He backed away from the sleeping beauty in the bed. Took to pacing the room to quell the tumult within. But she was everywhere. In his thoughts, on his lips, his skin.

It occurred to him there was a way to calm the tempest.

He'd take his frustrations out on the bloody Council.

●

Eli left the room and locked the door. He made his way back to the tunnels, found Crocker clearing away the goblets and straightening the chairs.

"Miss Gambit is resting but wishes me to ask a few questions."

"I told you everything when you came three weeks ago."

"I'm merely following the master's orders," Eli said by way of an excuse, for he wished to check for cracks in Crocker's story. "Is possible to duplicate a key?"

Crocker withdrew his handkerchief and mopped sweat from his brow. "Every key can be copied. But a master locksmith would have trouble duplicating those keys."

"Because of the indents along the shank?"

"It takes expert precision to align the markings, but it's not impossible. That's why Mr Daventry insists the lock is changed yearly. It was last replaced in December."

Eli knew the answer to his next question but sought confirmation. "And there's no possible way the doors were left open?"

A muscle in Crocker's cheek twitched. "All doors were locked. Mrs Gale noticed the entrance to the tunnel was open. The cloaked intruder hid in the Sanctum. When I entered, he made a dash for the tunnels and slammed the Sanctum door shut."

"Effectively locking you inside the chamber."

"By the time I'd activated the switch to override the lock, the scoundrel had fled. I roused every member of staff, scoured the gardens and surrounding land. There was no sign of him, but he'd dropped the coded letter on the gravel path."

"You're certain the thief was a man?"

Crocker shrugged. "It was dark. He hid behind the hood of a cloak. But it had to be a council member in possession of two keys."

"And if you had to pick a traitor out of all those on the Council, who would you choose?" Eli suspected Swanson or Truscott. Did the latter make a fuss merely to disguise his guilt?

"I'm paid to guard the Sanctum, not play constable."

"Miss Gambit will insist on a name."

"Then Miss Gambit must ask me the question." Crocker moved to the entrance and scanned the tunnel before adding, "When he left, Truscott said he suspects you're involved. He said a man willing to take orders from a woman is no man at all."

Eli's blood boiled. He'd put up with Truscott's pomposity for far too long. The man had served Themis for three decades, but Eli prayed the boasting buffoon was the traitor.

"Then I shall make sure Truscott is the next person I question."

Eli left Crocker to his work and entered the house in search of the fool. He marched into the drawing room and found Truscott and Cantrell lounging on the sofa, drinking brandy.

"You should be ashamed of yourself." Eli unleashed his anger at Truscott. "You've served Themis for thirty years, yet you behaved like a pathetic boy in the schoolroom today."

Truscott stared down his nose. "As you rightly said, I serve Themis. Someone is out to destroy our organisation, and Daventry's only defence is to send a damn woman."

"Miss Gambit is a skilled enquiry agent with a memory better than a seasoned academic. She's currently studying the coded letter dropped by the intruder." The lie was necessary, for it allowed Eli to gauge Truscott's reaction.

Cantrell sat forward. "The intruder left a clue to his identity?"

"More than a clue. I believe it's a coded list of instructions written by a council member, detailing what items to steal from the Sanctum."

Out of two hundred volumes lining the bookcases, the intruder knew to find the false frontage, knew the position of the latch, knew to take the portfolio containing details of their latest cases.

"When Miss Gambit breaks the code, we'll have an idea

who was behind the theft." Using the lady as bait was a risk. But there was no other way to lure the devil out of the darkness. It was Eli's job to play protector.

"It's clear to see why you have no objection to her appointment," came Truscott's snide remark. "Either you find yourself captivated, or you're the intruder trying to keep one step ahead."

Eli remained calm. "They say those quick to point the finger elsewhere are merely disguising their own guilt." He longed for the day Truscott proved unworthy. "You're overseeing Mary Harcourt's case. Stop behaving like a petulant child and do something useful. Surely you have new evidence to impart."

Embarrassment stained Truscott's cheeks. "Yes, there's new evidence. The girl demanded a physician examine her to confirm she's given birth to a child. Lord Meyer's council brought evidence proving Mary and a footman had intimate relations. The footman stated that Mary stole the jewels because she was trying to persuade him to leave his position and flee London."

"The footman still works for Lord Meyer, I assume." Had the Lord forced the servant to make a confession? "I need his name."

"James Tinsley. He's worked for Lord Meyer for three years."

"Then he has every reason to lie."

"As the evidence mounts, it's becoming increasingly difficult to believe Mary's story," Cantrell offered.

It was an odd remark. They never accepted a case without being assured of the condemned person's innocence. Why doubt Mary now?

"And Lord Meyer knows nothing of our involvement?" Eli asked. The men of Themis kept to the shadows, helped behind the scenes, but someone had turned traitor. Had the devil approached Meyer and offered his services?

"I serve Themis, not a pompous aristocrat," Cantrell countered. "Just in case you're in any doubt."

Eli gave a curt nod. "Has anyone investigated the servants who work for the Meyers?" If they were loyal enough to lie, they were loyal enough to hide a baby.

"The servants come from all corners of the country." Truscott sounded defensive. "The housekeeper and the butler hail from London, but they've no family to speak of. Lady Meyer is with child, which negates Mary Harcourt's claim that the woman is barren."

Loathe to admit it, Cantrell was right. Mary would likely hang for theft unless someone could prove the Meyers were lying.

"Has Lady Meyer been examined by a physician?"

"Yes, in Brighton. Lady Meyer saw the family physician whilst visiting her mother. Considering the nature of the case, I've written to the doctor asking he provide written proof of her condition."

Eli rubbed his jaw while contemplating the dilemma.

Despite the evidence, every instinct said Mary Harcourt had been manipulated and used diabolically. Or was it that Eli had such little faith in people, he expected all peers were lying leeches.

"Miss Gambit will want to investigate the Meyers herself." Eli observed both men's reactions. Cantrell gave nothing away. Truscott wore his usual contemptuous sneer. "Daventry ordered her to look at all recent cases."

"Then we'll assist her in any way we can," Cantrell said. "Based on the unusual nature of events, might I suggest we reconvene here next week?"

With luck, they'd have caught the traitor by then. If not, it would provide another opportunity to investigate the Council.

"I shall put your proposal to Miss Gambit. Perhaps then

you might have more information on the traitor in the Home Office."

Cantrell shifted uncomfortably in the seat. The man prided himself on his competence. Hated having nothing new to report.

Eli scanned the drawing room. "Where might I find Young and Swanson?"

"In the dining room, busy making notes for Miss Gambit." Cantrell checked over his shoulder before continuing. "Regardless of a witness coming forward, I cannot credit Swanson's explanation about the stolen key. If I had to point the finger, I'd say Young and Swanson are in cahoots."

Cantrell was quick to cast suspicion elsewhere.

"But Crocker encountered only one intruder in the Sanctum."

"Perhaps the other escaped. Perhaps the men drew sticks, and the loser entered the Sanctum."

"I'm sure Miss Gambit is pondering the possibilities as we speak." In between fidgeting in bed, nibbling her bottom lip and preparing to tempt a confirmed bachelor to sin.

Eli left the men to drink their brandy and whisper behind his back. He found Young and Swanson seated at the long table in the dining room. The fire burning in the stone hearth proved a welcome sight, and so Eli crossed the room and warmed his hands.

"I came seeking respite from Truscott's complaining," Eli grumbled. He would work to create suspicion amongst the men until they caught the person laying siege on Themis. "I find his opinions intolerable."

Ink pen in hand, Young looked up from the sheaf of papers spread over the oak surface. "We swore to follow the constitution," he said in his usual relaxed tone. "But I am surprised at Daventry's decision. Truscott will never tolerate a woman at the helm."

"He has no choice." Eli studied Swanson. Head bowed,

the man continued dipping his nib and scrawling on the paper. "Miss Gambit is a skilled investigator and will find those involved in the theft of the sacred seal."

"For the sake of Themis and the innocent people we protect, I pray she does," Young said. "Can we be of any assistance?" He gestured to the mass of notes. "We're recording everything we can remember about the case at Belton's Emporium, but I cannot see how it's related."

At present, Eli was just as clueless.

Perhaps he should return to London and investigate the cases himself, with Miss Gambit's help, of course. His mind flicked to the woman asleep in bed. A warning voice in his head said he should race upstairs and make sure Truscott wasn't hammering on the chamber door, demanding her presence downstairs. Or worse, the snake in the grass wasn't looking to steal back the coded letter.

"Tell me what evidence there is against the boy who's suspected of killing his stepfather." Eli recalled the youth's name. "David Scrivens. Why would a lanky, fourteen-year-old take on a hulk of a man in his forties?"

Swanson sprinkled pounce over the wet ink, then looked up. "His mother says her husband used to beat the boy. The constable who took him into custody states he had twenty-three bruises on his body. The mother argues her son acted in self-defence."

"And yet Scrivens argues the shopkeeper locked him in the pantry."

"The boy is innocent," Swanson snapped. He'd first brought the boy's plight to the Council's attention last month. Had already taken witness statements and made a catalogue of notes. "The shopkeeper, Mr Belton, claims Scrivens had a manic episode after his stepfather's angry outburst. He says he wrestled the boy into the pantry for fear he would murder someone else."

"And they were the only customers in the shop," Eli stated.

Swanson nodded. "Belton ran into the street and shouted for a constable. He grabbed a passerby and made him watch over the body while he raced to find help."

"Time is running out," Young said, looking dejected. "The shopkeeper has gained some notoriety. Every person in London considers him a hero. It will take a miracle to save Scrivens. We were hoping to examine the copies of the witness statements again, but they were amongst the case files stolen from the Sanctum."

It made no sense. The person who entered the Sanctum had to be a member of Themis. But why would a once honourable man want to see a boy hanged?

"What's the name of the witness who watched over the body?" Perhaps he killed Scrivens' stepfather, and the shopkeeper helped frame the boy. No. It seemed improbable.

"He's the brother of a baron. The magistrate accepted his account without question." Young rummaged through the papers. "I have his direction here if Miss Gambit wishes to question him. If she can find any cracks in the witness statements, we may get a reprieve."

"Where is the Emporium?"

"Surrey Street. South of the river. Across Blackfriars Bridge." Young handed Eli a sheet of paper. "The witness has a house in Salisbury Square but often retires to his brother's estate in Shoreham."

Shoreham?

Did Miss Gambit not take the stage from Shoreham?

Eli read the name scrawled at the top of the page and jerked his head back in shock. He masked his odd reaction by saying, "Good God, I can barely read your scribble."

Young grinned. "The man's name is Hanaway. Jacob Hanaway."

# CHAPTER 9

THE LIGHT RAP on the bedchamber door woke Rachel from her drunken stupor. She opened her eyes and glanced around the room. The scent of Mr Hunter's cologne lingered in the air, but there was no sign of the beguiling man who'd possessed her dreams.

The caller knocked again before sliding a key into the lock.

Rachel hugged the pillow and feigned sleep. Had she been sober, she would have taken the Skean Dhu from her satchel, for she always slept with a knife close to hand.

Instinct said the person entering the room wasn't Mr Hunter. The footsteps were light, the movements hesitant. Through lowered lids, Rachel scanned her surroundings, looking for the mystery visitor. To her relief, she noted it was Mrs Gale. The housekeeper roamed from corner to corner, conducting a thorough inspection. Perhaps she'd come to ensure the room was satisfactory. That, or she was searching for something important.

But what? The coded letter?

Mrs Gale left as quickly as she came, sneaking out of the room like a thief in the night. Seconds later, muffled voices in the corridor preceded the rattle of another key in the door. Rachel knew to expect Mr Hunter before he burst into the room as if the house were ablaze.

She feigned sleep again, for no other reason than to watch him at her leisure. But he raced to the bed and pressed the pads of his fingers to her throat.

"Miss Gambit." He lifted her lids and stared at her pupils.

Rachel gasped. "What on earth are you doing, sir?"

He must have caught Mrs Gale sneaking out of the room. Did he fear the housekeeper had come to suffocate her while she slept?

"Making sure you're alive."

He could be in no doubt she was breathing. His touch had her pulse thumping so fiercely she could hear the loud drum of her heartbeat. There were pipers as far afield as Skye marching to the rhythm.

"I passed Mrs Gale in the corridor." Concern marred his tone. "Did she enter your room?"

"Yes. She let herself in with a key. I faked sleep and watched her stalk about the place. She touched nothing, took nothing. Perhaps she came to check on the maid's work."

"Perhaps." He sounded doubtful. Wearing a frown of suspicion, he glanced around the room before facing her. "How are you feeling?"

"Much better." She rubbed her temple to ease the ache. "Have no fear. I'll not shame myself by asking you to waltz again."

The memory of him holding her close slipped into her mind.

The memory of that one sweet kiss burst to the fore.

She shot up so quickly the pounding behind her eyes made her wince.

Mr Hunter placed a steadying hand on her arm. "I'd have let you sleep but have important news."

"Before we continue, I must apologise for the way I

behaved earlier." She couldn't concentrate, not when embarrassment consumed her thoughts. Heat rose to her cheeks as she silently practised an apology. "Forgive me if I was a little forward of manner."

Mr Hunter arched his brow in amusement. "There's no danger of anyone calling you a wallflower, Miss Gambit."

She smiled. "No danger at all, sir."

"Does that mean you don't really like me?"

"Oh, I like you immensely. You're exceptional on all levels."

"Always so candid, Miss Gambit." He averted his gaze briefly, a sign emotions swam behind his cool reserve. "While I distrust compliments, I find myself having complete faith in yours. As for being forward, there's no need to apologise for something beyond your control."

"Making you kiss me was wholly inappropriate."

The Latin phrase engraved on his flask sprang to mind. Acts, not words—that was the motto. After her brazen actions, he could be in no doubt she craved his company.

Mr Hunter shrugged. "It wasn't a kiss by the usual standards."

Not a kiss? What in heaven's name did he mean?

"I beg your pardon?" Rachel swung her legs off the bed and stood. Mild cramp left her wriggling her toes in her boots. "I didn't realise there was a list of criteria."

"We brushed lips. We didn't kiss."

"You opened your mouth." She had next to no experience but was certain it qualified. "You moved it against mine, albeit a mere fraction."

"A kiss is an expression of desire, a sign of affection or love. We shared none of those things. You pressed your mouth to mine because you'd downed too much wine. Lust played no part."

Yes, she'd acted on impulse, but there had been an element of affection. And he had definitely kissed her back.

"When you returned this brushing of mouths, Mr Hunter, you were sober. Why reciprocate? Why not call me out for being a drunken harlot?"

He hesitated. "Perhaps I wished to avoid hurting your feelings."

"So you do think I'm a harlot."

"Of course not." He crossed the room to the drinks table and pulled the stopper from a crystal decanter.

Rachel followed him. "Brandy isn't the cure."

"The cure for what?" he said, splashing liquor into a tumbler.

"For the pain. For the emotions raging within."

He cast her a sidelong glance and sipped his drink. "Says the lady who suffers from cramp because she holds herself tense even in her sleep. That's why you're so restless. Perhaps a dose of brandy might help you relax."

"I am relaxed."

A mocking snort escaped him. "Every muscle in your body is strung as tight as a bow. It's as if you're waiting for the Hanaway brothers to come bursting out of the armoire, pistols at the ready."

The mention of those odious men raised her hackles. "After spending years fighting for my sanity, forgive me if I'm a little apprehensive. And you're hardly one to talk. You're like an automaton with a serious drink problem."

"Ah, now we get to the truth. You think I'm a tosspot."

"You think I'm a harlot."

"No, I don't."

"You do."

"If I thought you were a harlot, I wouldn't have hired you." He studied her over the rim of his glass. "Admit you made a mistake. You weren't thinking clearly when you pressed your mouth to mine."

No, she'd lost all rationale. Thoughts had given way to emotions. Logic had played no part in her desire to be close to him. And yet he was determined to prove it meant nothing. Mr Hunter was afraid. Afraid someone would fool him again. Afraid to believe a woman's words and actions.

"I'm not sure you want to hear the truth, sir."

"According to Sophocles, the truth is the strongest argument."

Oh, this man was a living monument to contradiction. "You respect the truth yet resist all efforts to speak it. Tell me who hurt you, and I'll tell you my deepest fears, my darkest secrets."

His resistance to reveal anything about himself was like an iron wall between them. Rachel took a leap of faith and decided to speak first. As a gentleman, he would feel duty-bound to reciprocate.

"The need to protect myself began whilst journeying on *The Canton*." Her chest tightened at the memory. She imagined herself back in the cargo hold, huddled behind tea crates, fearing every creak of the boards brought Mr Purvis. Tears threatened to fall, but she held them at bay.

Mr Hunter gave her his full attention. "Something happened aboard ship?"

"I witnessed Mr Purvis stealing from the passengers. When he caught me watching, he threatened to throw me overboard if I told anyone." Day after day, night after night, the man stalked her, kept her in his sights, grabbed her arm so tightly she had bruises for days. "He made me accept a share of his booty. As his accomplice, I was certain to keep his secret."

Mr Hunter inhaled deeply. "There were few survivors. I pray he perished in the shipwreck."

Rachel clutched her throat as guilt surfaced. "My darkest secret involves what happened to Mr Purvis as *The Canton* went down."

Intrigue flashed in Mr Hunter's striking blue eyes, but he

shook his head and said, "You don't need to explain. Painful memories are best left buried."

"You're wrong. They're more painful when left to fester." She snatched the tumbler from his grasp, swallowed a mouthful of brandy and hissed a breath. "I killed a man, Mr Hunter. While clinging to the wreckage, I bit Mr Purvis' hand when he tried to clamber alongside me. I sunk my teeth into his flesh until I drew blood. I watched him fall into the water, later read that he was named amongst the dead."

Tears filled her eyes. She would likely burn in hell for letting him perish. But the dreadful years spent at Lady Hanaway's home had been more than adequate punishment.

"One could say the storm and the captain's ineptitude killed the man," Mr Hunter assured her. "In the end, it was a fight for survival."

"I'll never forget the look on his face. The fear filling his eyes." Teardrops landed on her cheeks and slid down to wet her lips. "It's why I accepted Mr Daventry's offer to join the Order. If I save a life, surely it will count for something."

Mr Hunter took the glass from her hand and placed it on the silver tray. He drew her into an embrace, stroked her hair. "Had the man been kind to you, you would have saved him."

She had never been held. Never been comforted. Had never felt a soothing touch. Not when being dragged from the sea, a bag of cold, shivering bones. Not after walking seven miles alone on a deserted country road in the dead of night. Not after every harrowing ordeal when she had lain in bed and wept until morning.

"We reap what we sow." Mr Hunter continued whispering words of comfort. "Mr Purvis' case is a classic example. In that respect, he killed himself."

She looked up, met eyes as blue as a glorious summer sky. "I couldn't trust him. He would have let me drown to save himself. Had I helped him, I wouldn't be standing here now. I'd be dead."

"What a travesty that would be. The world needs courageous women. Women willing to stand up for their rights. Women like you."

"Ah, you're a revolutionist, Mr Hunter."

"My father was a military man. He fought many wars abroad, yet the biggest challenges people face are here at home. One might say I followed in his footsteps. I seek to save the lives of my fellow countrymen but not through the spilling of blood."

His eyes brightened when speaking about his father. His voice sang with pride. Was it grief that left him so cold and detached or something else?

"You must miss him dreadfully."

"Everything changed when he died." He stared at nothing, evidently lost in the memory. "I'm a private man, Miss Gambit. What I tell you must remain between us." He could have released her, but he kept his arm around her waist as if needing a crutch.

"Sir, you can trust me to keep your secret." All sadness abandoned her at the prospect of Mr Hunter opening his heart.

His lengthy sigh spoke of untold pain. "Like most men, I lived quite recklessly in my early twenties, kept mistresses, gambled and drank to excess. But my parents urged me to settle down. I was to wed Miss Portland the month my father died. We'd known each other since we were children. It was what our parents wanted, and I believed myself in love with her."

It wasn't the shock of hearing Mr Hunter say he'd loved someone that stole Rachel's breath, but the slither of jealousy coiling inside.

"But you didn't marry?"

"No. Felicity wanted to wait until a suitable mourning period had passed." Contempt marred his tone. "She liked being the focus of everyone's attention."

Rachel hid her surprise. Mr Hunter seemed the sort who despised vanity.

"Did a tragedy befall her?" Had his love died before becoming his wife? "If it's too painful to continue, I understand."

Mr Hunter met her gaze. Hatred turned his blue eyes dark and threatening. "Felicity had another reason to delay. She was in love with my brother Dominic, but they were so scared of my father's reaction they'd kept their love a secret. When he died, they were compelled to act on their desires."

His fiancé loved his brother?

Rachel's heart ached for him. The deceit, the betrayal, was undoubtedly the reason for his cool reserve, his disinterest in forming relationships.

"I'm sorry, Hunter. It must have been so painful to hear their confession." To lose two people he loved in one fell swoop must have hurt deeply.

"They didn't confess. I might have had more respect for them had they sat me down and explained their feelings. I found them together in the orangery." He released her, rubbed his eyes as if desperate to eradicate the harrowing vision. "Making love on the day we should have wed."

He turned away, set about pouring himself another brandy.

Compelled to comfort him, she said, "I'm glad you found them, else you'd be married to a woman who doesn't love you, and you deserve much better than that."

He tossed back the contents of the tumbler and faced her. "I'm glad I found them, too, else I'd be a damn sight more miserable than I am now."

"Is that even possible?"

"Probably not."

"I presume they're still alive."

The corners of his mouth twitched. "I didn't murder them in the orangery if that's what you're suggesting. I left without saying a word, left my family home, left Chichester. I've not spoken to them or been back since. But they're married now and have a child. My mother writes often."

Rachel swallowed past the lump in her throat. "To know one's love is unreciprocated is painful enough. To suffer such a betrayal ... well, I know why you prefer to live alone, work alone."

"It wasn't the love celebrated by poets. It wasn't the love that makes one's heart ache, nor an all-consuming desire that cannot be tempered. In truth, my brother's deceitfulness hurt most."

Rachel doubted a love that powerful existed.

She hoped teasing him would draw him out of the doldrums. "Just like my kiss wasn't a kiss at all. It, too, lacked that special something."

His expression softened. The air between them shifted as if charged by a wild current of energy.

"I lied. The kiss was short but far from lacking. I lied because ... because I felt something. I've felt nothing for so long it caught me off guard."

He'd lied?

He'd appreciated the kiss after all?

The rush of euphoria was impossible to hide. "Without the wine, I would never have been so bold, but I've thought about kissing you since you pinned me to the door in your bedchamber. I like you, Hunter, and have no regrets."

"While I'm in the mood, I'll tell you another secret." He captured her chin, drawing her mouth closer to his. "You failed the test at Vauxhall, not because of your error in the Dark Walk, but because I like you, Miss Gambit. I've liked you from the moment we met."

Excitement fluttered in her belly. "You mean I'm not incompetent?"

"Not in the least. You're the most competent woman I've ever met." The teasing devil drew her mouth closer still. His hot breath breezed over her lips. "But while the kiss proved satisfying, it failed to convey the depth of my desire."

"A kiss should be a true expression of one's feelings."

"Indeed, perhaps we should kiss again." He stroked her jaw, caressed her neck, touched her with a tenderness that belied the dark hunger in his eyes.

"It's the only way to know." Anticipation raced through her body as she came up on her tiptoes.

The first touch of his mouth sent her world spinning. While she found the woody scent of his cologne alluring, breathing in the earthy smell of maleness left her giddy.

The kiss began like the gentle flow of water from a mountain stream. So pure. So natural. Their mouths moved with effortless ease as if Mother Nature had planned this union. But lust's undercurrent ran deep. The first touch of their tongues swept them into a torrent of unbridled passion.

One minute she was taking his tongue deep into her mouth. The next, he'd pressed her back against the drinks table, grinding against her in such a rhythmical fashion there was no question he could dance. But this was by no means a waltz. This was an erotic mating of two eager souls.

"God, I love how you taste." He set his hot mouth to her throat, searing the sensitive spot below her ear. "Does every inch of your skin smell of orange blossom?" He sucked her ear lobe.

Good Lord! His words were like a siren song, alluring, deliciously dangerous.

"Mr Hunter," she panted, clinging to the last threads of sanity. "It's fair to say the kiss revealed the true depth of our feelings. It's fair to say we felt something."

She felt more than something. The hard evidence of his erection was like a steely rod against her thigh. His essence penetrated her reserve to leave her sex pulsing. She was so aroused she was in danger of hiking up her skirts and letting him ravish her senseless.

But that wasn't what affected her most. No. She felt so safe with Mr Hunter she was in fear of losing more than her virginity. She'd likely lose her heart.

"Mr Hunter," she said when he moved to claim her mouth again.

"Forgive me." He pulled back and looked at her beneath heavy lids. "It was supposed to be one kiss, not a rampant prelude to something sinful."

Rachel dabbed her fingers to her brow. "Well, it seems we both passed the test."

"The test?"

"To discover if our harrowing experiences have left us cold."

A confident grin formed. "Trust me, Miss Gambit, you know how to heat a man's blood."

"Likewise," she said but then caught herself. "I mean, you know how to heat a woman's blood." Nerves had her muttering gibberish, and so she returned to the matter of his pressing news. "Now we've established there's no barrier to conveying our emotions, we should concentrate on the case. What is the important news that cannot wait?"

He stepped back, his expression grave. "There's something you need to know before we proceed with our enquiries." His deep tone carried the weight of his burden. "Something that will invariably cause you distress."

Rachel gulped. "Something to do with the case?"

What on earth could it be?

"While you slept, I questioned Truscott about new evidence relating to Mary Harcourt." He told her about Mary's request for an examination and the footman's damning statement. "When I questioned Young and Swanson about their case, they told me the shopkeeper at the emporium dragged a man off the street to act as a witness." He pursed his lips, seemed reluctant to reveal what he'd discovered.

"Yes. Why would I be distressed about that?"

"Because the man's name is Jacob Hanaway."

For a moment, the world stopped spinning on its axis.

"Jacob Hanaway!" The cold hand of fear snaked up Rachel's spine. Nausea roiled in her stomach. She liked to pretend the Hanaways were no longer of this world. That they'd been mauled by wild dogs or killed by a deadly disease. "But that's impossible."

"That's the name written in the notes."

"No! No! There's been a mistake." She started shaking.

Memories flooded her mind. Vile memories. Wretched memories.

She could cope with anything. Anything except facing the Hanaways again.

Good God! Did Mr Daventry know Jacob Hanaway was a witness? Did he not think to warn her?

Mr Hunter captured her trembling hands. "Young doesn't make mistakes. As part of our ongoing investigation, we'll need to interview the witnesses."

Interview Jacob Hanaway?

Never!

"Then you'll have to speak to Mr Daventry and hire another agent." The urgent need to flee left her shuffling her feet. The need to put a thousand miles between her and talk of the Hanaways saw her tug her hands from Mr Hunter's grasp.

"There's nothing to fear with me by your side."

"You don't understand, Hunter. A meeting between the Hanaways and me won't end well. They'll hunt me down, find out where I live. I'll not spend the rest of my life looking over my shoulder."

"Surely they've outgrown their evil games."

"Their need to see me dead or in Bedlam is not a game. On my twenty-fifth birthday, I inherit twenty thousand pounds from Lady Hanaway. Should I perish or be declared of unsound mind before November, the money returns to the estate."

It was yet another reason why she'd joined the Order. If she could survive until then, the money would pay for a new life in the Americas.

"You can't hide forever. Jacob Hanaway has a house in town. You could run into him on any street corner." His tone was a mix of compassion and frustration. "Let me help you deal with the matter, once and for all."

"Deal with the matter?" Unease clawed at her shoulders. "The only way to deal with the matter is to murder them both."

"If it's a case of self-defence, I'll do whatever's necessary."

Rachel considered this masterful man, with his chiselled jaw and dangerous eyes. With the physique of a gladiatorial champion, he was more than a match for the portly Jacob Hanaway.

"I'd like to hear what you think we should do next." He gestured to the chairs positioned around the fire. "I have a plan and hope you're of a similar mind."

Welcoming the distraction, she crossed the room and sat down.

"Mr Daventry suggested we interrogate the Council at length, but I disagree." She doubted a man of Themis would confess to being a traitor. "We must focus on a motive. Why would a council member betray his brethren?"

"Because he's being blackmailed."

"It's the only logical explanation," she agreed, trying not to stare at his muscular thighs as he sat open-legged in the chair opposite. "And the best way to get to the truth is for us to investigate Lord Meyer and the shopkeeper from the emporium."

A devilish smile crept over his face. "Agreed. I suggest we leave immediately. It will send the villain into a panic. And there's nothing more to be done here."

Rachel wondered if Mr Hunter had another reason for wanting to leave so abruptly. Did he regret the kiss and long for a distraction? Did he fear for her life? He'd raced into the bedchamber as if expecting to find her as cold as a cadaver on a mortuary slab.

"What about interviewing Mr Crocker? And should I not at least hear Mr Swanson's version of how someone stole his key?"

Mr Hunter shrugged. "As we don't know the identity of the villain, we can't know who's lying and who's telling the truth."

"So we leave for London and focus on two suspects. Is Lord Meyer lying?" Had he fathered a child with Mary Harcourt? They'd need to confront the lord, question his staff. "Did the shopkeeper really lock the boy in the pantry, or did he have a reason to murder the victim?"

It occurred to her that leaving for London meant residing in Mr Hunter's home. After sharing such a passionate kiss, how would they fare living under the same roof? Would Mr Hunter retreat to his lair, the dark, forbidden place where he prowled semi-naked? Would he subject her to more tests, where she had to resist the urge to kiss him again?

A lady could live in hope.

# CHAPTER 10

THREE DAYS HAD PASSED since they'd left the disgruntled council members at Trēowith and returned to London. Three torturous days spent with the delightful Miss Gambit. They had compiled a list of Lord Meyer's staff, visited the cook's sister in Romford, the chambermaid's mother in Windsor. Neither were hiding a newborn babe.

Much to Miss Gambit's relief, they discovered Jacob Hanaway was visiting his brother in Shoreham. They had been granted permission to interview David Scrivens in Newgate. The lad kept to his story. In a blinding rage, the shopkeeper snatched a longsword from behind the counter and drove the blade into his stepfather's chest.

For three nights, they'd returned home tired and exhausted. They'd shared intimate evening meals in the dining room, sat before a roaring fire, drinking port and discussing the case. For three torturous nights, Eli had paced the boards in his bedchamber, fighting the urge to give in to temptation and seduce the woman who had broken through his barricade.

Now, they had taken command of the study. Eli sat rigidly

behind his desk while Miss Gambit lounged on the small sofa, her stocking feet dangling over the padded arm.

She continued flicking through her notebook.

Eli was supposed to be reading the copy of Belton's statement given to him by the magistrate at the Hatton Garden office, but Miss Gambit kept wiggling her toes, an action as enticing as a lover's beckoning finger.

"Hunter?" She didn't face him, but continued examining her notes.

"Yes?" he said, as if focused on work and not the attractive turn of her ankles.

"Based on the number of bruises on David Scrivens' body, he must have taken regular beatings. When we visited him in Newgate, he flinched at the mere mention of his stepfather."

Since kissing her, he had developed the ability to predict her thoughts. "You mean he lacked the strength and the courage to fight back."

As she straightened, he glimpsed a shapely calf. "Many times, I've thought about murdering Jacob Hanaway. But I would have poisoned his food, drugged him, suffocated him in his sleep. I wouldn't have the strength to wield a longsword, let alone drive it into his chest."

Regardless of whether or not it served the case, Eli would venture to Shoreham and beat Jacob Hanaway to within an inch of his life.

"Scrivens is shy of six feet, weighs less than eight stone." Eli suspected the lad had been starved as well as beaten. "His limbs are like spindles. Let's make a plea to the magistrate. We'll have him wield the weapon and try to thrust it into a grain sack."

"Yes, I'm confident he'll struggle to perform the task."

Pride filled his chest. "Well done, Miss Gambit. I'm surprised Young or Swanson hadn't thought of it before." Both men seemed keen to save Scrivens, yet a re-enactment would have proven the lad was too weak to carry out the task. They were not usually so incompetent.

Miss Gambit closed her notebook. "I know we planned to question Lord Meyer today, but perhaps we should visit Belton's Emporium. Did you find any discrepancies in his statement?"

Eli shifted in the seat. "I've not read past the first paragraph."

Miss Gambit frowned. "Then what have you been doing for the last thirty minutes?"

Creating a host of fantasies in his mind. Fantasies involving an imposing black poster bed and a golden-haired angel come to tame the devil. Fantasies involving sucking tiny toes and finding other ways to ease the unbearable ache.

"Thinking." It wasn't a lie.

"Well, read through the statement while I race upstairs and make myself presentable."

"You look fine as you are." A golden wisp of hair had escaped her simple up-do to stroke the elegant column of her throat. Her pale pink gown carried an innocence so opposed to the mischievous glint in her eyes.

"Fine, as in it doesn't matter what I look like? Or fine, I look quite remarkable today?"

"You always look remarkable."

She narrowed her eyes, waiting for him to follow with a witticism, but blushed when she realised he'd spoken in earnest.

"If you're not careful, sir, you'll get a reputation for being charming, not dangerous."

"I doubt it. I'm only charming when I'm with you."

The air between them thrummed with the same electrifying energy he'd felt many times since sharing a kiss. It was exhilarating and terrifying at the same time.

A nervous laugh escaped her. "The last time you gave such

a compliment, you kissed me like you'd been deprived of affection since birth."

Yes, and he'd thought about nothing else for days.

"I tasted the same desperation on your lips."

She stepped closer and braced her hands on the desk. "Well, what's to be done about it, Mr Hunter? Are we to continue passing pleasantries while secretly wishing for a more intimate relationship?"

"Daventry will disapprove."

"Does he need to know?" She shrugged as if there was nothing illicit about conducting an affair. "You're in love with your work and have sworn never to trust another woman as long as you live. I plan to leave for the Americas when I gain my inheritance, start a new life in a new world."

*The Americas!*

A boulder of a lump formed in his throat. When this was over, he'd assumed they would still be friends. Indeed, he didn't want to think of her thousands of miles across the ocean.

"If I were to have a dalliance with anyone," she continued, "I'd want it to be with you. There's no man I respect or admire more."

The compliment touched him deeply. "Not even Lucius Daventry?"

"He doesn't count. Besides, I have no desire to kiss him."

"But you have a desire to kiss me?"

She smiled. "We'll talk about our growing attraction during dinner this evening. For now, we must take a trip across Blackfriars Bridge and visit the emporium. If we've time, we will call at Lord Meyer's abode."

Reluctantly, Eli pushed all romantic inclinations from his mind. He reached for the note Daventry's man had brought an hour earlier.

"Daventry has friends in high places. This is a letter from the Home Secretary, granting us permission to question all the witnesses, including Lord Meyer. He'll have no option but to comply with Peel's request."

Most of the time, it wasn't what a suspect said that made one doubt his version of events, but the way his eyes shifted, the way he held his body tense. Without Peel's letter, there'd be no way to study Meyer.

Miss Gambit clapped her hands. "Then let's be on our way. The quicker we achieve today's objectives, the quicker we can discuss our personal affairs."

●

Of the many shops along Surrey Street, only one had a queue of customers that stretched almost as far as Blackfriars Bridge. A tangible excitement hummed in the air. Ladies giggled hysterically, captured by a frenzy that left them in a mad state of agitation.

Eli led Miss Gambit to the back of the queue. "We'll not reveal ourselves to Belton until we've seen what's causing the commotion."

Miss Gambit craned her neck and observed the crowd. "To some, murder scenes are more fascinating than rare finds in a museum. Mr Belton will have seen an increase in profits since the horrific incident."

One glance at the Quality in the queue said Miss Gambit's observations were correct. Those waiting in line came from the middle and upper echelons. Carriages rolled to a stop outside the curiosity shop. The elegant occupants received preferential treatment and breezed past the eager souls desperate to gain entrance.

"Look, Hunter." Miss Gambit clutched his upper arm with a familiarity that no longer unnerved him. "That lady swooned straight into her beau's arms. He's had to carry her to the carriage."

The sight should have left him pondering what frightful

scene they'd find inside Belton's Emporium. Instead, Eli imagined playing the gallant hero to the inquisitive beauty beside him. He imagined scooping her up into his arms as he'd done at Vauxhall, carrying her to the safety of his bed.

*Hellfire!*

In a matter of days, he'd lost all sense and reason.

"Do you think Mr Belton has staged a re-enactment of the crime?" Her fingers wrapped around his bicep. Her essence burned through his coat sleeve, through the fine cambric shirt.

"Judging by the hysteria, it's the only explanation."

The gentleman in front glanced over his shoulder. "Like my wife, I presume yours has no interest in Belton's trinkets."

Eli looked at Miss Gambit. "Mine has a fascination with the macabre."

*Mine!*

Possessiveness surged inside him with the force of Poseidon bursting from the sea. Eli would never marry, never trust a woman with his heart. So why did he feel a need to claim Miss Gambit as his own?

Miss Gambit quickly fell into the role. "My husband is the best of men, sir. He has no interest in trinkets or the macabre and stands here as the strong arm of support."

The gentleman arched a brow. "A man will endure the fiery pits of hell for his lady love." He turned back to his wife and clasped her hand.

The comment sent Eli hurtling back to the past. Betrayal flowed like poison in his veins. His bitterness had nothing to do with losing Felicity. Theirs was not a love that moved mountains. Theirs was not love at all.

Eli was still lost in thought when they reached the front of the queue.

A stocky man dressed in mourning and with dried blood splatters on his face greeted them. "Who dares step into the shadows of Lucifer's lair?" His dramatic voice rang with intrigue. "Who dares venture inside to witness a scene of sheer brutality?" He held out his grubby hand, leant forward and whispered, "That'll be two shillings apiece, gov'nor."

"Two shillings to enter the emporium?" Eli challenged.

"Since the murder, I've had to hire staff to cope with the crowds. A man has to make a living." He gave a sly wink. "Don't you want to see the gruesome scene?"

Ah, so this stout fellow was Mr Belton.

"Indeed." Eli paid the fee and escorted Miss Gambit into the emporium.

Gone were the china plates, landscape paintings and knickknacks filling the sideboards. Long black curtains hung from rails on the ceiling to make dark, narrow walkways. A young boy dressed in an oversized tailcoat and dusty top hat greeted them.

"Welcome to Belton's Emporium." The boy gave a sweeping bow. "Scene of the brutest murder committed this—"

"You mean the most brutal," Miss Gambit said.

"That's wot I said." The boy resumed his performance. "Scene of the most brutest murder committed this century." He raised a lit lantern and beckoned them to follow him through the makeshift tunnel.

Miss Gambit reached for Eli's hand. "Don't let me go, Hunter."

"I'm here as the strong arm of support, remember."

As he clasped her hand, pressed his palm to hers with nary a hair's breadth between them, his mind skipped forward to them catching the traitor. Soon he would have to let her go. Soon they would say their goodbyes, part ways for good. Eli would return to his empty house and empty life, and Miss Gambit would sail away to new horizons.

"Was the second day in January when the devil appeared," the boy recited as he led them through the tunnel. "Like all good Christian folk, the Beltons were busy workin' behind the counter when Satan came to threaten their livelihood." They stopped at a small trestle table, and the boy picked up a tatty, blood-stained waistcoat. "This 'ere belonged to the cove wot met a grisly end."

It did not. Miss Gambit had insisted on examining the victim's clothing when the magistrate refused to let a woman inspect the body.

Miss Gambit glanced at the stained garment. "Then you should take the waistcoat to the Hatton Garden office as evidence. Keeping it here means you're hindering an investigation. That in itself is a crime."

The boy paled. "Well, it ain't the real waistcoat."

"Then you shouldn't advertise it as such."

A high-pitched squeal came from somewhere behind the curtains.

"Pay it no mind, miss." The boy jerked his head for them to follow. "The ladies always scream when they see the body."

"The body is in the mortuary," Miss Gambit countered.

The lad shrugged. "It ain't the real body."

"Is there anything here that isn't staged?" Eli asked.

"The bloodstain is real."

"Then take us to the bloodstain."

They weaved through the dark walkways and came to a trunk of rusty old weapons. With his lantern raised, the boy pointed to red marks on the boards.

"So the victim was stabbed here?" Eli asked.

"That's what old Belton said."

Eli considered the scene. The stab to the heart required precision and upper body strength. The youth who had suffered systematic abuse at his stepfather's hands possessed neither.

"For there to be this amount of blood, the perpetrator must have thrust the sword into the victim's chest and removed it instantly." An impossible feat for someone as slight as David Scrivens.

"Best ask Belton. I'm paid to take punters around, gov'nor."

"Where is Mrs Belton?"

"With the body. It helps calm the ladies. Belton wants us to get through the punters quickly and don't want anyone swoonin' and holdin' up the queue."

Because money mattered more than seeking justice for a murdered man.

With a firm grip on Miss Gambit's hand, Eli pushed past the boy and strode to the end of the walkway. A stout woman stood over a tailored mannequin. Trousers stuffed with straw acted as the victim's legs. The head was fashioned out of a grain sack filled with old clothes. Belton had thrust a longsword through the padded chest and must have hit it with a mallet to secure it to the boards. Blood pooled around the entrance wound and trickled onto the floor.

Mrs Belton began her dramatic narrative, but Eli raised a hand to silence her. "Newspaper reports say your husband wrestled Scrivens into the pantry."

Taken aback by the comment, it took her a few seconds to nod. "Yes, the blighter was like a rabid dog, snarling and snapping and foaming at the mouth. He'd have killed us both had we not acted so quickly."

"Where is the pantry?" Miss Gambit said.

"Through the door behind the counter."

"May we see the murderer's temporary prison?"

Mrs Belton frowned. "It ain't on the tour." She tried to usher them on. "Move along, else you'll hold up the queue."

"Did you see Scrivens stab his stepfather?" Eli asked.

The woman winced and recoiled. "Oh, it was a gruesome sight to behold, sir. It haunts my dreams, torments my waking hours, too. I can still see the devil charging, can still hear the sword slicing through cloth and skin."

Being a woman of keen mind—unless when in her cups— Miss Gambit pounced on the glaring inaccuracy.

"Scrivens took the sword from the trunk of weapons, did he not?"

"That's right, dear. Best we keep them locked in a cupboard from now on."

"The body was found next to the trunk. So why would Scrivens need to charge at his victim?"

Mrs Belton's eyes widened, and her double chin sagged. "Well, it's obvious, ain't it?"

Miss Gambit shrugged. "Not to me."

"He charged to the trunk and snatched the sword. Yes. Yes. The blighter had been pestering his stepfather to buy one. That could be why he killed the man."

Scrivens pestering a man who beat him most days? It was highly unlikely.

It was Eli's turn to apply a little pressure. "The murder weapon measures three and a half feet. Judging by the width of the trunk and the other weapons stored inside, the sword is too long and had to be stored elsewhere."

This time, Mrs Belton gulped. She stood dazed, her face a perfect picture of guilt. Then panic set in, and she called for her husband.

"Harold! Harold! Come quickly!"

The man, whose neck was as wide as Eli's waist, came bounding through the tunnel. "What is it, woman? I've got a queue a mile long. There'll be riots if no one's guarding the damn door."

Mrs Belton stabbed her finger at Miss Gambit. "These people ain't leaving."

Mr Belton gave a frustrated sigh then firmed his jaw.

Fixing them with a menacing glare, he leant closer. "Now listen 'ere. Be on your way else I'll have to remove you myself."

Blood pumped through Eli's veins as he squared his shoulders. "I could kill you where you stand, Mr Belton. Best not let matters get out of hand." For fear of them packing up shop and fleeing into the night, Eli decided not to accuse the couple of murder and perjury. He raised his hands in mock surrender. "But we've seen enough and will be on our way."

With a guiding hand on Miss Gambit's back, Eli led her out of the emporium. He waited until they reached his carriage, parked on the opposite side of Surrey Street, before relaying his suspicions.

"Now I'm certain Scrivens is innocent of the crime."

Miss Gambit climbed into the carriage. "Mr Belton is guilty, and his wife is his accomplice. We just need to discover why and be able to prove it in court."

Eli told his coachman to take them to Lord Meyer's abode in Upper Brook Street, then settled opposite Miss Gambit. As always when they were alone together, his thoughts drifted from the case to the woman who haunted his dreams.

*If I were to have a dalliance with anyone, I'd want it to be with you.*

Eli could commit to nothing more, yet every nerve in his body said it wouldn't be enough. Indeed, one taste of her lips had left him with an undeniable craving only she could sate.

"Hunter? Did you hear me?"

"Yes, but what motive could they have for killing a customer? And why would a member of Themis think it so important they'd risk their life and reputation to steal the case notes?"

"Now Mr Daventry has returned from visiting Lord DeVille, we should ask if his agents could investigate Mr Belton's background. Honora and Eliza haven't been assigned cases. Perhaps they could help."

"I assume they're the ladies Daventry hired."

"Yes, but he's very particular about who they work for." She gave a curious hum. "When you told him you wanted to hire an agent, did he mention the other ladies?"

"No, he insisted on sending you."

Daventry demanded Eli give her an opportunity to prove her worth.

"Perhaps he knew we'd work well together. I'm rather forward of manner, and you're quite reserved. We complement each other. It's what's needed in a case."

Eli thought to tease her. "You think me reserved? I'm more than free with my affections when I'm with someone I like."

A coy smile played on her lips. "Based on the wild kiss we shared at Trēowith, it's clear you like me, Mr Hunter."

"Based on the kiss we'll inevitably share soon, you can be certain of that, Miss Gambit."

## CHAPTER 11

"LORD MEYER IS at his club and isn't expected back until late this evening. Might I suggest you visit his secretary and make an appointment?" The butler was in the process of closing the door when Mr Hunter shoved his booted foot against the jamb.

"Lady Meyer is at home." Mr Hunter thrust the letter from the Home Office at the snooty fellow. "I must insist she grant us an audience. I would hate to tell Peel you've been uncooperative."

The butler's gaze swept over the official letter. "I'm afraid her ladyship's delicate condition prevents her from receiving visitors. As I said, I advise you write to his secretary to make arrangements."

"This is not a social call," Rachel countered. "We will return with a constable if necessary." She gestured to the elegant houses along the row. "I'm sure her ladyship would find it more distressing to have men charging into the street, clacking their rattles and beating down the door."

"Perhaps she has another reason for refusing to speak to us," Mr Hunter added. "Perhaps she has something to hide."

A soft, feminine voice breezed through the hall. "It's all

right, Gibson. You may show them in. This is Mayfair, not Billingsgate Fish Market. I'll not have arguments on the doorstep."

"Yes, my lady." Gibson pasted a smile and opened the door. "Please follow me."

Lady Meyer didn't greet them in the hall. Rachel caught a glimpse of a pale blue gown as she glided into the drawing room to await the introductions.

Gibson led them into a room decorated in garish salmon pink. He introduced them and stated their business while Lady Meyer looked on with a regal bearing. The lady was no older than thirty and was so beautiful, one couldn't help but stare in awe.

"Won't you sit down?" The lady gestured to the damask sofa.

The Empire cut of her gown disguised her swollen stomach. Only when she placed a gentle hand on the bump was it apparent she was with child.

Being a lady of sophistication, she preferred to discuss general topics before moving onto the serious affair of her maid's duplicity. They spoke about the weather, about the theatre and the recent production of *The Wheel of Fortune*.

"Did you not think it a marvel of comedy genius, Mr Hunter?"

"I find nothing amusing about revenge, madam."

"Did Penruddock not learn to forgive?"

"Penruddock was a weak-minded fool."

The lady looked at Mr Hunter as if she wished to strip back every layer and devour what lay beneath. She spoke to him in a low, seductive voice that would have many a man dancing to her tune.

Mr Hunter was not dazzled by her beauty. He did not fall over himself to impress. He kept the same unreadable expression he wore with all strangers. Not once did his eyes betray him. Not once did he glance at the swell of the lady's breasts almost bursting the seams of her gown.

His evident inattention left Lady Meyer a little at odds. She brought a limp hand to her brow and asked Mr Hunter to help her move to another chair.

"It's less draughty here." She gripped his hand and lowered herself down gracefully despite being so heavy with child. "Thank you, Mr Hunter. It's reassuring to know you're as strong as you look."

Mr Hunter ignored the compliment. "Perhaps you'd like a shawl."

"No, no. I shall be fine now."

"If you're able, I'd like to ask you a few questions about your maid, Mary Harcourt. You may find the subject distressing, but I'd like to understand the facts."

"Of course." Her tight smile belied her affable tone. "May I ask how you're connected to the case? Gibson said you're from the Home Office."

"We've been instructed to inspect the work of those at the Great Marlborough Street police office." Mr Hunter spoke in the detached voice of a government official. "We seek to examine the procedures they used when conducting their investigation."

Lady Meyer's gaze swept over Rachel. "To my knowledge, women do not work at the Home Office."

"I'm not employed by the Home Office, my lady." Rachel had no intention of revealing the true nature of her profession. She reached into her reticule and removed her pocket book and pencil. "I'm employed by Mr Hunter merely to take notes." And to judge Lady Meyer's reactions.

"I see." The lady's approving smile said she liked unconventional men.

Mr Hunter sat forward. "Forgive me if my questions cause distress, my lady. But we're here to ensure justice is served."

The lady seemed captivated by Mr Hunter's muscular

thighs, and it took her a moment to tear her gaze away. "Nothing is more distressing than betrayal. Had Mary come to me with her problem, I may not have thrown her out."

Mr Hunter firmed his jaw. "Her problem?"

"Mary's dalliance with the footman. The girl lacks morals. Her ridiculous tale about us stealing her baby stems from the loss of her own child."

"Mary gave birth to the footman's child?"

"No, she miscarried."

Fearing Mr Hunter might miss the opportunity to challenge Lady Meyer, Rachel said, "If Mary suffered due to the loss of her child, surely that accounts for her mistake in taking the jewels. Grief affects people in surprising ways and often leaves them dazed and confused. Clearly, prison isn't the place for her."

Lady Meyer smirked. "Mary is a liar and a thief." Her mouth twisted in disgust. The expression saw a beautiful woman become an ugly hag. "Dishonesty must be punished. You may fight against convention, my dear, but those of us in the upper echelons must set an example."

"And yet one cannot reach the highest realms without understanding compassion."

Mr Hunter smiled. "You quote Socrates, Miss Gambit."

Rachel shrugged. "In a fashion."

"Are we not digressing?" Lady Meyer sneered at Rachel yet moistened her lips for Mr Hunter. "Are you not here to assess whether the constables at Marlborough Street followed protocol?"

"Indeed." Mr Hunter fixed her with his impenetrable stare. "Again, I ask you to forgive my blunt manner, but nowhere during the early proceedings did you mention Mary's indelicate situation."

"I mentioned it to Sir Oswald, the magistrate at Marlborough Street. He took a little too much port and may have forgotten to record the details." A frustrated sigh left her lips.

"I don't know what all the fuss is about. It's a simple case of theft."

Forgotten to record an important piece of evidence? Highly unlikely.

"Mary claims she gave birth to your husband's child."

Lady Meyer's mocking snort rang with insincerity. "That's preposterous. Have you seen Mary? She's short and dumpy and is as dull as a winter's morn."

Rachel interrupted again. "Why would Mary hide the jewels under the boards? Why not take the first mail coach out of London? From the report, they'd been stolen a week before they were found in Mary's room. What prompted you to search there?"

Lady Meyer looked at Rachel as if she were something foul stuck to her shoe. "I thought you were here to take notes, not impress your colleague. Let me give you some advice. Men dislike interfering women, Miss Gambit. A lady should attract a man's eye, not test his patience."

"Yet I value her opinion," Mr Hunter replied. "There is nothing more attractive to a man than a woman with a keen mind and honest heart."

Heat filled Rachel's chest. Mr Hunter was a remarkable man, though she would have liked him to say she was as beautiful as the goddess sitting opposite.

"Please answer her question," he pressed.

"I cannot begin to know the workings of a criminal's mind. I can only presume she meant to persuade the footman to leave, too." Lady Meyer gestured to the pocket book. "Write this down, Miss Gambit. If Mary admits to the crime, admits she lied about the baby, I'm willing to press for transportation rather than the noose."

Oh, the lady was a conniving devil. They'd have no option but to put the proposal to Mary Harcourt. When facing a choice between a dangerous voyage and the scaffold, the maid would be easily swayed.

"No judge in the land will permit your interference," Mr Hunter said.

Lady Meyer's smile dazzled. "Men always bend the rules to please me."

"Not all men," came Mr Hunter's sharp reply. "Might you summon your footman, James Tinsley? We wish to ensure his statement is watertight. Confessing to a constable is slightly different from confessing to a bench of miserable men in periwigs."

"The footman in question is away at present, visiting his sick mother in Lincolnshire." The lady gripped the gilt arms of the chair and pushed slowly to her feet. "He's not due to return until next week. Kindly leave your direction, Mr Hunter, and I shall send word when he is free to attend you."

How convenient. The only person to verify Mary Harcourt's story had probably been bundled away under cover of darkness. She'd not be surprised to find the fellow dead in a ditch.

Mr Hunter stood. "Then I shall make an appeal to the magistrate and issue a warrant should he fail to return. A key witness in a case should be available for questioning."

"Sir Oswald agreed he might go. James hasn't committed a crime."

Rachel slipped her pocket book into her reticule and stood, too. A thought struck her, and she intervened one last time.

"It's common knowledge you choose your footmen for their handsome appearance." It was just an assumption, but based on the way she looked at Mr Hunter, Lady Meyer sought constant male attention.

Lady Meyer stared down her pert nose. "Appearance is everything."

"Then one wonders why your footman was so taken with Mary. Did you not say she is short and dumpy and as dull as a winter's morn?"

The lady's arrogant bearing faltered. "Who can say what brings two people together?" Her bottom lip quivered. "When one is deprived of affection, one lowers one's standards."

"In court, they may decide the same is true of your husband."

Lady Meyer bristled at the accusation. "What poppycock! You've outstayed your welcome. Gibson will see you out." She flounced from the room in a huff of pale blue satin.

Gibson appeared, to throw them out and warn against returning without an appointment.

"It's fair to say the Meyers have a less than perfect marriage," Rachel said, settling into the black leather seat in Mr Hunter's carriage. "The lady has a courtesan's charm and is far too amorous in her attentions."

"The lady is so hungry for affection she'd throw herself at anyone."

"You caught more than her eye." A stab of jealousy hit her between the ribs. "She hoped you would satisfy more than her curiosity."

"I imagine any breathing male would suffice."

"You do yourself a disservice, Mr Hunter. Not only are you loyal and dependable, you've a rugged appeal any woman would find attractive." Rachel cleared her throat and quickly sought to change the subject. "And thank you for defending my character. I may not have Lady Meyer's allure, but an honest heart is the true measure of one's worth."

A sinful smile touched his lips. "Lady Meyer is ugly inside and out. You steal my breath whenever our eyes meet."

The air suddenly thrummed with an intensity that overpowered the senses. Amorous thoughts filled her head, thoughts that had her staring at his mouth, had her yearning to taste him again.

"You know how to soothe my insecurities, sir."

"It's time we dispensed with the formalities. Call me Eli."

*Eli.*

She whispered it silently, aware the sound stirred something deep inside.

"And you must call me Rachel."

"Rachel." He spoke her name as if it were a mystical word with the power to weave miracles. "You've a logical mind, Rachel. Perhaps you might explain something I'm having difficulty understanding."

"I'll help if I can." She loved hearing her name on his lips.

He straightened, stroked his hand down his thigh. "We have much to discuss. Lady Meyer is lying. The Beltons are lying, too. We'll need our wits if we're to prove they all have something to hide. I cannot trust my brethren, and we'll need the luck of the gods to find the traitor."

Rachel frowned. "Yes, so what troubles you?"

"We have a mammoth task ahead, yet every moment we're alone, you're my only focus. How is it a man who's locked his heart away in an impenetrable chest at the bottom of the ocean can suddenly feel it beating?"

Rachel sat there, struggling to take air into her lungs. "You've become my priority, too. It's been so long since you let anyone in, Eli. You're bound to suffer these odd emotions. We've become friends, and you didn't plan for that."

"Friends? This morning you wished to conduct an illicit affair."

She shrugged. "I'm curious by nature. Something exists between us, something I've never felt before. After what I've experienced, I should be the least trusting person, but I have unwavering faith in you."

"Would it not be foolish to partake in a relationship that had no future?"

"Like you, I might have died many times." She'd not drowned off the Dorset coast or suffocated in a coffin in the cellar, but the Hanaways had nine months left to achieve the task. "I'd be a fool to live for anything but today."

"How do you know I almost died?"

"When you stalked me around your bedchamber, half-naked, I saw your scar. Did it happen during your work for Themis?"

"No." His deep sigh spoke of unpleasant memories. "The months after I left Chichester are a blur. Most days, I consumed more than my weight in wine. I was staggering through an alley in the rookeries when Daventry called for me to stop a thief. The blackguard lashed out with a butcher's knife."

"That's how you met Lucius Daventry?" The master of the Order had a knack for appearing at just the right time.

"Indeed. I could have throttled him, but he saved my life in more ways than one. It's the reason I agreed to meet you at Vauxhall."

Mr Daventry had been quick to come to her aid, too.

"If you'd had a Skean Dhu in your boot, you might have fought back."

He smiled. "Remind me never to confront you in a dark alley."

"If you did, I doubt we'd be fighting."

"No?" Mischief danced in his eyes. "What would we be doing?"

"Talking." She gave a coy shrug. "Kissing."

Never had she been so bold, but lust clawed in her veins, and she had to do something to ease the infernal ache. The need to feel his tongue thrusting into her mouth proved a strong incentive, too.

Said tongue slipped over his lower lip, reminding her how masterfully he'd devoured her mouth. "I'm tired of playing the hunter. With you, I have an overwhelming desire to be the prey."

Rachel swallowed. No doubt many women longed to have Eli Hunter at their mercy, to have him in their bed. The man was all muscle and brooding glances, but it was his loyal character and their undeniable connection that made her heart race.

"You want me to capture you in my snare?" she teased.

"I need to know you want me, Rachel."

"But I don't know the first thing about pursuing a man."

"Improvise."

"How do I know my attentions will be reciprocated?"

He laughed. "Trust me. You'll know."

She studied him, not knowing where or how to begin. Somehow, she couldn't help but think this was another test. A means for him to learn to trust someone again, a means of opening his heart.

"Thank you for making your position clear." Battling the urge to kiss him, she settled back in the seat. "An expert hunter uses the element of surprise, captures his prey unawares. I shall contemplate my next move carefully."

His blue eyes darkened with disappointment. He must have hoped she'd scramble onto his lap, slip her tongue over his and mate with his mouth. But she would bait him first. Lure him with her womanly wiles.

"So, you mean to make a plan of action." His gaze raked slowly over her, leaving a scorching trail in its wake.

Rachel smiled. "I plan to follow your advice and improvise."

# CHAPTER 12

THE BOARDS in the corridor creaked beneath the weight of footsteps, drawing Eli from a light slumber. Ordinarily, he would grab a weapon and hide behind the bedchamber door, ready to defend or attack, but Rachel had been so coy in manner during dinner this evening, he knew she'd been plotting something in that pretty head of hers.

His heart thumped wildly at the prospect of her entering his private domain. Had she thought of something important relating to the case? Or was this midnight liaison an attempt to catch him unawares?

Eli waited until the doorknob turned before feigning sleep.

A vision of loveliness slipped into his chamber. A vision of pristine white cotton and flowing golden hair. Amid the glowing embers of the fire and flickering lights of the candle lamps, he saw her curvaceous silhouette through the fine material. Hell, the plain nightgown was more alluring than sheer silk.

Rachel closed the door and padded over to the bed.

Lying naked with the bedsheets stretched across his abdomen, Eli wondered if she'd notice the rapid rise and fall of his chest, notice the outline of his shaft growing more prominent with each breath.

She took a moment to inspect his unconventional bed. Erotic images entered his head when she stroked the solid post, but he was the prey, not the hunter, and so could do nothing but wait with eager anticipation.

The minx trailed her fingers along the sheets as she moved towards him. "I know you're awake, Eli."

He opened his eyes and drank in the magnificent sight. "I'm rather glad I am. I'd not have missed this for the world."

"This?" She arched a brow.

"This unexpected yet welcome intrusion." Transfixed by her mussed hair and pouting lips, he suddenly wished he was the one in control, the one intent on seduction.

"I'm not here to ravish you," she said, yet her gaze slid over his bare chest, hot and needy. "I've come to negotiate." She touched him then, the soft pads of her fingers settling on his arm. "And to discuss the next move in this case."

He hoped the next move was her slipping her hand beneath the sheets to caress his aching cock. The glazed look in her eyes said she'd had a similar thought. Instead, she climbed onto the bed and sat beside him.

"Concerning our next move, the possibilities are endless." He gripped the bedsheets to protect his modesty and sat up. He tried not to stare at her bare feet, but beneath the night-dress were bare legs and a jewel of a treasure. "We find James Tinsley and prove the Meyers are lying. We tell the Council we're making progress with the coded letter. We—"

"I have made progress with deciphering the code. With *ing* being a common ending, I now know which symbols relate to those three letters."

"Excellent. I'll have a footman deliver a note to Truscott's London abode, warning him you're close to solving the riddle." Truscott would soon spread the word to the other council members, and the traitor would panic. "As to the matter of what to do next, we could accost Mrs Belton when she's alone and drag the truth from her lying lips."

"We could." She touched her hand to her chest and inhaled deeply. "Or we could do the one thing I've sworn never to do."

Eli grinned. "Make love to a man who sleeps in Lucifer's bed?"

Her eyes widened. "While you make the illicit sound appealing, I meant take a husband."

It was Eli's turn to inhale sharply. "Take a husband? Surely you're not referring to me?" Despite the all-consuming need to possess this woman, he, too, had sworn never to marry.

"Not legally." She laughed. "We'll pretend we've wed."

"Feign marriage? For what purpose?" Was there a genuine reason behind the suggestion, or was entering his room in a state of dishabille part of this huntress' plan? "And what has it to do with negotiating?"

"Logic says we should question the physician who examined Lady Meyer. Why would Mary claim her mistress is barren when it's evident she's with child? As her lady's maid, she'd have been the first to notice." Rachel shuffled closer. "And if we're going to Brighton, we may as well visit Shoreham. In one quick trip, we might solve a host of problems."

"Shoreham!" Surely not. "Visit Jacob Hanaway?"

She shivered visibly at the mention of the man's name.

"But you refused to entertain the idea." Whenever Eli broached the subject, she hid behind her barricade and told him to hire another agent. "You said you'd rather die than face him again."

Her shoulders sagged. "I know what I said, but the Hanaways could be out searching for me as we speak. If Jacob Hanaway thinks I'm married, he'll have to accept the terms of his mother's will." She gestured to his bare chest. "One look at your impressive physique and Satan would skitter into the shadows."

Just to tease her, Eli smoothed a hand over his pectorals. "I'm glad you thought of a use for me." Though it wasn't the use he'd hoped for. "So, we'll visit Shoreham. You'll question the witness while I threaten him to within an inch of his life."

"Yes." She seemed keen to meet the bastard who'd taken her to hell and back. "After visiting Brighton and Shoreham, I thought we could take a slight detour before returning to London."

Unease slithered in his chest. Unease became a rolling sense of trepidation. A man didn't need James Cook's grasp of geography to understand her intention.

"You mean we should call at Chichester?"

She cast a mischievous grin. "Wouldn't your mother like to know you've married a harlot who works as an enquiry agent?"

Though his blood turned icy in his veins, Eli couldn't help but laugh. "She'd prefer the truth. My virginal bride is the most astute, most courageous woman in all of London. A cunning minx who thinks I'm blind to her scheming."

"You'd say such things to your mother?"

"If I agreed to visit Chichester. As it stands, I have no intention of venturing within ten miles of the place."

She looked disappointed, but not defeated.

"Perhaps you might reconsider." The lady touched his leg. The sheets were so thin she may as well have been touching his bare thigh. "Perhaps knowing you're willing to confront your past will help me confront mine."

"So now you resort to blackmail?"

She threw her hands in the air. "Has it occurred to you I'm willing to face my biggest fear so you might find the courage to return home again?"

It was a tremendous sacrifice, a selfless act, he knew, but going home was a step closer to forgiveness, and he enjoyed wallowing in resentment.

"Rachel, they stole everything that night."

"That night and every night since. You sleep alone in this monstrous bed. You isolate yourself from family and friends. You avoid intimate connections."

"I've been intimate with you."

"It's different with me. I forced you into this partnership, forced the friendship, forced the kiss, and now you want me to play the hunter and force myself on you. Why?" She answered for him. "I'll tell you why. You're afraid to trust me. You're too scared to take a risk. You're terrified someone will hurt you again."

Had he been anything but naked beneath the sheets, he'd have shot off the bed in protest. Yet everything she said was true.

"People have hurt me too, Eli. But it's unhealthy to live with hatred in your heart." She slid off the bed and faced him, braced her hands on her hips, drawing attention to every delicious curve. "Either this friendship works on a mutual level with equal effort on both parts, or you'll have to hire another agent."

This was the sort of complication he'd hoped to avoid. Now his emotions were engaged he didn't want to continue the investigation without her.

"What are you saying? That if I don't visit my mother, you'll leave?"

"I'm asking you to let me in, Eli." The words were tinged with desperation. "I'm asking you to help rid us both of our demons. The choice is yours. I shall leave you to sleep on the matter. But no, I'll not turn my back on you or the case. I shall accept whatever decision you make."

She left the room.

Eli didn't call out to her. His mind was in the midst of a civil war. Every nerve in his body was primed for a confrontation with the Hanaways. He longed to put an end to Rachel's misery. To ensure she broke free from the traumas of the past. Despite that, he couldn't bear the thought of seeing his mother, facing his brother, didn't want to witness a scene of domestic bliss.

And yet something had shifted in the ether.

He was not the same man he was a week ago.

Rachel Gambit had breathed life into his withered heart. She had stirred dormant emotions. Renewed his faith in womankind. He was on a journey of discovery and would be a fool to change course now.

With Rachel at his side, could he conquer his fears?

With Rachel at his side, could he confront his traitorous brother?

●

*Henfield Park*
*Shoreham*

Built in the Elizabethan era, Henfield was once a noble home with noble occupants. Rachel could not say the same about the dilapidated mansion house or its owners today.

The previous Lord Hanaway had sired two angelic boys who were taught that women were objects to torment and abuse. Months before his demise, the lord had an epiphany and sought to mend his wicked ways. Still, everyone was shocked when he left his unentailed properties and worldly possessions to his long-suffering wife—not his heir.

Thrilled to have her freedom, Lady Hanaway became a spendthrift. A woman swayed by a sad tale. One who wasted money on extravagant hobbies and lived life to excess. Spending was a means to punish her husband, and she did so with an aristocrat's aplomb.

"Are you sure this is the right place?" Mr Hunter stared out of the carriage window at the overgrown gardens and crumbling boundary wall. They'd passed through rusty iron gates, charged along the weed-infested drive, crashed through large ruts in the road.

"Lady Hanaway wanted her husband's home to rot away like his corpse." Rachel finished the sentence despite the barrage of horrible memories. "She wished to force her sons to marry well, hoped being indebted to their wives would make them subservient, iron out the ruthless streak."

"Instead, she controlled them and fed their hatred of women."

"A parent's caring deed can often cause more harm than good." Rachel's father had acted out of love when he'd kept them in the dark about his financial affairs. "Did your mother remain in contact with your brother after he betrayed you? Does she see her grandchild?"

The questions raised Eli's hackles. "Yes. She refused to take sides."

"Is that the reason you stay away?" Her loyalty must have hurt him as much as his brother's betrayal. "Did your mother not invite you to visit?"

"Visit Hunston Hall?" A mocking laugh escaped him. He shook his head and dragged his hand through his dark brown hair. "Hunston belongs to me, not my mother. Dominic and Felicity live there with their child. My brother planned to follow in my father's footsteps and have a military career, but Felicity pleaded with him to reconsider."

Rachel's heart sank. "Good Lord. You support the brother who married your betrothed?"

He shrugged. "What else am I to do?"

No wonder he was bitter and angry.

No wonder the wounds had never healed.

"Eli, why didn't you say so last night? I might have understood why you were so reluctant to return to Chichester."

"Because you were right. Hatred is poisoning my future."

Eli's carriage rumbled to a halt outside the entrance to Henfield.

In her absence, the house had fallen further into decay. Ivy had ravaged the facade. Rachel wished the creeping tendrils would wrap themselves around Jacob's neck and suffocate the last breath from his lungs. Cracked window panes and dirty stonework said the house had been neglected since Lady Hanaway's passing.

Still, fear, and the overwhelming need to support Eli as he battled his demons, had her crossing the carriage to press a chaste kiss on his lips.

He showed his appreciation by catching her around the waist and pulling her into his lap. "Is that my reward for honesty, Rachel? A kiss to stitch the wound?"

She cupped his cheek. "It's an apology for making you suffer. A means to distract my mind from the terrifying task ahead."

His expression darkened. "The Hanaways won't hurt you. Not as long as I've breath in my lungs and blood in my veins."

Being so strong and dependable, Eli Hunter had the power to bring an end to anyone's nightmare—except his own. But one look at the neglected mansion said the Hanaways would do anything to prevent her from inheriting their mother's money.

"I'm scared, Eli."

It would have made more sense to visit Brighton and then take the coastal road to Shoreham and Chichester, but she couldn't question the doctor while terrified of meeting the Hanaways.

"After today, you'll never have to deal with them again."

The comment bolstered her courage. Still, her knees trembled as she trudged up the moss-covered steps and approached the rotten oak door. Seeing the gargoyle knocker brought bile to her throat. The grotesque figure had given her pause when she'd first arrived at Henfield. It should have served as a warning. Those who lived beyond the doors were ugly inside and out.

Bryson answered. The butler looked just as he had the day of Lady Hanaway's funeral: his lank white hair reaching his jaw, his lips a thin, disapproving line. As with all the staff at Henfield, he had been equally possessed by the devil's coldness. He considered Rachel through sunken eyes—seemed shocked that anyone would voluntarily return to the mouth of hell—before casting a wary glance at Eli Hunter.

"We come seeking an audience with Jacob Hanaway," Eli said in a stern voice. He presented the letter from the Home Office. "We come at Peel's behest to investigate a crime where your master is named as the only witness." He gestured to Rachel. "I believe you know my wife."

Bryson didn't bother to read the document. He didn't acknowledge her, didn't smile or welcome her home.

"Wait here." Bryson left them on the doorstep for two minutes. When he returned, he merely said, "Follow me."

At the pace of those in a funeral procession, the butler led them through the gloomy hall, through the long gallery with its carved Jacobean panels and gilt-framed portraits. The untrained eye might be fooled into thinking the house belonged to cultured, well-bred gentlemen. But one sniff of the earthy aroma in the air said damp and decay lay behind the facade. Indeed, Henfield's heart was rotten to the core.

Eli Hunter seemed unaffected by the miserable surroundings. He had not raced through the cobwebbed corridors in the dead of night, scared out of his wits. He had not been forced to kneel on the stone floor until the cold chilled his blood. He had not woken each morning wondering if this was the day he would die.

Her heartbeat thumped in her throat as they approached the drawing room. The fortitude that had given her the courage to fight back surfaced the moment she strode into the room and caught sight of the men, men she would murder without guilt chipping away at her conscience.

Like a wolf spotting a lonely lamb, Jacob Hanaway

grinned. "Rachel, what a pleasant surprise. You've been a stranger these last three years." He did not stand as a sign of respect, but gave an indolent wave at Mr Hunter. "I see you've brought a friend."

Eli straightened to an intimidating height. "She's brought her husband, though we come in a professional capacity, not for a reunion."

With his chubby hands resting on his paunch, Peter Hanaway studied them. At six and twenty, Peter was older than Jacob by two years, though the brothers were so alike in looks they could be twins. Both had curly brown hair and unkempt side-whiskers, both had lips so thick and wide they didn't need spoons to slurp their soup.

"Yes, Bryson said you're here at Peel's behest." Peter scanned Eli's black attire. "You speak and dress like a gentleman's son, yet are in the unfortunate position of having to work for a living. Perhaps that's why you failed to address me with the respect befitting my station. Rachel must have informed you I'm a baron."

Eli's mocking snort echoed through the room. "I know who and what you are. I'm the eldest son of Major General Edmund Hunter, a decorated war hero. With a yearly income in excess of thirty thousand pounds, I have no need to work. Like my father, I serve king and country but prefer to do so within the realms of government."

Rachel hid her surprise. Thirty thousand? Good grief. Surely he was exaggerating.

The brothers' eyes bulged.

"I'm here for two reasons," Eli stated. "The first being to question Jacob Hanaway about the murder at Belton's Emporium in Surrey Street, London. As a witness for the prosecution, he is legally bound to make himself available for questioning."

Jacob relaxed back in the tapestry covered chair. "As the brother of a baron, the rules do not apply to me."

"You're mistaken." Eli stared down his nose. "You will answer my questions, Mr Hanaway, or I shall take you into custody. Be warned. You may break a few limbs in the struggle."

Rachel found the strength to speak up. "I should do as he says. My husband is a dangerous man. A man looking for any excuse to inflict pain on the devils who tormented me for years."

Jacob glanced at Eli's broad shoulders and paled. "Tormented you? They were childhood pranks. Thanks to my mother, your inheritance is more than adequate compensation."

"Unless Rachel is unfit to inherit," Peter added.

"As her husband, I shall do everything in my power to ensure she gets the full entitlement. Should anything untoward happen, I shall kill you both." He paused. "That's not a threat. It's a promise."

"Have no fear, husband. I've spent the last three years training for the event." Rachel slipped her Skean Dhu from her pelisse pocket. She drew the blade from the sheath and addressed the rogues who lacked the manners to offer them a seat. "Perhaps you'd like a demonstration of my skill."

With a quick whip of her wrist, she threw the blade at Jacob Hanaway. It whizzed through the air, missing his ear by an inch, and became embedded in the oak panel behind.

Jacob's eyes almost rolled out of their sockets.

With a look brimming with admiration, Eli turned to her and whispered, "I find myself suddenly aroused, my love. What other tricks can you perform that might stir a man's blood?"

"If I told you, it would spoil the surprise." Clenching her fists at her sides to stop her hands from shaking, Rachel marched across the room and retrieved her weapon. She stopped in front of Jacob's chair. "I'm no longer the girl you terrified. You'd do well to remember it."

Peter Hanaway took it upon himself to be the voice of reason. "Enough! Say what you need to and be on your way. Jacob will answer any questions relating to this business of murder."

Jacob gritted his teeth. "There's nothing much to say on the matter. The man dragged me off the street. I stood over the body until he returned with the constable."

"Where was Mrs Belton while you were watching the body?" Eli said.

Jacob shrugged. "Shouting at the boy locked in the pantry."

"Shouting what?"

"That he's a thief and a murderer and would swing for his crimes."

"A thief?" Rachel returned to Eli's side. "You made no mention of it in your statement. A boy's life hangs in the balance. Every snippet of information is of vital importance."

"Why should I care what happens to a criminal? I'd have missed the stage to Shoreham and so told the constable the basic facts."

Rachel frowned. "The stage? You hate using public transport."

"I cannot afford to keep a coach in town because my bloody mother left you my inheritance." Spittle flew from his mouth and landed on the tatty rug. "I can barely afford to run the house in Salisbury Square. Had I known you were in London, I'd have paid a house call to beg for funds."

"And I'd have thrown you out after bloodying your nose," Eli countered. "Did Mr Belton have blood on his clothes?"

"On his clothes, hands and face," Jacob said after muttering an obscenity. "By all accounts, he tried to stem the flow of blood."

"So the sword had been drawn from the body?"

"There was no sign of the weapon."

Rachel wondered how the Beltons managed to wrestle a sword-wielding murderer into the pantry.

"There may be a clause in Mother's will," Peter Hanaway interjected in a sly tone, "preventing Rachel from inheriting now she's married. Perhaps a trip to town is in order."

Nausea roiled in Rachel's stomach. The men would step on hot coals to get their hands on her inheritance. Jacob had mocked David Scrivens, but he was just as capable of stealing, just as capable of murder.

"There is no such clause. Accept your mother favoured me and sought to teach you both a lesson."

Hatred flashed in Jacob's dark brown eyes. She had stared into those depthless pools many times, fearing what he would do next. He would do nothing while in the presence of Eli Hunter. But she suspected the brute would be on the next stage to London.

Jacob hauled himself out of the chair. "The money is not yours until November, Rachel. I'm not one to rest on my laurels. Where might our solicitor send his correspondence?"

Rachel remained tight-lipped.

"Blackstone House," Eli said as if challenging the man to break into his home in the dead of night. "On the Uxbridge Road. You can send your correspondence there."

Panic tightened her throat.

Sheer terror sent her thoughts scattering.

Eli clasped her hand and held it firmly. He bid the gentlemen good day and drew her towards the drawing room door.

"With luck, I'll see you soon, Rachel."

Jacob's comment brought them to a halt.

Rachel couldn't summon the words needed to put the rogue in his place.

Eli cast a confident grin. "Rest assured, we'll be waiting."

# CHAPTER 13

ANGER SEETHED INSIDE. Eli knew enough about evil people to know Jacob Hanaway was the devil's spawn. Inflicting pain on others bolstered the brute's confidence, and it was clear he would not rest until he'd gained Rachel's inheritance.

Rachel sat in the carriage seat opposite, her gaze glued to the window, for she had not looked at Eli since leaving Shoreham.

"Say what you need to, Rachel. Don't spare my feelings."

She managed a sidelong glance. "Perhaps it's best I don't."

"Aren't emotions more painful when left to fester?"

She sighed. "I'm angry, Eli. And I'm so scared my stomach hurts. I don't want to say something I'll regret."

"Angry because I told Jacob Hanaway where to find us?"

"Angry because he'll raze your house to the ground with us both inside." And yet fear had her shaking in the seat. "He'll do anything to reclaim the inheritance."

"Was it not your idea to come here?" he said softly.

"It was a mistake." She covered her face with her hands. "I thought it would deter him, but it's only stoked the flames of vengeance."

On the contrary, it was the best course of action. The

attack would come sooner rather than later, and Eli would be prepared. Besides, they had learnt something from the visit. In calling the boy a thief, Mrs Belton had a motive for murder.

"It wasn't a mistake. We'll deal with him and be done with it."

She looked at him incredulously. "I don't inherit until November. It's February, and we'll surely solve the case soon. What am I supposed to do for the next nine months?"

She was supposed to trust him to solve the problem.

"Hanaway is driven by hatred. I guarantee we'll have dealt with him and solved the case within the week." Or pretty soon after, depending on what Dr Baker said when they questioned him about his examination of Lady Meyer.

"And if not?"

If not, Eli would be her shadow.

Daytime. Nighttime. Any time she needed him.

"Rest assured, I'll deal with Hanaway." He would consult Lucius Daventry, have Hanaway beaten by a thug in a dank back alley. Have the resurrectionists murder him and dispose of the corpse.

Silence descended.

The carriage trundled along on its way to Brighton. According to the notes Truscott made whilst at Trēowith, Lady Meyer's doctor lived in West Street.

"It's but six miles to Brighton," he said, attempting to distract her mind and have her focus on the case. "We must decide how to deal with Dr Baker. According to Mary Harcourt, Lady Meyer cannot be with child." Yet they had seen evidence to the contrary.

Rachel thought for a moment. "Either Dr Baker examined Lady Meyer and can confirm she is with child, or he agreed to give false evidence. I doubt he'll confess to perjury."

"Let's assume he's lying. Let's assume Lady Meyer is too."

"We could trick him into confessing." Rachel's countenance brightened. "Your carriage is unmarked. Let's pretend Lady Meyer sent us because she needs a document confirming her condition. I'll say I'm her lady's maid. You can play the footman sent to keep me safe."

It could work. "We'll need to be vague in our approach."

She gestured to his black attire. "And you'll need to change out of those clothes, change into something in keeping with your lowly position."

Eli straightened his cravat. "Do I not look like a servant in his Sunday best?"

"A servant could never look so commanding."

●

At the mention of Lady Meyer's name, they were ushered into the doctor's small townhouse and told to wait in the study. Having swapped clothes with his coachman, bar the greatcoat, Eli looked more like a man in service than a hunter on the prowl.

The doctor strode into the room, his attention absorbed by the book in his hand. He glanced up and barely gave them a moment's consideration. He didn't welcome them, didn't ask about their journey or offer to send to the kitchen for refreshments.

"Lady Meyer sent you," the red-haired man in his forties stated. He stole a look at Rachel. The lecherous glint in his eyes said he thought her pretty.

"Yes, sir." Rachel dipped a curtsy. "I'm her lady's maid. A replacement for Mary Harcourt." She spoke in a broad East London accent.

"Mary Harcourt? Ah, a terrible business. When one considers your predecessor, you should have no problem pleasing your mistress." He dropped the book on the desk, flicked his coattails and sat down. "And who's this stern fellow?" he said, studying Eli's broad shoulders.

"The new footman, sir. Hired to replace James Tinsley. Lady Meyer was glad of his confession, though best I say no more on the matter."

"Quite right. Let's pray the fellow is content in his new position."

"He wasn't keen on leaving, sir, but it will all work out for the best."

"Lady Chadwick is less demanding. He should have no complaints."

Lady Chadwick? So Tinsley wasn't nursing his sick mother.

Eli was forced to suppress a surge of admiration. Rachel Gambit was an expert in manipulation. A force to be reckoned with. Having met Jacob and Peter Hanaway, he understood why.

Rachel curtsied again. "We're not supposed to talk about that until after the trial. Best I tell you why we've come."

Dr Baker did not offer them a seat. Perhaps he imagined after such a long journey, they wished to stretch their legs. Perhaps the man was an arrogant ass who thought himself superior on all levels. Either way, Eli couldn't wait until they revealed the true purpose of their visit. He couldn't wait to see Dr Baker squirm.

"So, you've come at Lady Meyer's behest." Dr Baker sat forward.

"Yes, it's a delicate matter, sir. But Lady Meyer wants a letter for the magistrate saying you examined her and she is with child."

Dr Baker paled. "A letter? We agreed she could mention the examination, but I made no arrangements to provide written proof." He thought for a moment. "Tell your mistress I'm sorry, but I'll not put my name to paper."

So he hadn't examined Lady Meyer. Else what had he to hide.

"Oh, but I can't leave without it, sir." Rachel feigned tears.

"Her ladyship needs it desperately. She said I'll lose my position if I return home empty-handed."

"We need written proof," Eli pressed. "A sworn statement."

Being a man with a short temper, Dr Baker pushed out of the chair. "Tell your mistress that's not what we arranged." He snatched the tiny handbell from the desk and rang for his housekeeper.

The stout woman entered so swiftly she must have had her ear pressed to the study door. "You rang, sir."

"Show these people out, Mrs Green."

Eli cleared his throat. "You'll do nothing of the sort, Mrs Green." He did not disguise his voice. "Else, I shall knock every door on this row and tell your affluent neighbours Dr Baker is to be prosecuted for giving false evidence."

Dr Baker's cheeks flamed. "Prosecuted? You'll not threaten me in my own home. Tell Lady Meyer she can go to the devil. Tell her, should they call me to the witness stand, I'll not lie for her."

In his confusion, the doctor presumed they were issuing threats on Lady Meyer's behalf.

Eli smiled inwardly. "You'll tell them you didn't conduct the examination confirming she's with child?"

"I'll tell them I didn't conduct the examination. Tell them she is presumed barren, and therefore the whole story must be a lie."

Barren? In using a clever disguise, Lady Meyer proved she was a skilled deceiver.

"We'll need that in writing, sir," Rachel said.

The man threw his arms in the air. "How many times must I tell you? I'll not sign my name to anything that might incriminate me. Now get the hell out of my house."

"I'm afraid you've no choice." Eli removed Peel's letter from his pocket and slapped it on the desk. "We don't work for Lady Meyer. We work for the Home Office. We're seeking a reprieve for Mary Harcourt. You'll either make a statement in writing, or we'll report your offence to the local magistrate and have you transported to London in a prison cart."

With a trembling hand, the doctor took the letter and dropped into the chair. He read Peel's words, knew he was considered a witness, which meant he would have to take the stand and give his version of events.

"Why did you lie for Lady Meyer?" Eli knew the answer. It was the reason Sir Oswald forgot to record important details. Both men were dazzled by her beauty. "What story did she weave to gain your confidence and trust?"

The doctor dragged his hand down his face and groaned. "The same story all temptresses use to get a man to do her bidding. She roused my pity, acted the injured female needing a strong man's support. Led me to believe she enjoyed my company."

Had Lady Meyer batted her lashes and whispered sweet nothings?

"You'll tell us what she told you," Eli demanded. "You'll tell us, or you'll tell the magistrate."

After some thought, Baker gave a sigh of resignation. "She told me about Mary Harcourt, said she couldn't stand the shame of anyone thinking her husband had seduced the dumpy maid. She said Mary stole the jewels and lied about the affair. That's when she asked if she could mention my name, say I'd examined her and could confirm she was enceinte. She appeared to be with child, and so I saw no issue."

"But you said she was barren?"

"After a dreadful riding accident ten years ago, she was considered so, but doctors make mistakes."

"You made a huge mistake." Eli frowned. "You presumed no one would question your word."

"She said her staff would testify to her condition and so no one would question my involvement."

He wasn't wrong. Had Mary's case not been brought before the Council, no one would have contested Lady Meyer's word.

"You gave no thought that an innocent woman would hang?"

"A thief deserves to hang."

Rachel stepped closer to the desk. "Lady Meyer hid the jewels under the boards in the maid's room. The only woman who deserves to hang is the liar you've protected."

Baker's head fell into his hands, and he bemoaned his stupidity.

"You cannot undo your mistake." Eli imagined there were a host of men who'd fallen foul to Lady Meyer's wicked wiles. Indeed, why hadn't Truscott sent a man to question the doctor? "But you can make amends. Draft a statement informing Peel that Lady Meyer spoke in error. That she tricked you into believing she's carrying her husband's child."

And if she had tricked the doctor, she had tricked the authorities. If Mary Harcourt had told the truth about the lady being barren, perhaps she'd told the truth about giving birth to Lord Meyer's child.

The doctor began a rambling conversation with himself. "Yes, I could lay the blame at her door. Yes, I could say I've heard about her lies and felt compelled to set the record straight." He took to nibbling his fingernails. "Yes. Yes. That might work."

Eli coughed into his fist. "Write the statement, Dr Baker, so we can be on our way. We have another call to make today."

In truth, Eli hoped the doctor spent hours mulling over his account. He hoped the man ran out of ink, then paper, and didn't finish until nightfall. It was imperative they returned to London to continue the investigation. With luck, there would be no time to visit Chichester.

But being in a state of agitation, the doctor finished within minutes.

"There!" Baker thrust the letter at Eli. "I trust that will suffice."

Eli scanned the document. "Excellent. Sign it. Fold the letter and press your seal into the wax."

With a huff of frustration, Baker did as commanded.

Eli slipped the note into his coat pocket. "I doubt we'll have cause to visit again. We've all been deceived at some time in our lives. Let's hope you've learnt that honesty prevails."

Baker lamented his involvement in the sorry affair and then rang for his housekeeper, who came bustling into the study to escort them out to their carriage.

Eli opened the carriage door for Rachel before pulling out his watch and checking the time. "It's a three-hour drive to Chichester. We'll not reach Hunston Hall until seven."

Rachel considered him through narrowed eyes. "I'm happy to travel through the night if you're desperate to return to London."

His heart sank to his stomach. "I'm not thinking about myself." The lie would eat away at him, too. "I'm thinking about my coachman."

"Then we find a coaching inn and stay the night." She touched him gently on the upper arm. "Every part of your body is fighting against the idea of going to Chichester. But trust me, Eli, you'll be glad you've taken the plunge."

Eli arched a challenging brow. "Are you glad we visited Jacob Hanaway?"

"Not at present, but I'm sure I'll look back on this journey and be glad I conquered my fear."

Fear was the right word. Eli was afraid he'd lose his temper, afraid of rejection, of receiving a frosty reception. He was afraid he would see Dominic and feel the loss more profoundly. Afraid to acknowledge he was no longer part of the family. Preferred to live in ignorance.

"Are you worried you might still feel something for Felicity?" Rachel tilted her chin as if the answer would hurt as much as a savage blow. "Perhaps you'd rather remember her in a poor light, for it makes the pain easier to bear."

Had they been alone in a private room, he would have captured her proud chin and kissed away her obvious insecurities. Still, the question forced him to face the fact that Rachel meant more to him than Felicity ever had.

"I'm not worried in the least. There is nothing between us. I'm willing to push my own anxiety aside to prove my affections do not lie with a woman from my past."

She swallowed deeply. "Where do they lie?"

With a woman who made him breathless at the mere thought of kissing her again. With a woman who filled his every waking thought, visited him in his dreams.

Eli smiled. "You're an enquiry agent for the Order, Miss Gambit. I'm sure you're able to draw a logical conclusion."

●

Hunston Hall sat amid the darkness, the facade a flushwork of flint and stone that made the house appear like a dull, lonely figure on the landscape. Candlelight streamed through the lower windows. A welcome sight to a weary traveller. To Eli, it brought a deep sense of despair.

Upton stumbled back in shock when he opened the front door. The butler had served the family for three decades, and no doubt had lost count of the days since he'd last seen the master.

"The family are in the drawing room, sir." Upton gave Rachel a surreptitious glance. "Shall I inform them of your arrival, or do you wish to catch them unawares?"

Eli patted the fellow on the upper arm. "We shall wash

before greeting my mother. Have a pitcher of warm water sent up to my chamber." He needed a moment alone with Rachel to calm his volatile spirit. "And a decanter of brandy and two glasses."

Upton grimaced. "Begging your pardon, sir. I can have a maid prepare another room. Your brother and sister-in-law occupy that bedchamber."

*What the blazes!*

"On who's authority?" he snapped.

"Your mother's, sir."

Rachel slipped her hand into his and squeezed gently. "I'm sure your mother will understand why we're a little dusty and dishevelled." She spoke to Upton. "Please announce us at once."

Noting Eli had no issue with Rachel giving orders, Upton bowed. "Of course, madam. If you'll kindly follow me."

Eli gritted his teeth. He may have been absent for three years, but he knew his way to the bloody drawing room.

The slow, methodical trudge along the hall was like the walk to the scaffold. In a few short steps, his life flashed before his eyes. Hunston Hall had been his home since birth, yet the thought of living under the same roof as Felicity filled him with revulsion.

Upton paused outside the drawing room. "Shall I announce you formally, sir?"

"Yes." Why the hell not?

"May I enquire as to your companion's name, sir?"

"Companion? Rachel is my wife." The words left his mouth before his brain engaged. Indeed, she looked almost as shocked as Upton.

"I thought we were going to wait before telling your family?" she said, masking her surprise.

Eli shrugged. "I think we'll tell them now."

He had the utmost faith she'd play the role like a seasoned

performer. And the devil on his shoulder desperately wanted to create a stir.

All conversation died when Upton entered and cleared his throat.

"What is it, Upton?" Eli's mother snapped. "You look so pale one fears you've seen a ghost."

"May I present Mr and Mrs Hunter, madam?"

"Have you been at the port again, Upton?" Eli's mother laughed. "Go and smell his breath, Dominic."

At the mention of his brother's name, Rachel looked at Eli and whispered, "We can leave now if you'd rather. But know I'll support you in whatever you decide."

The heart that had withered years ago blossomed like a bud in spring. Heat filled his chest. After the trauma of visiting the Hanaways, he owed it to Rachel to tackle this problem. Else how could he ever move forward?

Eli gripped her hand and strode into the drawing room. "I can assure you, Upton hasn't touched a drop." Good God! He felt sick with nerves. "I imagine he would have been less shocked to see a ghost."

A heavy silence descended.

Eli refused to look at the couple lounging on the sofa, but Felicity's lavender perfume hung thick in the air, assaulting his nostrils, clawing at his throat.

Violet Hunter pushed to her feet. Her hair was more grey than brown now, the crinkles around her eyes more prominent. Little else had changed.

"Eli!" She clasped her hands to her chest. "You should have written. You should have told me you were coming home."

Home!

It was anything but. Indeed, he felt like a nun in a whorehouse.

"I'd have had your room prepared," Violet continued.

"According to Upton, my room is occupied."

His mother paled. She cast the figures on the sofa a side-long glance.

Eli did not.

"It's the largest room in the house," came her mumbling excuse. "Little Edmund struggles to sleep and likes to be close to his mama. It's a temporary arrangement. Yes, just temporary." It was then Violet noticed Rachel, noticed their crumpled attire, and recalled Upton's lofty announcement. "Did I hear correctly?"

"Allow me to introduce Rachel, my wife."

A man who valued honesty shouldn't lie, least of all to his family, but he could hardly say he'd hired her to catch a traitor. And he didn't want them thinking his life was meaningless, empty. That he spent his nights alone embittered by the past.

"Good evening." Rachel's tight smile said she was equally nervous. "Forgive us for not giving you prior warning, but we were in the area and thought to inform you of our wonderful news."

"In the area?" Violet observed their shabby attire. "When did you marry? And why did I not hear of it until now?"

"Looking at properties," Eli said. "We married a week ago."

Violet frowned. "Properties?"

"For a family home where we might raise our children."

"But Hunston is your home."

Eli cleared his throat. "Hunston is your home, Mother. It's Dominic's home, not mine. Please tell me you don't expect us all to live as one happy family."

Violet groaned. "For goodness sake, Eli. Surely you're not still angry about what happened all those years ago. It's done with now. You read my letters. You know how happy they are."

Anger and resentment burned inside. Eli looked at Dominic's handsome countenance, expecting to see the charming smile that captivated most women. Thankfully, his brother's pained expression went some way to cooling the inferno.

Dominic stood. "Perhaps we might speak privately."

"We all know what happened. We can discuss it here."

Rachel hugged his arm. "Maybe you should speak alone."

Eli turned to her and took comfort in her compassionate blue eyes. "You know my reputation, Rachel. You know I need you beside me to smother fury's flames."

Dominic stepped forward. "What do you want me to say, Eli? That I'm sorry? That I've missed your company these last three years? That I never meant to hurt you?"

Eli shrugged. "It would be a start."

"All those things are true. But I should have come to you, at least tried to explain."

Felicity stood, and Eli forced himself to look at her.

The glossy red curls that had felt like silk between his fingers were styled for a relaxed evening at home. Her figure had altered since bearing a child, her willowy frame being fuller now. She looked tired, wore the same sad pout that usually had men scrambling to give her attention.

He expected to feel something, anger, inadequacy, regret.

He felt nothing.

"Would you like to see your nephew, Eli? He's sleeping upstairs in his crib."

Typical Felicity, using manipulation to control a situation. If Eli refused, he'd look like a heartless devil who didn't deserve a woman's love. He'd be the villain of this piece, not the victim.

"Of course."

Rachel released his arm. "You go. I shall wait here."

He felt something then. A burning need to protect Rachel from the wolves. A reluctance to put any distance between them, no matter how short.

"Would you care for refreshment, Rachel?" Dominic said, playing host. "We have sherry, or I can ring for tea."

She smiled. "Thank you, may I have a small sherry?"

"Certainly."

Felicity crossed the room. "Come, Eli. Edmund looks so angelic when he's sleeping." She led him upstairs to the bedchamber that belonged to him but had been captured by the enemy in his absence. "Hush. Tread carefully."

Eli entered the room. He peered at the beautiful child sleeping peacefully in the crib. Edmund had Dominic's dark hair, Dominic's dimple, Dominic's chunky thighs. That didn't stop Eli feeling a rush of affection for the boy.

"He's a handsome chap. Do you have plans for another?"

Felicity shrugged. "Dominic's not the same since you left. He used to be so attentive, but guilt eats away at him, and he misses you, Eli. He misses you terribly. We both do. You left in such a hurry, I never got a chance to explain."

This wasn't a means to introduce him to his nephew but for her to complain about her husband. An opportunity to plead for forgiveness.

"Fate brought you here tonight, Eli."

"No. My wife suggested I come." And yet fate had brought Rachel to Vauxhall. Fate had bound their lives together. Fate or Lucius Daventry. Eli often thought they were one and the same. "I understand the situation perfectly. We were made to believe we suited, Felicity. We did not."

"You loved me desperately and would have married me."

"I thought I loved you but was wrong in that assumption, too."

Her mocking laugh almost woke the baby. She set her hand to the boy's chest and rocked him gently.

"We were made for each other. In a moment of folly, I lost sight of that." She faced him, moved closer. The hand that had soothed the baby came to rest on Eli's chest. "Your brother seduced me. He'd always wanted me for himself, and I was swayed by his constant attention."

Eli suspected it was the other way around.

She smoothed her hand over the hard planes. "You've changed. There's a darkness behind your eyes that's so beguiling. There's an air of authority about you that's so appealing. More fool me for being so susceptible to flattery."

"Please don't tell me you married the wrong person, else you'll have destroyed a family for nothing." He gripped her hand to remove it from his person just as the door creaked open, and Rachel and Dominic entered.

Rachel took one look at the cosy scene and fled.

Hellfire!

Eli released Felicity's hand. "Goodbye, Felicity. I doubt I'll have cause to see you again." He hoped never to lay eyes on this conniving temptress.

"Of course you will. Now you're married, you will come and live at Hunston. Things will be just as they were before."

Eli reached into the crib and stroked Edmund's tiny fingers, then he crossed the room to speak to Dominic. "Should you wish to discuss our estrangement, Mother has my direction."

"I've been to London, visited that address, watched and waited." Dominic's voice was choked with emotion. "It's clear you don't live there, Eli."

No, he'd not wanted anyone to find him.

"It's a house I own and lease, though the butler knows to forward all correspondence. If you decide to come, tell him who you are." He glanced at Felicity. "Come alone."

Eli wasn't sure why he'd extended an olive branch. Perhaps he pitied Dominic. Perhaps there was no longer room for hatred in his heart. It didn't matter.

"Excuse me, I must find my wife."

Eli left the room, but Rachel wasn't waiting on the landing. He hurried downstairs, but she wasn't waiting in the hall nor the drawing room. Seized by panic, he shouted for Upton.

"Mrs Hunter left the house," Upton pronounced.

"Left the house?"

"Yes, sir. In somewhat of a hurry."

"Did she say where she was going?"

Upton shook his head. "No, sir, though I got the impression she wasn't coming back."

# CHAPTER 14

"Rachel!"

The word pierced the silence, forcing her to stop and turn around. Eli was sprinting along the gravel path, his breath bursts of white mist disappearing into the chill night air.

He closed the gap between them. "It's cold out. Come back to the house." He touched her gently on the upper arm. "We'll talk there. It's not what you think."

"I need to walk for a while to calm my temper." There was no polite way to relay the conversation that had taken place once Eli had left the drawing room. "Your mother thinks Felicity should give me lessons in decorum."

"Decorum?"

"She thinks I should visit Felicity's modiste in town." It had been a constant barrage of suggestions. A deluge of critical comments aimed at Rachel. Hence why Dominic suggested they venture upstairs to see Edmund. "Felicity is to have her maid style my hair. Felicity should remain in control of the household management as she's an excellent hostess."

Rather than apologise for his mother's indelicacy, Eli laughed.

"It's not funny. I sat there feeling like an urchin brought in out of the cold. By all accounts, Felicity is the perfect daughter-in-law."

"My mother hides behind a facade. Felicity is anything but perfect." Eli laughed again. "I thought you were angry because you saw me holding Felicity's hand."

"I'm hurt, not angry." She hugged herself to chase away the cold and calm her emotions. Witnessing the intimate scene had hurt more than she cared to admit.

But what right had she to make demands? They were friends who'd shared a kiss, business associates who should have more serious things on their minds than enjoying a flirtation.

"It's clear you still care about her, Eli."

"Care about her?" He jerked his head back. "I don't give a damn about Felicity. I was in the process of removing her hand from my chest when you walked in. Like Lady Meyer, Felicity craves male attention. She never spoke about her son, only complained about her marriage."

Honesty swam in his wide eyes.

Honesty rang in the determined tone of his voice.

"You did look annoyed." She glanced at the grand house, noting it was as grim as its occupants. "Do you regret coming here tonight? Do you wish I'd not persuaded you to confront your past?"

"Not in the least. I see Felicity for what she is—a damn liar and schemer—a woman so insecure she needs constant reassurance." He sighed. "I've invited Dominic to visit me in town. There's much to say, but I'll not suffer Felicity's interference."

"You did? That's wonderful news." Rachel forgot about her problems. Pride warmed every cold extremity. Where was the stern man she'd met at Vauxhall? The man who insisted on keeping everyone out?

"It's a start."

"Dominic spoke to me in the hall. He asked what he could

do to earn your forgiveness, told me how much he misses you."

He had begged to come visit them, begged for a chance to make amends. When possessed by lustful cravings, few stopped to consider the consequences of their actions. Thankfully, Dominic had found the courage to atone.

"I can't promise I'll forgive him. But a week ago, I hadn't the strength to visit Chichester." Eli's piercing blue eyes softened, and he reached for her hand. "Thank you. Thank you for unlocking the door to my prison."

"You unlocked the door. I merely gave you the key."

A slow smile formed as his gaze raked over her body. "Let's find a coaching inn and rest our weary heads. We'll leave for London at first light. On the journey, we'll decide how to tackle Lady Meyer."

Stay at an inn?

Would he hire one room or two?

"Won't your mother be disappointed you're leaving?"

"Hardly. She's given Dominic my room." He drew her closer, his voice turning deep and mischievous. "We'll leave without telling anyone. Sneak away under cover of darkness, like a secret elopement."

He made a simple journey sound like a thrilling adventure.

And yet, they were not giggling and laughing with excitement during the short carriage ride to the inn. Tension hung thick in the air—a desperate need to ease the inner ache. A restless energy had them shifting in their seats. Every pause for breath, every heated look fed the hypnotic attraction.

The Swan Inn was a hive of activity. The commotion in the adjacent field acted as a much-needed distraction. Amid the crowd, people sang folk songs and danced to a fiddler's tune. A bonfire kept the revellers warm. Some drank ale and watched the entertainment from a row of wooden benches. A woman with a pretty wreath in her hair proved the focus of everyone's attention.

"Either they're taking part in a pagan ritual, or it's a wedding celebration." Rachel found the sight enchanting. The air of gaiety was so opposed to the awkward ambience they'd encountered at Hunston Hall.

Eli escorted her across the yard but stopped at the gated entrance to the field. "For centuries, this has been a popular place for celebrations. You see the row of silver birch." He slipped his arm around her shoulder, pulled her closer and pointed to the blanket of trees in the distance. "The Druids called them Goddess Trees. They represent love and fertility and new beginnings."

New beginnings? Meeting him had definitely been the start of something wonderful, something magical.

She looked into his striking eyes. "Is that why we've stopped here? Do you wish to pay homage to the silver birch? Do you wish to pray for a fresh start?"

"I'd pray for love. I've already experienced an awakening." His intense gaze searched her face. "I'm not the man I was the day I met you. I'm not the man I was two hours ago. You've changed that."

She cupped his cheek, longing to kiss him. "I'm not the same woman I was the day I met you. I've lost all need for bravado. I'd like to say I've learnt to trust someone, but you made it so easy, Eli."

"Together, we've faced our fears."

"Yes." She swallowed deeply as his gaze dropped to her mouth.

Love was in the air. But all hope he might kiss her vanished when a young couple spotted them, grabbed their hands and forced them to join the celebrations.

A piper took up his flute to play a lively tune.

Everyone jumped to their feet to dance. The country reel wasn't one Rachel knew, but she looped around in a figure of eight, linking arms with strangers, twirling until she was dizzy, laughing until her stomach hurt.

She saw Eli wearing a wide grin as he gripped a toothless woman around the waist and swung her around. Those magnificent blue eyes, which upon first glance had stolen her breath, were bright with laughter. He looked happy, carefree, so handsome she couldn't concentrate on the music.

The ache in her chest felt different from the one pulsing in her core. She knew the latter as lust, knew the deeper yearning warned of a complicated emotion.

The dance ended, and the piper took to playing a ballad.

Eli found her in the crowd. "Would you care to dance, Rachel?"

"I thought serious men didn't prance about like popinjays."

He laughed. "I owe you a waltz after the terrible way I treated you at Vauxhall. Besides, it will be nice to dance with you while you're sober."

She wasn't sober.

Everything about him left her in a giddy stupor.

"Let me check my dance card, sir." She pretended to gather an object dangling from her wrist. "It seems we've danced twice already. Both times at Trēowith."

He frowned, but recognition dawned. "You mean we performed a sensual waltz with our mouths."

"Yes, in perfect harmony, as I recall. A third would seriously damage my reputation."

"I don't see the problem. I hope to ruin you completely."

Her heart raced. "And when will this ruination occur?"

"When you ache for me as I ache for you." His velvet voice slipped over her, teasing the fine hairs on her nape. "I've sworn to protect you, but I'll not trust myself to be alone with you tonight." He brushed a lock of hair behind her ear. "I've reached the point of no return, Rachel. I cannot keep my hands off you a moment longer."

The thought of giving herself to him was so appealing.

"Then make love to me, Eli. Take my virginity. Let me

remember this night until I'm old and grey and can barely recall the days. Let us have one night where we forget our troubles."

One night of pure, unadulterated bliss.

He said nothing. The heat in his eyes spoke a thousand words. He clasped her hand, threaded his fingers with hers and led her to the coaching inn.

Every nerve in her body rang with anticipation as she watched him pay for one room. They remained silent as they trudged upstairs, though his thumb caressed hers as he kept a firm hold of her hand.

The room was dark. She stood by the door while he lit the lamps.

Eli turned to her. "Are you sure this is what you want?"

"I've never been more sure of anything."

"It's been years since I took a woman to bed." He cleared his throat. "Forgive me if my performance falls short."

"I know next to nothing about the experience." Unlike Madame Dubarry, she was hardly an expert in pleasure. "Forgive me if nerves make for an uncomfortable coupling."

"Perhaps we're overthinking."

"I don't imagine our minds will have a great role to play once we slip into bed. Maybe we should begin by doing something to settle our nerves. Take turns playing hunter and prey."

He smiled. "Who's to begin?"

"I will. I'll play the huntress."

The huntress, the seductress, they were one and the same. The pressing question was, where to start? She recalled the flash of excitement in his eyes during their witty exchange at Vauxhall. Eli Hunter found confidence attractive. He admired honesty, directness. He admired her figure, for she had caught his covert glances many times.

Rachel began slipping the buttons on her pelisse. "According to Roman mythology, Diana is the goddess of hunting." She shrugged out of the garment and let it fall to the floor. "She's also known as the virgin goddess."

"I see a stark similarity."

She took slow steps towards him. "Diana is the moon bringing light to the darkness. She is enlightenment, the bearer of truth." She reached up and threaded her arms around his neck. "The truth is, I've never wanted a man the way I want you. When you kiss me, I transcend this ugly world full of doubts and fears. When you kiss me, you transport me to a place where hopes and dreams flourish."

He captured her around the waist. "Let's visit that idyllic place now."

He bent his head, settled his mouth over hers, moved in the slow sensual way that left her limp in his arms. The first slide of his tongue had lust pooling low and heavy. Knowing she was quickly becoming this mighty hunter's prey, she chose to remind him who was in control.

Rachel tore her mouth from his. "Strip off your clothes."

The sudden command made him blink, though shock soon gave way to a wicked grin. "All of them?"

"Every stitch." She stepped back.

He shrugged out of his coat. "Have you ever seen a man naked?"

"Only Madame Dubarry's lover. She chased him out of her bedchamber for falling asleep during the act." Rachel couldn't help but laugh at the memory. "The poor fellow had no time to gather his clothes."

"If he'd fallen asleep, one suspects his manhood was flaccid." Eli threw his waistcoat and cravat onto a nearby chair.

"It reminded me of the sausages at Smithfield Market, all skinny and shrivelled and pale."

"Rest assured, you'll not see the same tonight."

Eli drew his shirt over his head, and all amusement faded. Her mind returned to the night he'd prowled towards her in nothing but his trousers. She'd wanted him, even then.

Rachel moistened her lips and stared. Every muscle had been carved by a master craftsman, planed to perfection, every inch of bronzed skin sanded until it was silky smooth. Her gaze dipped to the only sign of imperfection—the jagged scar warning this man was as dangerous as he was handsome.

"Do you want me to continue?" he teased.

"Absolutely."

He dropped into the chair and tugged off his boots. When he stood, he stalked towards her, captured her hand and pressed her palm to his chest.

"Feel how my heart beats for you."

It thumped wildly.

"I fear it might burst through your chest. Your skin is so warm."

"My blood burns in my veins." He drew her hand over the rippling muscles in his abdomen, down to the scar. "This reminds me how thankful I am to be alive."

"I can't imagine a world without you."

He fixed her with his heated gaze. "They say forewarned is forearmed. Do you want to know what to expect when I step out of these breeches?"

She swallowed past her nerves and nodded.

Tentatively, he slipped her hand over the solid length bulging against the material. He was so hard, so thick, and yet she could feel him growing larger with each stroke.

"Don't be afraid. The night you sat at my supper booth, I knew we'd complement each other perfectly. We'll fit together perfectly now."

"Let me see you." Her voice broke. A huntress should be a fearless creature, not a quivering bag of nerves. "Let me touch you."

Eli inhaled sharply. He released her hand, fiddled with the buttons on the waistband and pushed his breeches past his lean hips.

It wasn't the scar that held her riveted but the rigid shaft springing free. Like the man himself, it stood firm, a powerful presence in the room.

"Touch me," he said, his voice strained. "Then it's my turn to play the hunter. It's my turn to make demands."

Eli showed her how to hold him, how to slide her hand back and forth to bring the ultimate satisfaction. Oh, she loved having him at her mercy, loved seeing him gasp for breath, loved this glimpse of vulnerability.

"Enough, love," he panted, firming his hand around hers and forcing her to stop. "Next time, you can pleasure me to your heart's content, but I doubt I'll last much longer, and I'm keen to bury myself inside you tonight."

Excitement surged through her. "Then it's time for a role reversal." She released him and raised her hands in mock surrender. "It's my turn to be the prey."

●

Eli couldn't take his eyes off her, couldn't wait to lay her down on the bed, drive deep into her body and make this woman his. Seeing her dancing beneath the stars, so wild and carefree, had been his undoing. To that mind, the journey from curiosity, to friendship, to lust, to an infinitely more profound emotion began the moment he'd set eyes on her at Vauxhall.

He recalled those quiet moments while he waited in the supper booth. Mere seconds before she appeared, he'd felt the subtle shift in the atmosphere, the gentle whispers of his heart, the sudden stirring of his soul. He'd tried to suppress the instant attraction, might have succeeded had she not appeared hours later, a vision of loveliness in his bedchamber.

Now, as he observed the coy smile on her lips, watched her pull the pins from her hair and shake her golden locks free, his heart rejoiced, and his soul sang.

"Would you like me to undress, Eli?"

While he'd like nothing more than to watch the erotic

show, he'd die if he didn't touch her. "Love, I want the pleasure of removing every inch of clothing myself."

"Where will you start?"

"With your boots." Then her stockings. Then the soft
flesh above the tied ribbons. "Come, sit down."

He drew her to the chair. As she sat, her wide blue gaze
settled on his cock, at a perfect angle to slide into her mouth.
The mischievous glint in her eyes said she was considering
touching him, considering setting those luscious lips to the
swollen head, keen to taste him.

"Minx! I can read your thoughts."

"Then I'm surprised you're kneeling and grabbing my
ankle."

He laughed. "If you could read my thoughts, you'd know I
have something else in mind." Indeed, he'd need her aroused
if she was to find pleasure in their lovemaking tonight.

With deft fingers, he removed her boot. Slowly, he
smoothed his hands from her calf to her thigh, tugged the
ribbon and rolled the wool stocking down to her ankle.

"I—I'm only wearing wool because it's so cold out."

He grinned. "My only focus is what lies beneath the stockings." He removed the other boot, but slipped past the
ribbon to caress her bare thigh. "Your skin is so smooth and
soft." He edged higher. "It's my turn to touch you intimately,
Rachel."

The flash of heat in her eyes said she'd touched herself
before.

Hell, the thought kept his cock rigid. "You understand my
intention?"

She nodded as her breathing quickened.

"I don't want you to remain silent." He watched the rapid
rise and fall of her chest as he traced a circle on her inner
thigh. "I want to hear your thoughts, want to hear your little
pants and moans when I touch you here." He stroked his
fingers over her sex.

"Oh!" She gripped the arms of the chair.

"Why the surprise? You've touched yourself before."

"Yes, but … but it's entirely different."

"You mean you like the feel of my fingers." He continued massaging in teasing circles. "You like being at a man's mercy."

"I like your fingers," she panted. "I like you pleasuring me, Eli."

"I know. You're so wet already."

Entranced by her little whimpers, he watched in awe as she rode his hand. "How about I change the rhythm?" Eli played her like a maestro, a mix of slow and fast tempos that had her begging for release.

"Eli … it's too much and too little at the same time."

Hell, he was so hard it hurt.

"Don't … don't stop."

He stopped only to push one finger inside her velvet heat. "You feel so damn good. You're so tight you hug me like a glove." He spread her wider with a second finger, pushed deep.

"I need you, Eli."

Those simple words tore a growl from his throat. Desperate to feel her squeezing his cock, he rubbed his thumb over the aching bud. She came apart shuddering against his hand, her inner muscles clamping around his fingers.

He expected her to sag in the chair, but the minx pinned him with her hungry stare.

"I need more, Eli. I need to feel you, all of you. Hurry."

He stood, his erection a mighty thing, so hard the veins pulsed along the length. "I need you out of those damn clothes." He needed to see every naked inch, press his mouth to every bit of milky white flesh.

Quickly pulling her to her feet, he started unfastening the

row of buttons on the back bodice, resorted to dragging her dress over her head along with her petticoat.

He turned her around to untie the front-fastening stays, but Rachel wouldn't stop touching him, wouldn't stop caressing his chest, stroking his cock.

"To hell with it!" He lost patience, scooped her into his arms and carried her to bed. "Next time, I'll strip you naked and resist the urge to watch you come."

"Next time? How presumptuous."

"A man can live in hope." He pushed her chemise up over her thighs and settled between her legs. "Just say the word if you want me to stop."

She responded by opening her legs wider and gripping his hips. "You do want me, Eli? You want to make love to me?"

His instinct was to laugh at the absurd questions, to remind her of the throbbing cock pushing against her entrance. Instead, he kissed her deeply.

"You're the one I think of at night," he whispered, dragging his mouth from hers. "You're the one who leaves me breathless." His words rang with a tenderness that was so unlike him. "It's you, Rachel. Only you."

Instinctively, she wrapped her legs around his waist. "Then have me."

Aching with need, he pushed slowly into her tight body. Hot, wet flesh surrounded him, hugging his cock like they were made to fit together. Hell, he fought the urge to drive hard, to slam into her, to let her feel every inch of his devotion.

"There's no easy way to do this."

"The desire to feel all of you will override any pain."

He kissed her, slipped his tongue over hers as he thrust to the hilt. They gasped in unison, gasped into each other's mouths. Buried balls deep, he waited for her to grow accustomed to the feel of him, watched as she caught her breath, revelled in the slow, sensual smile that said she liked feeling full.

"Move slowly," she breathed.

"Like this, love." He pinned her to the bed with his gaze as he withdrew, rolled his hips and pushed into her silky heat.

"Just like that." She relaxed more with each teasing thrust, but it wasn't long before she gripped his back and rocked against him, wasn't long before he was pounding hard.

She came again, hugging him so tightly he managed to withdraw with nary a second to spare. And as they lay together, a tangle of limbs, breathless from their lovemaking, Eli knew one thing with absolute certainty.

The case would soon be over.

But there wasn't a chance in hell he could let her go.

# CHAPTER 15

THEY LEFT the coaching inn at dawn. An overturned carriage blocking the road near Guildford meant it was five o'clock that evening when they eventually reached London. The visit to The Wild Hare to discuss their progress with Lucius Daventry resulted in him arranging a meeting in Hart Street the following morning.

The housekeeper, Mrs Gunning, greeted them on arrival. "They're all waiting in the drawing room, dear. I'll hurry along and fetch refreshments."

"All?" Rachel asked, aware the hum of conversation emanating from the room meant Mr Daventry wasn't alone. "Mr Daventry has summoned other agents?"

"He's called all those available."

"I see." Rachel's stomach churned.

Was the master disappointed with her progress? Did he plan on letting another agent take the case? Her heart ached at the thought of leaving Eli.

Rachel tried to look on the bright side. At least she'd have an opportunity to speak to Eliza and Honora. Since her intimate encounter with Eli two nights ago, she'd struggled to rouse a logical thought and desperately needed a woman's advice.

Rachel glanced at the handsome man who had stolen her heart. It had taken every effort not to join him in bed last night. She had heard him pad along the corridor, stop outside her door. But something prevented him from knocking. Something made him retreat to his room and sleep alone.

"No need to wait," Mrs Gunning said when she noticed Rachel lingering.

Eli opened the door. "After you, Miss Gambit."

He did not step back but gestured for her to squeeze past his muscular frame. Being within inches of him left her pulse pounding in her throat.

He bent his head. "We've much to discuss, you and I."

She met his intense gaze and nodded.

After the traumas she'd encountered with the Hanaways, she had sworn never to place herself in a vulnerable position again. Foolishly, she'd believed herself in control of her emotions. Stupidly, she'd not thought love could be so complicated.

She gathered her composure and scanned the faces of those in attendance.

Mr Daventry was seated on the sofa, engaged in a private conversation with Dante D'Angelo. Eliza and Honora occupied the two chairs opposite and were chatting amongst themselves.

"Ah, Hunter. Miss Gambit." Mr Daventry stood. "Take a seat."

Mr D'Angelo pushed to his feet. "So you've stayed the course, Miss Gambit, survived Hunter's rigorous tests."

Eli tutted. "The tests at Vauxhall proved Miss Gambit has gumption."

"Judging by what's happened during this investigation, you've had many opportunities to study her performance."

From the mischievous glint in Mr D'Angelo's eyes, he was teasing.

The gentle sigh from Eli's lips suggested he was mentally appraising a different performance. "Miss Gambit is exceptional in every regard."

Rachel stole a glance at Eliza, who was currently examining the width of Eli's thighs. Silent messages passed between them: Rachel's plea for help and Eliza's nod of acknowledgement.

Mr Daventry motioned for them to sit on the empty sofa positioned around the low table. "I've informed your colleagues of the current state of affairs."

"You've told them about my position in your organisation?" Eli sounded surprised. He waited for Rachel to sit before settling beside her.

Heavens! She'd never concentrate with him sitting so close. The heat of his body and the alluring scent of maleness roused memories of their lovemaking.

"I trust my agents, Hunter, and you need their assistance. There are too many lines of enquiry, and I want the traitor caught before he sells us all to the devil."

"You're supposed to be in your sickbed," Eli countered.

Mr Daventry shrugged. "This meeting is more important than fooling the Council. And I expect Miss Gambit to have solved the case within the next few days. As I've already updated our colleagues on your progress, perhaps we should hear from Miss Dutton." He turned to Eliza. "What would be your next line of enquiry?"

Eliza's eyes widened. Like Rachel, she was desperate for her first case. "You mentioned two keys are required to enter the Sanctum."

"Yes. But they're not like any keys you've seen before," Eli said.

"Then I would visit the locksmith. We must make certain the man didn't copy the key. Or no one stole the cast."

"Agreed." Mr Daventry took the pencil off the table and scribbled in his notebook. "I shall accompany you. The man is sworn to secrecy and will refuse to tell you anything." He turned his attention to Honora. "Miss Wild? Do you have any suggestions as to how we might approach the case?"

Honora looked through spectacles perched on her nose. "Based on the conversation Rachel had with the doctor, we should attempt to find the footman. It shouldn't be difficult to locate the whereabouts of his potential new employer."

"Lady Chadwick," Rachel added. "Perhaps he might shed light on whether Mary did give birth to a child."

Mr Daventry nodded. "An excellent idea. You'll be responsible for locating the footman, Miss Wild."

"Me?" Honora clutched her hand to her throat.

"Have faith in your abilities," the master said. "You've a logical mind and must overcome your fears. I may have a case for you, and so this will be your test. You'll take my man Bower. He'll be on hand should you need assistance."

Honora nodded though took to nibbling her bottom lip.

"D'Angelo? What are your thoughts on the case?"

The man with the dangerous persona sat forward. "While I doubt we can trust Jacob Hanaway's word, Belton accusing the boy of theft rouses suspicion. I shall check Belton's background. Perhaps he's been plagued by thieves and thought Scrivens' stepfather had stolen something from the emporium."

"See if Mr Belton owes money to lenders or gaming hells," Rachel said. Few men would think to capitalise on a murder. Most would find the whole business disturbing. "Mr Hunter and I will use the information from Dr Baker to intimidate Lord Meyer's staff. Their mistress is a liar, and they need to know they'll face a perjury charge for supporting her story."

"I thought to give you different assignments," came Mr Daventry's shocking announcement. His gaze shifted to Eli, then to Rachel. "One of you can question Lord Meyer's staff. The other can spy on Truscott now he's returned to town."

He wanted them to work separately!

Every fibre of her being fought against the idea.

Eli appeared to find the notion equally distressing. "There's every chance Jacob Hanaway will come to town. Having persuaded Miss Gambit to question the fellow, I'll not leave her open to an attack."

Mr Daventry considered Eli's comment. "Miss Gambit, you're skilled enough with a blade to defend yourself against the oaf. Do you feel it necessary to remain at Blackstone, to have Hunter be your protector?"

Rachel's chest tightened at the thought of leaving Blackstone, leaving Eli. But she had to choose her words carefully. Mr Daventry was a perceptive man.

"Jacob Hanaway will seek me out, sir. I believe he planned to wait until my first meeting with the solicitor before attempting to get rid of me. Now he knows where to find me, I doubt he'll have the patience to wait." The man was definitely of unsound mind.

"All the more reason you should return to Howland Street and Miss Trimble's care. D'Angelo will keep watch on the house."

Desperation scratched at her throat. "Sir, Jacob Hanaway will probably set the house ablaze. In all honesty, I would feel safer with Mr Hunter. At least until we've solved the case and determined Jacob's intention."

"Very well. A few more days can't hurt. With Blackstone being on the outskirts of town, no one will know you're there."

She resisted the urge to sag in relief. "The case occupies every waking hour. We spend very little time at Blackstone."

Eli relaxed back in the seat. "Any news from the Hatton Garden office regarding the re-enactment of the crime?"

Daventry nodded. "I received word a little over an hour ago. Scrivens lacked the strength to wield the heavy weapon, let alone drive it into the grain sack."

Thank heavens!

"Then surely they must release him." Rachel knew it was more complicated than that. They needed to find a motive for Belton killing the man first.

"The prosecution will seek to discount the evidence. We need something more substantial." Mr Daventry addressed the room. "We must work quickly and will reconvene here tomorrow." He stood. "Before you leave, Hunter, I'd like a private word."

Despite being curious as to why Mr Daventry wanted a private word with Eli, Rachel was relieved to have a moment alone with Eliza and Honora.

They congregated on the pavement outside the Hart Street office, waited for Mr D'Angelo to bid them good day and climb into his conveyance before bursting into conversation.

"What's going on between you and Mr Hunter?" Eliza was as direct as the Great North Road. "His gaze lingers whenever he looks at you. There's a softer tone to his voice when he mentions your name."

There was no point hiding the truth. She could trust these women with her life. "We're attracted to each other. We've kissed, and we've …" Both women were astute enough to fill in the missing words.

Honora clasped her hand to her mouth.

Eliza seemed shocked but then laughed. "I knew it. And I imagine Mr Daventry knows it, too, hence why he suggested giving you separate assignments. No wonder he kept Mr Hunter behind."

Panic gripped Rachel by the shoulders.

Would Mr Daventry forbid Eli from pursuing a relationship? Would he threaten to remove Eli from the Council? Threaten to dismiss Rachel from the Order for fraternising with a client?

"I'm in love with him," Rachel blurted. "I'm in love with Mr Hunter." She exhaled deeply and then laughed. "Oh, it sounds ridiculous. Me. In love. But he lives in my dreams, commands every waking thought. What else can it be?"

Honora got over her shock. "It could be infatuation. Perhaps Mr Daventry is right. A separation would give you time to consider your feelings."

"My whole body hurts at the thought."

"It's an addiction, then," Eliza offered. "If one can become addicted to laudanum, one can become addicted to kissing."

All the words one associated with addiction—craving, dependency, an uncontrollable fixation—described how she felt about Eli Hunter. Perhaps Honora was right. One had to remove oneself from temptation to overcome the addiction.

"I'm definitely addicted to the taste of his mouth."

"Rachel!" A blush stained Honora's cheeks.

"I can see why." Eliza sighed. "He's quite captivating."

"Perhaps I'm over-thinking. It will all be over in a few short days, and we will go our separate ways. Mr Daventry will assign me another case, and Mr Hunter won't have time to meet at a coffeehouse, let alone conduct an illicit affair."

Yes, then she would realise it wasn't love. And she would remember it as two lonely people seeking a moment's solace.

With a renewed sense of faith, the knowledge that she wasn't drowning in a sea of romantic notions, Rachel straightened. "Have you heard anything about your potential assignments?"

Eliza tutted. "No. Lord Greyson visited the office three days ago. He wanted to hire an agent to find his half-sister. After hearing the sad tale, Mr Daventry told him we were all occupied with cases and sent Mr Sloane."

Rachel thought it odd. "Mr Sloane is already dealing with a matter of fraud. How will he find the time to work two cases?"

Eliza shrugged. "I heard Mr Daventry tell that fool Lord Roxburgh that if he wishes to hire an agent to help find his conscience, I was available."

"Roxburgh?" The lord was handsome and witty, but he was a rake and a gambler and a man any principled woman should avoid. "Has Mr Daventry forgotten your father gambled away your fortune?"

"It can't have slipped his mind."

Honora shook her head. "As if you could ever conceive working with such a degenerate. If Mr Daventry is so undiscerning, one wonders what he has planned for me."

Rachel suspected it had something to do with the master's recent visit to Kent. "Lord DeVille wishes to hire an agent. Mr Daventry went to see him at his cliff-top mansion in Whitstable."

Honora's eyes widened, but she dismissed the notion she might be a candidate. "He won't send a female agent to stay in Whitstable."

"No. Probably not."

There was no time to continue the conversation. Eli appeared looking as if he hadn't a care in the world. He smiled as their eyes met. Clearly, Mr Daventry hadn't threatened him or given him an ultimatum.

He gestured to his black carriage parked on the opposite side of the street. "If you're ready, Miss Gambit, we should visit the Meyer household and frighten them into confessing."

Rachel tried to ignore the swarm of butterflies tickling her stomach. "I'm ready to leave now. Do you have Dr Baker's confession?"

Eli tapped his coat pocket. "Indeed."

Rachel hugged her friends and bid them farewell. Once seated inside Eli's carriage, she broached the subject uppermost in her mind.

"Did Mr Daventry warn you against consorting with his agent?"

Eli smiled. "He apologised for the inconvenience of having you stay at Blackstone. He said he hoped the matter would be concluded quickly, mentioned you returning to Howland Street soon, presumed I longed for some semblance of normality."

"And he had no clue we've been intimate?"

The word failed to convey the powerful surge of emotion she'd experienced when Eli Hunter moved deep inside her. He'd claimed her body and soul that night.

"If he did, he never mentioned it. He asked about our progress with the coded letter and suggested you spend the evening studying the symbols."

"I'd planned to do just that upon our return to Blackstone." She had to find something to occupy her mind while attempting to break free from her addiction.

"Daventry said the fact Swanson lost his key and failed to interview Jacob Hanaway rouses some suspicion."

"Mr Truscott failed to interview Dr Baker."

Eli gave a curious hum. "Yes, I can forgive Swanson, as he was likely in a panic after someone stole his key. But Truscott is one of the most experienced men on the Council. It's strange he didn't make the trip to Brighton himself."

They sat in silence for a time, undoubtedly considering their passionate night in a coaching inn, not the evidence.

"How did Mr Crocker come to be the custodian of Trēowith?" she asked.

"He worked for Viscount Alderney, was sent by the peer's youngest son to visit Mr Trentham and collect on a promissory note. Crocker watched Trentham count the money and place it in a leather pouch. When Crocker returned with the pouch, it contained nothing but slips of paper. Trentham accused him of stealing the contents."

Rachel sighed. "It must have been difficult to prove Mr Crocker's innocence." In such cases, the servant was always presumed guilty.

"Daventry's father-in-law, Atticus Atwood, dealt with the case. An investigation into Trentham's financial affairs showed the man was on the verge of bankruptcy. Had he not paid on the promissory note, Alderney's son would have called him out."

"And so he saved Mr Crocker from the noose."

"Indeed."

But what if Mr Crocker had stolen the money? Could he have deceived the Council? Could he have lied about the intruder? He had access to the Sanctum once the members had left the room.

As instructed, Eli's coachman slowed the carriage to a stop on the corner of Park Lane and Upper Brook Street, adjacent to Hyde Park. Rachel shuffled forward, but Eli placed a stalling hand on her knee.

"Today, our minds are occupied with the case. Tonight, we need to discuss what happened between us at The Swan Inn."

Her heart skipped a beat at the memory of their passionate lovemaking. "There's nothing to discuss." Talking would only feed her addiction. "We took advantage of the moment."

"I took your virginity. Don't imagine that means nothing to me."

What did it mean? Surely he didn't feel obliged to offer for her now.

"You didn't take it, Eli. I gave it freely. And you already know why."

"And that's all you have to say on the matter?" He raised a

questioning brow. "Might we take advantage of the moment again, do you suppose?"

She shrugged, yet given a chance, she would gladly throw herself into his arms. "I imagine so. Should we both feel the inclination." She glanced out of the window and quickly changed the subject lest she tell the man she was addicted to his smile, his smell, his taste, his touch. "We should focus on what we plan to say to Lady Meyer's butler."

Eli opened the door and exited the carriage. "We'll continue the conversation this evening. As to how we'll approach Lady Meyer's servants, I think we'll avoid a direct confrontation."

"What have you in mind?"

Eli helped her to the pavement. "There's no one more loyal than a man's butler, and I'd rather avoid Lady Meyer overhearing our conversation. I suggest we venture into the mews and speak to a groom, have him relay the information to the rest of the staff."

"You should give him your calling card. If they recall important information, they might send word to Blackstone. And explain the seriousness of lying to a magistrate."

"Agreed. The Woods' mews service those houses on the north side of the street." He offered his arm, and she gripped it without question. "It's but a hundred yards."

Touching him was like that first desperate nip of laudanum. It warmed her insides, settled her nerves, relaxed every muscle. It induced a hypnotic trance where sentiment reigned supreme.

Lord Meyer commanded the third carriage house on the row. The double doors were open. A young lad with a freckled face and a dirty cap was busy scrubbing the wheels of a town coach.

Eli coughed into his fist to get the lad's attention. "I'm looking for Lord Meyer's head groom."

The boy dropped his brush into a bucket and whistled to

someone inside. A slim fellow with bushy side-whiskers and a long nose strode into the yard. He scanned their attire and waited for them to state their business.

"We come with news your colleagues might find interesting," Rachel said.

The fellow frowned. "If yer from Spitalfields Orphanage, we ain't takin' on any more help." He gestured to the lad, who looked no older than ten. "The boy works like a dog, so he does, but the master won't take another."

"We're not from the orphanage." Despite the man reeking of stale sweat, Eli beckoned him closer. "It's concerning Mary Harcourt. We're investigating her case on behalf of the Home Secretary and have evidence to confirm your mistress is lying."

The fellow listened but said nothing.

"We come to warn them that if they continue to pervert the course of justice by supporting Lady Meyer's lies, they will be considered accomplices to her crimes." Eli retrieved the letter from Peel and showed it to the head groom.

"Ain't no point givin' me that. I can't read a word."

"But you can see the official stamp?" Eli tucked the letter back in his pocket and removed a silver case. "Take my card. Give it to anyone who wishes to retract their earlier statement." Eli thrust his card into the groom's hand. "We understand the staff may have been forced to lie. A confession will mean they escape arrest. I'm sure I don't need to tell you that the punishment for perjury is transportation or the pillory."

The man's ruddy cheeks turned ashen as he fingered the card.

Rachel decided to press him further. "We know what happened to James Tinsley. We doubt he took the stage or hired a hackney, which means he travelled in Lord Meyer's coach. It means you know where he is."

For fear Dr Baker had been duped into thinking the

footman had gone to work elsewhere, Rachel made no mention of Lady Chadwick.

"I can't afford to lose this job."

"You're likely to lose more than your job if the magistrate discovers you know something that might shed light on the truth." Rachel tutted. "Have you no conscience, sir? Do you not care that an innocent woman may hang?"

"Aye, it don't sit right with me." The fellow leant closer and assailed them with his foul breath. "James, the footman, he didn't want to say them things." He took a quick peek over his shoulder. "The mistress made him an offer he couldn't refuse. His mother was in the workhouse over in Cleveland Street and took sick. The mistress hired them a cottage on the road out past Mile End."

"In exchange for his testimony?" Eli said.

"Aye. All he has to do is tell a story about the maid, and Lady Meyer will let them stay at the cottage and will provide food and medicine."

"Tell a story about Mary Harcourt?"

He nodded. "I hear the gossip but ain't been party to what's go on."

After a brief silence, Eli gestured to the card in the groom's grubby hand. "The staff have two days to come to me with their confessions. After that, it may be too late to save Mary, too late for them to escape punishment when the truth comes to light."

The groom nodded.

"Two days," Eli reminded him. "No more."

They left the man to his work and returned to Eli's conveyance.

"We need to send word to Howland Street. Tell Honora about the cottage near Mile End. Have Mr Bower take her to search for James Tinsley."

"We'll stop on our way back to Blackstone."

"But it's only one o'clock." If they returned to the house

now, they'd be alone for hours. She'd become consumed by her addiction, and they'd find themselves in an intimate clinch. "We could venture out of town. See if we can find the footman's cottage. It will save Honora the trouble."

Eli gave her a knowing look. "Miss Wild needs to prove her worth if she's to get her own case. Surely you don't wish to hinder her chances of success."

He was right, of course.

"No. Finding James Tinsley will give Honora a much-needed boost of confidence." Rachel tried to think of another excuse to waste a few hours. "We could visit Belton's Emporium, examine the bloodstains. If David Scrivens drew the sword from the body and had it in his hand when the Beltons wrestled him into the pantry, there should be a blood trail."

"An excellent point. One we will broach when we have evidence to prove Belton had a motive for murder." He narrowed his gaze and rubbed his jaw. "It seems you're keen to avoid spending time alone with me. Daventry gave you the option of working separately. You don't have to stay at Blackstone."

Oh, her head was a muddled mess.

He'd said honesty was the best argument, so she decided to convey some semblance of the truth. "Eliza and Honora fear I'm a little obsessed with you. They're worried this dalliance won't be as straightforward as we'd originally thought."

"They are?" Eli relaxed back in the seat and folded his arms across his broad chest. "You told them about the night we spent together at The Swan?"

Heat crept up her neck to warm her cheeks. "Not in so many words, but they are very astute."

"They are." His amused smile reached his eyes. "But let's agree to speak plainly. You're worried that you're growing too attached to me. You're scared because we've spent a night together, and you didn't expect to find your emotions engaged. You fear once we reach Blackstone and we're alone together, this obsession will override all rhyme and reason."

Her pulse raced. Was she so transparent?

"Something like that. How can you tell?"

His smile turned sinful. "Because we're suffering from the same ailment."

# CHAPTER 16

BASED ON THEIR RECENT CONFESSION, Eli decided to leave Rachel alone in the study while she examined the letter written in strange symbols. The fact he wanted to sit with her and watch her work proved more disturbing than his desire to carry her to his room to make love.

Eli was in his bedchamber, contemplating how he might persuade Rachel to sleep in his bed tonight, when Jacobs appeared in the doorway.

"This arrived for you, sir." Jacobs offered the silver salver. "The hackney driver is waiting outside for your response."

Eli took the note from the salver. He knew it came from the butler at his leased property in Harley Street. That it meant someone from Hunston Hall had arrived begging for an audience.

He peeled back the folds and read Dominic's request to meet. His brother had wasted no time in coming to London. No doubt he had much to say. No doubt he dragged guilt behind him like a lead ball chained to his ankle.

"Jacobs, give the hackney driver a note with my direction."

The twitch of Jacobs' brows confirmed his surprise. "Yes, sir."

Eli's first instinct was to head to the study and inform Rachel.

She looked up from the scribbled notes littering the desk. "Dominic is in London? So soon? Though after his heartfelt plea, I'm not surprised."

"With Harley Street being a little over a mile from here, we can expect him shortly." Nerves pushed to the fore, though Eli would rather speak to his brother at Blackstone than under Felicity's watchful eye in Chichester.

"Will we tell him the truth? Will we say we're colleagues and lovers, not husband and wife? Will he not find our arrangement shockingly unconventional?"

Eli shrugged. "I see no reason to correct the misconception."

"It was a lie, not a misconception. You're estranged from your brother because of his deceit. You'd be a hypocrite to let him believe I'm his sister-in-law."

She was right, yet his stomach churned at the thought of telling Dominic the truth. "I don't want him to think less of you, less of us." He gulped past a lump in his throat, past a fear of putting his feelings into words. "I want him to know I care about you, care deeply, not think this is some sordid affair."

"I'm sure he'll see that we care about each other."

Or were both infatuated to the point of madness.

Only time would reveal their true feelings.

"There should be no more lies between you and your brother, Eli. Tell him you mentioned marriage because you wanted to protect my reputation."

He wasn't sure why he'd introduced her as his wife. It had felt as natural as taking air.

"You're right. I'll leave you to your work and send Jacobs

to fetch you once I've told Dominic what I really think of his betrayal."

She nodded. "I'm here if you need me."

"Likewise." He inclined his head and left the room.

Knowing she was close brought immense comfort. Indeed, things would soon change, and yet he wanted everything to remain the same. Not exactly the same. His bedchamber would become their bedchamber, and he would never sleep alone again.

Dominic arrived, and Jacobs escorted him to the drawing room.

Eli did not bow to his brother nor give him an affectionate pat on the arm. "I know I offered an olive branch, but I didn't expect you to snatch it so quickly."

"I've waited three years for the opportunity." He observed Eli's attire. "Are you in mourning?"

"Black used to suit my mood." With it being a particularly cold day, Eli gestured to the fireside chairs. "Sit down. Will you take coffee?"

"Please." Dominic scanned the burgundy walls, the walnut bookcases, the paintings of horses and hunting dogs. "Does Rachel not object to the masculine ambience? Felicity insists on a palette of pastels."

Eli's stomach twisted into knots at the thought of Felicity taking command of his family home. "Rachel doesn't live here." Not yet, at least. "I'm afraid I have a confession to make. As a man who detests lies, I can't think what came over me."

Dominic sat down, a frown marring his brow. "You live separately from your wife? Is that not considered irregular?"

"Rachel is my colleague, not my wife." Eli tugged on the bell pull, then sat down. "We work to prove some of those awaiting trial in Newgate are innocent of their crimes. We save them from the hangman's noose."

Dominic shook his head, confused. "But why say she's your wife?"

"We were in Shoreham interviewing a witness. Rachel thought I should visit Chichester and attempt to heal the rift. The lie fell easily from my lips."

A knock on the door brought the maid, Clara. Eli ordered coffee.

"But you look at her as if she's a rare find, a priceless gem," Dominic said once Clara had departed. "To be truthful, you have the look of a man besotted."

*You? Truthful?* he wanted to say.

Eli paused but decided to admit to his feelings for Rachel. "I am besotted. We're attempting to solve complicated cases. When we have, we'll deal with our blossoming relationship then. She's in the study if you'd like to see her. Then again, you've come seeking a private audience. To explain why you failed to warn me I might find my betrothed bouncing naked on your lap."

A vision of them frolicking in the orangery burst into Eli's mind. Usually, the image left him cursing them to the devil, had bitterness writhing in his veins. Today, he felt nothing. No, not nothing. Relieved.

Dominic sat forward. "Eli, I wanted to tell you so many times, but Felicity said you'd load a pistol and fire a lead ball between my brows. That or you'd likely shoot yourself."

"Murder my own brother? Despite everything you've done, you know that's beyond the realms of my capabilities."

"But a man can lose his mind when he loses the love of his life."

"The love of my life?" Eli hoped they heard his mocking snort in Chichester. "If I loved Felicity, I would have beaten you to a pulp. What you did was a gift. Sadly, it took me three years to realise." It had taken the words of a wise woman, a loving and compassionate woman, to show him the light.

"A gift?"

"Be assured, your betrayal cut deep, but you saved me from making the biggest mistake of my life. I agreed to marry Felicity to please Father. The mind is a powerful beast, and I convinced myself I felt something."

Dominic sat back in the chair. "I'm not in love with Felicity, either." He dragged his hand down his face and sighed. "She has a way of dousing passion's flames. The constant complaining slowly killed any emotional connection."

The news came as no surprise. It didn't rouse anger, only pity.

"Thankfully, that's your cross to bear, not mine."

Silence descended.

Clara arrived with refreshments. She placed the silver tray on the sideboard and served the drinks. Before leaving, she stole a quick glance at Dominic and then Eli, surely noting the striking similarities. They were alike in looks, nothing alike in character.

"I doubt you'll ever trust me, Eli, but I hope we might be close again."

"I forgive you." The words came as a shock to Eli, more so to Dominic. Yet he felt suddenly lighter. "I'm willing to try to rebuild our relationship, to be an uncle to your son, but I dislike Felicity, and I'll never again visit Hunston."

Dominic's smile faded. "But Hunston is your home, your inheritance. Father trusted you to take care of his beloved estate."

"I hate Hunston. Having invested the money left to me, my property portfolio gives me a sizeable income." Eli paused, mulling over a sudden idea. "I've decided to give you the deeds to Hunston, though should you die before your son is of age, I shall be named his trustee."

Dominic's mouth dropped open. "But you can't. Father wanted—"

"Father wanted me to marry Felicity, so it's fair to assume his judgement was flawed." Every cell in his body confirmed it was the right decision. He wanted free of it, free of the burden and the shackles that bound him to the past. "Besides, it's time you made your own way in the world and stopped tugging on my purse strings. I'll not be responsible for Felicity's extravagant spending."

Dominic reached for his coffee cup, and the china rattled on the saucer. Such was the state of the man's nerves. "I don't deserve your generosity."

"No, you don't. But you're going to make something of Hunston Hall. You're going to make your son proud. He will continue Father's legacy."

They sat and spoke about the potential of building new tenant cottages, of purchasing the land to the south and raising cattle. Eli agreed to lend his brother ten thousand pounds at five per cent interest, agreed to have legal documents drawn up with a solicitor.

Dominic asked if he might see Rachel.

Eli escorted his brother to the study, informed her that he'd explained the true nature of their relationship, relayed the news that Dominic was now the proud owner of Hunston Hall.

Rachel didn't spout flowery nonsense but spoke directly. "Eli does you a great honour. His benevolence is a credit to him. No other man has the strength of heart to forgive such a betrayal."

Desire coiled low and heavy in Eli's loins. A burning heat flooded his heart. Never had anyone spoken with such faith in him. The realisation that he loved her came over him in warm waves.

Dominic inclined his head. "Eli has always been an exceptional man. One day, I hope to prove I'm worthy of his faith and kindness." Seemingly keen to change the subject, he gestured to drawings scattered over the desk. "Eli said you're trying to identify which symbol corresponds to which letter."

"It's a case of looking for patterns."

"May I see the symbols?"

"Of course." Rachel handed Dominic the letter. "Please tell me you understand some of what's written."

Dominic fell silent while concentrating on the drawn images. "I'm not entirely sure, but I think a few may be alchemical symbols, some astronomical." He pointed to a circular shape with an arrow pointing northeast. "I'm certain this is the astronomical symbol for Mercury."

Excitement sparked in Rachel's eyes. Eli was more annoyed at his brother for rousing her interest than the fact he'd fucked Felicity.

"Do you have any books on astronomy or alchemy, Eli?"

"No. My interests lie in art and philosophy, though I believe—" He paused. Damnation! The conniving devil. "I believe Swanson has an interest in medieval alchemy."

"Mr Swanson?" Rachel's mouth dropped open. "He lost his key and knows how to decipher some of the symbols in this cryptic note. It can't be a coincidence."

Dominic chuckled. "To say I'm fascinated by your work is an understatement. There must never be a dull moment."

Eli met Rachel's gaze. "Every new revelation steals my breath, leaves me desperate to learn more."

She smiled. "I find myself equally captivated."

Perhaps reading the thrum of sexual tension in the air, Dominic returned the letter to the desk and made his intention to leave known. He bid Rachel farewell, said he looked forward to meeting her again, spoke as if she held a permanent place in Eli's life.

"There's another startling difference between us," Dominic said when Eli escorted him out to the stable yard. "I like your wife immensely."

Eli laughed. "Rachel is remarkable, but she's not my wife."

"Not yet. One suspects it's only a matter of time before you accept your fate." Dominic paused. "You seem happy, Eli. Happier than I've seen you before."

Eli took a moment to still his mind, to listen to the wild drum of his heartbeat, to feel love's life force flowing through him.

"I'm in love with her. I need to decide how I might fit into her future plans. She means to start a new life in America." If only he could persuade her to stay.

"She seemed rather comfortable in your study."

"Who can say what fate has in store? A week ago, I never thought to see you drinking coffee in my drawing room."

Dominic apologised again and promised to spend his life making amends. They hugged for the first time in years, and Eli made him swear not to inform Mother or Felicity of his address in town.

Eli stood alone in the dim stable yard long after his brother's carriage rattled away, long after the groom handed him a lit lantern to navigate his way back to the house in the dark.

He didn't return to the house but walked through the garden, contemplating whether to reveal the true depth of his feelings. He'd found the strength to open his heart, to trust someone, and now his greatest fear was losing the only person he'd ever truly wanted. The only woman he'd ever truly loved.

●

"Eli," Rachel whispered through the darkness. She held the lantern aloft and moved along the garden path. "It's cold out. Come inside. Where are you?"

She scoured the shadows, wondering why he'd not returned to the house, knowing he wouldn't leave without giving her prior warning, suspecting something was amiss.

She shivered—from the chilly air, from the fear that Jacob Hanaway had found his way into the garden, had caught Eli unawares and ... and ...

"Eli!" Gripping the handle of her knife, she edged into the blackness.

The door in the boundary wall creaked open.

A light appeared, a dancing glow in the dark.

"Rachel!" The voice she longed to hear reached her through the gloom.

Her pulse settled when he came into view, unharmed and looking as handsome as ever. "You've been out here an hour. I feared you'd tripped and banged your head."

"Or Jacob Hanaway had buried me in a shallow grave." He closed the gap between them, slipped his arm around her waist and pressed a lingering kiss to her forehead. "Forgive me. I went for a walk in the field beyond the house and lost track of time."

"You must be cold to your bones. You were so long, I asked Jacobs to have a fire lit in your chamber, have a hot bath drawn."

The hand at her back moved in slow, caressing strokes. "You must have been worried. You've left the house without your pelisse." His lips curled into a wicked grin. "Perhaps a hot bath for two is in order."

Excited by the prospect of making love to him, she smiled coyly. "Will there be enough room? Perhaps I should wash you, massage your tight muscles."

"As I'm keen to see every inch of you, I suggest you bathe first."

She couldn't hide her eagerness but suddenly recalled their earlier conversation. "Is it right that we continue to feed this obsession?"

"I think we both suspect it's more than an obsession. But I want you, and you want me. We're not hurting anyone. I can only speak for myself, but I've never been happier."

Oh, her heart was so full of happiness it might burst.

"I never thought I could feel this way about anyone." She yearned for his company, longed to feel his mouth on hers, craved his touch. "Let's go inside and discuss it somewhere warm."

Eli led her into the house. They extinguished their lanterns and left them outside. The slow climb upstairs had anticipation thrumming through her body, just like it had the night at The Swan Inn. Except the footman was still lugging buckets, still filling the bathtub, the maid still busy stoking the fire.

Rachel stopped outside Eli's chamber door. The servants knew this was more than a business arrangement, but she would not be so blatant about their affair.

"I'll retire to my room until you've bathed." She still carried her knife and needed to store it away in its sheath. The distant chime of the long case clock reminded her dinner would be served in an hour. "We're to dine at eight. Perhaps we can leave our conversation until then."

He reached for her hand. "I can't wait that long."

"Then I'll return in ten minutes," she whispered.

During those ten minutes, and fearing a repeat of her struggle to undress while aroused, she stripped off her clothes and slipped into her cotton nightgown. She heard the servants retreat, knew Eli's loud cough meant the coast was clear.

When she entered his lair, she found him perched on the edge of the bed, stripped of everything but his breeches. Her mouth watered at the sight.

"Close the door."

"We've an hour until we're due in the dining room." She shut the door and turned the key in the lock. "It doesn't leave us much time to bathe."

He stood. "I sent word to Jacobs. Cook will prepare a tray in two hours and have it brought to my room. There's plenty of time to bathe."

Rachel noted the steam rising from the tub. "At this time of year, a lady usually bathes in her shift, but it seems so warm in here." Warm, because flames danced in the grate, flames flickered in the lamps, flames of lust licked her skin.

"Then remove your nightgown."

Pushing nerves aside, she reached for the hem, gathered the garment to her waist, then pulled it over her head. She threw it onto the floor and stood before him, naked as the day she was born.

Eli hissed a breath, his greedy gaze teasing her nipples to peak.

He slipped off the bed, removed his breeches to reveal his jutting manhood.

"Step into the water, Rachel. A good hunter uses the element of surprise, captures his prey unawares. I shall consider my next move carefully."

She did as he asked. The water was warm, soothing.

He came forward, scooped water from the tub with his cupped hand and trickled it over her breasts. "I'm going to wash every inch of you." A sinful grin formed on his lips. "Then I'm going to lick you dry."

Her knees almost buckled. "And I shall do the same to you."

"Not tonight. We'll save that for next time." He set his mouth to her nipple and sucked gently. "And yes, I'm being presumptuous, but I can't get enough of you." He lavished the other nipple with the same attention, licked around the areola.

Rachel pushed her fingers through his dark hair and tugged hard. "Yes. Oh, yes. Soon it will be my turn to play the hunter."

He looked up at her, his eyes glazed with desire, while flicking his tongue over her nipple.

"Don't stop, Eli."

He dragged his mouth away, cupped more water and wet her abdomen. The feel of his mouth on her skin sent tingles to her toes. Then he gripped her buttocks and swirled his tongue around her navel.

Her head fell back, a moan leaving her lips. But then he

moved lower, slipping his tongue between her folds and sucking softly on the aching nub. He made her come like that, his face buried in her nest of curls, his mouth and tongue working its magic.

He pushed his fingers inside her as she shuddered, showering her in pleasure.

"We'll bathe together once you've taken me," he said in a husky voice, confirming he was just as aroused. "It's my turn to lie back and enjoy the view."

She understood his meaning when he settled back on the bed, his shaft standing upright and proud. Madame Dubarry had said a woman could experience a sense of freedom when riding a man. It seemed Rachel was about to see if the modiste's wise words had merit.

Still, that didn't stop her taking the head of his manhood into her mouth.

"Hellfire!"

She moved to sit astride him. "You said I should capture my prey unawares."

His strained expression matched his frustrated groan. "Take me inside you, love." Another needy moan escaped him when she sank slowly down onto his shaft. "God in heaven."

Oh, feeling full with him felt divine.

He gripped her hips and helped her find a rhythm, a tantalising rhythm where she appreciated taking every inch of Eli Hunter.

He never took his eyes off her, not when pleasure engulfed them, not when he whipped her onto her back and spurted his seed onto her belly. Not when she settled into his arms and silently whispered—"I love you."

●

The tinkle of the security bell dragged Eli from his slumber. He might have shot out of bed, but Rachel's legs were entwined with his, and her head rested on his chest.

He shook her gently. "Rachel. Rachel. Wake up."

She stirred, released a sweet moan, draped her arm around his waist and snuggled into him.

"Love. There's an intruder. Someone has entered the house." Entered via the rear door and tripped the wire, which ran all the way upstairs to trigger the small bell.

She raised her head and blinked numerous times. "An intruder." The words penetrated her sleepy head, and she jumped up as if he'd pricked her with a pin. "Intruder! It's Jacob Hanaway. Quick, Eli. He'll burn the house to the ground."

He reached for her hand. "One does not enter a house to burn it down. Find your nightgown. We need to creep downstairs and confront the devil. My robe is hanging in the armoire. Put it on. Hurry."

She leapt from the bed as if they'd not a second to spare, banging the boards in the process. She froze and met his gaze. "Sorry. I've cramp in my foot."

"I'll massage your feet when we've dealt with the scoundrel," he whispered, though struggled to tear his eyes away from her lush curves as she slipped into her nightgown. He dragged on his breeches and threw his shirt over his head.

The armoire door creaked, and she cast him an apologetic look. He gestured to the blanket on the chair and mouthed for her to wrap it around her instead. Thankfully, the hinges on his bedchamber door were well oiled. Eli opened the door, turned to see Rachel removing the blade and the etui from her reticule.

"Leave them. I'll protect you."

"And what if Jacob shoots you?"

She had a fair point.

They tiptoed downstairs, noticed the faint glow of candlelight through the partially open study door. The sound of rustling paper and banging drawers masked the occasional creak of the boards as they descended to the hall.

Eli crept to the coat stand, took the swordstick, then gestured for Rachel to follow behind.

The devil must have heard them because he snuffed out the candle and suddenly came hurtling out of the study. Eli drew his sword, but Rachel threw something in the villain's face that made him stumble back, drop a host of paper, and cry out in pain.

Eli shot her a quizzical glance.

"It's the lemon juice." Rachel grinned. "It works every time."

# CHAPTER 17

RACHEL WAS RATHER proud of herself, truth be told. Lemon juice stung the eyes, but one had to have a perfect aim for it to be a suitable weapon. Eli looked impressed, and so she gave a confident smile and pointed to the blackguard groaning on the floor.

"It's not Jacob Hanaway," she said with utter relief upon noting the man's thin frame. She picked up a piece of strewn paper and examined the markings. "It seems our intruder is keen to steal all evidence of the coded letter."

Eli closed in on the miscreant. He grabbed the fellow's wrists and dragged his hands from his face. Despite the darkness, Rachel recognised him instantly.

"If you're so desperate for information, might I suggest you call at a respectable hour." Eli hauled the Council member to his feet. "Truscott wishes to know whether you're close to breaking the code, Miss Gambit."

"And I would have happily told him had he made an appointment." After Mr Truscott's interference at Trēowith, Rachel wasn't at all surprised he'd taken matters into his own hands.

Mr Truscott shrugged out of Eli's grasp. "I knew it!" He

rubbed his eyes, but had trouble opening them fully. "The two of you are in cahoots." He glanced at Rachel's nightgown. "You're lovers."

"Don't be ridiculous." Rachel snatched the blanket off the floor. One couldn't protect one's modesty and hurl lemon juice with such precision. "Mr Daventry insisted I stay here for my own safety. Mr Hunter woke me to inform me of an intruder in the house. My poor maid is still snoring on her trundle bed if you'd like her to bear witness."

Jacobs appeared in his robe and nightcap. He raised his candle. "Forgive me, sir. I failed to hear the bell and only woke upon hearing the commotion. Am I to send for a watchman?"

"No, Jacobs. But if you'd light the lamps in the study and fetch a pitcher of water and a linen square, you may retire to bed."

"Very good, sir."

Eli turned to Mr Truscott. "Don't move."

Rachel knelt and gathered her scribbled notes. "You must see how this looks, Mr Truscott. You object to me investigating the theft of the case files, then you break into Mr Hunter's home and attempt to escape with the evidence."

"I came to steal evidence." He jabbed a finger at Eli. "Evidence he's the damn traitor."

Eli laughed. "Perhaps if you'd spent the last few days investigating the Meyers, you might be closer to learning the truth. As it stands, we met with Daventry yesterday, and he asked we visit you to discuss the case. You've saved us the trouble of traipsing halfway across town."

The glow of candlelight in the study preceded Jacobs leaving the room.

"As temporary master of Themis, Miss Gambit, you may sit behind the desk." Eli waited for her to take her position before forcing Mr Truscott to sit opposite and settling into the chair beside him. "Miss Gambit? Is there anything you'd like to ask Truscott?"

Rachel straightened. "Are you the traitor, sir?"

"Certainly not!" Mr Truscott's cheeks ballooned with outrage.

"Then perhaps you might explain why you failed to investigate Dr Baker." Rachel informed him what they had learnt in Brighton. "It took no more than ten minutes to gain the doctor's confession."

Mr Truscott rubbed his red eyes. "I sent a man to Brighton, but Dr Baker was away in Eastbourne. I wrote asking if he might comment on his examination of Lady Meyer but received no reply."

"The best way to learn the truth from a deceiver is to join the game," Eli said. "Now we have evidence to support Mary's statement."

Jacobs appeared with a pitcher and washbowl.

"Wet the linen, Jacobs, and give it to Mr Truscott. Then you may retire."

Jacobs obliged and left Mr Truscott pressing the damp cloth to his eyes.

"What has this to do with catching the man who stole the sacred seal?" Mr Truscott groaned. "Surely breaking the code is the priority."

Rachel explained the connection. "The thief's objective was to steal the files, not the seal. Therefore, the traitor must have an interest in one of the current cases."

"Lady Meyer's footman, the one who testified against Mary, is currently hiding in a cottage past Mile End," Eli informed the man. "We have an agent investigating as we speak."

Mr Truscott snorted. "Even if the footman retracts his statement, no judge in the land will call a peer's wife a liar. If we're to save Mary Harcourt, we must force Lady Meyer to confess."

"We?" Eli said with some amusement. "Am I to understand you no longer believe we're conspiring against the Council?"

"I doubt the traitor would work so hard to solve the case." Mr Truscott paused. "Unless you're diverting attention away from Belton."

"Belton is guilty of murder." Rachel felt the truth of it to the marrow of her bones. She was confident Mr D'Angelo would find the evidence needed. "Tomorrow, we seek to gain his confession."

Mr Truscott dabbed the cloth to his eyes. "Is the coded letter your only clue to finding the traitor's identity?"

"Yes." Rachel gestured to the pile of scribblings. "Hence why I've spent most of the afternoon trying to decipher the symbols." And most of the evening solving a more important riddle. She was in love with Eli Hunter. It wasn't infatuation or an addiction. It was a meeting of souls, hearts and minds.

With some hesitance, Mr Truscott said, "Might I examine the letter?"

Rachel sought Eli's approval, and he gave a curt nod.

"Of course. We have nothing to hide, sir. It's time you accepted we're on the same side." She reached under the desk and flicked the secret switch. The top drawer clicked open, revealing the coded letter. "We know some are alchemical symbols." Rachel handed Mr Truscott the document. "Some are astronomical symbols, and some are invented to make it difficult to decipher."

Mr Truscott studied the letter beneath the lamplight. "Yes, the circle with the dot and arrow is the symbol for Uranus. It was created shortly after the planet's discovery some forty years ago."

Unable to contain her excitement, Rachel found the list of deciphered images and added Uranus. "We assumed the first letter of the word is relevant."

"The upside-down triangle with the line cutting through

is the alchemical sign for Earth. I remember it from Greek studies at Eton. It's one of the primordial elements."

Heavens! Mr Truscott was extremely knowledgeable. Or was he the traitor feeding them false information?

Rachel filled in the corresponding spaces with the letter E and stared at the paper. "The first word contains four letters and can only be *meet*."

Mr Truscott shook his head. "Offhand, I cannot recall any more. But I may have a book or two at home relating to old alchemical symbols."

"That would be most helpful, sir."

Eli cleared his throat. "As I said, the best way to learn the truth from a deceiver is to join the game. I have an idea. Once we've broken the code, we'll construct a letter—one arranging another meeting. We'll send a copy to Lady Meyer and to every council member. Then we'll gather at the arranged point and see who appears."

It was an excellent idea. "Only those who know the code will be able to understand the message." And judging by the letters they had in the first line, it definitely referred to a secret liaison.

"I believe I owe you both an apology." Mr Truscott squirmed in his seat. The man disliked admitting he was wrong. "It's evident you've been working tirelessly to find the devil who stole the sacred seal." He pressed his hand to his heart as if about to make the pledge. "You must understand, my great grandfather first served Themis and instilled the importance of truth and loyalty in all things."

"My father was of the same mind," Eli said. "But our faith in loyalty can often blind us to the truth." He referred to the situation with Felicity. "We're your friends, not your enemy, and serve to protect Themis."

Mr Truscott pursed his lips and nodded. "Then I'll help in any way I can. From what I know regarding the case at

Belton's Emporium, I'd say Swanson and Young have been slack in their approach. Both men are usually so thorough."

"I must agree," Eli said.

Rachel listened with interest. The men couldn't have visited the emporium. Else they would know the sword was too big for the chest. And why hadn't they questioned the boy's ability to commit the crime?

"Young is suspicious of Swanson after the theft of the key," Mr Truscott added. "He said Swanson doesn't seem interested in proving the boy is innocent. Cantrell offered to work with Swanson, but Young refused and said he didn't want Daventry to think him incompetent."

One stolen key and Themis had become a hive of mistrust.

"With luck, we'll have solved the Belton case tomorrow," Rachel said.

"Assuming the traitor isn't colluding with Belton." Eli stood. He seemed keen to bring the conversation to an end. "I'll send word when we've finished at the emporium. When this is over, I suspect Daventry will want to reassess who has a place on the Council."

Mr Truscott nodded and came to his feet. "May I help with the letter? Help identify the symbols?"

Eli cast Rachel a wary glance.

"I'm afraid I can't let you take the letter, Mr Truscott, but will copy a few symbols for you to study at home."

He seemed appeased, so she snatched a piece of paper, drew three signs, and gave it to Mr Truscott.

"Well, sir, we have much to do tomorrow. I shall bid you good night."

"Yes, yes. I should let you get to your beds."

Thankfully, Mr Truscott failed to notice Eli's wicked grin or the twinkle in his eyes that said he longed to return to the privacy of his chamber.

Eli escorted Mr Truscott out of the house and returned to

the study ten minutes later. "Truscott underestimated me. He thought he could enter my home, rummage in my desk, and I'd be clueless."

"It's difficult to know if we can trust him." Standing in front of the desk, she turned to examine the words they had deciphered so far. "*Meet noon Monday*. They're definitely the first three words." She pointed to the last word in the sentence. "Do you suppose it's a place or a person's name?"

Eli came behind her. He slipped his arms around her waist and peered over her shoulder. "It will be a place. There aren't many in London beginning with G and containing nine letters."

"Thanks to Mr Truscott, we now know the sign for E." Rachel filled in the blank spaces. "It starts with green."

"Greenford." He kissed her shoulder. "Greenwich. Green Park."

"The fact the code contains astronomical symbols suggests it might be Greenwich, home of the Observatory."

"It's a logical assumption." Eli kissed the sensitive skin below her ear.

"Judging by the hard length pressing against my buttocks, it would be logical to assume you're not thinking about the Observatory."

"Not in the least. It can wait until tomorrow."

Excitement shivered down to her toes. "Is there something else you wish to study, Mr Hunter?"

"Yes. Clear the desk." He drew her around to face him, bent his head and brushed his mouth against hers. "I wish to make a thorough study of my favourite subject."

"Your favourite subject?" she teased, perching on the edge of the desk.

"Hmm. I always preferred anatomy to astronomy."

●

*Belton's Emporium*
*Surrey Street*

"Move along! The emporium is closed today." Mr Daventry's man, Mr Bower, waved his rattle and told those queuing in Surrey Street he was a constable from the Hatton Garden office and would arrest anyone causing a disturbance. His hulking frame was enough to terrify the most hardened villain. "Move along!"

"We'll not warn you again!" Mr D'Angelo sounded equally menacing. "Go home!"

A panicked Mr Belton turned to Eli. "What's this, sir? We can talk elsewhere. There's no need to close the shop." He called for the boy wearing the dusty top hat. "Mind the door. It's two shillings apiece. Two shillings, do ya 'ear?"

"We're closing the shop indefinitely," Rachel informed him. "It's the scene of a heinous crime."

"Aye, but they have the murdering devil behind bars."

"We'll discuss the matter inside, Mr Belton."

A handsome coach with a team of matched greys clattered to a stop outside. Mr D'Angelo exchanged words with the occupants, and the vehicle charged away.

"No! Wait!" Mr Belton darted across the pavement and waved frantically at the coachman. "We'll be open again in ten minutes. Come back."

Mr Belton had every reason to panic. Having met with Mr Daventry and Mr D'Angelo in Hart Street this morning, Rachel had learnt that the shopkeeper owed a substantial sum to a notorious moneylender in St Giles.

"We've permission to search these premises." Eli showed him Peel's letter, which looked tatty around the edges. "You'll come inside, Belton, or I'll drag you over the damn threshold."

Resigned to his fate, Mr Belton beckoned them inside

while Mr Bower and Mr D'Angelo attempted to disperse the crowd.

Eli rounded up the patrons in the makeshift tunnel, ushered them outside, then closed the door.

"What's all this?" Mrs Belton braced her hands on her hips as recognition dawned. "Not you again. We ain't got nothin' to say."

"Then I shall do the talking." Rachel removed her pocket book from her reticule—merely for effect—and flicked to her expenses sheet. "I shall present the evidence beginning with Mr Belton owing the Cartwright brothers five hundred pounds."

"What? I don't owe them a penny," he spat. "I paid them in full last night."

Last night? Typical.

Rachel kept a stern expression while scrambling for a way to unsettle these devils. "You paid the outstanding balance but failed to pay the interest."

It was a blatant lie.

Baring rotten teeth, Mrs Belton turned on her husband. "You said you'd paid 'em. You said we've nothin' to worry about no more."

"I did pay them. They've made a mistake."

"According to Mr Cartwright, the interest is two hundred pounds."

Mr Belton gulped. "He said the sum covered the interest."

"He lied."

"You idiot!" Mrs Belton punched her husband's arm.

"Shall we move to the next piece of evidence?" Eli said now they were rattled. "The spate of thefts that occurred in December. You reported the crimes, and your neighbours say you complained about a group of light-fingered rogues who work out of The Clifford Inn in Holborn."

The milliner next door had informed Eli of the fact only this morning.

Mr Belton shrugged. "They've caused mischief up and down this street."

"It ain't got nothing to do with the murder," his wife protested.

Eli stepped forward. "It has everything to do with the murder. The first witness to the scene has changed his statement and swears you repeatedly called David Scrivens a thief after locking him in the pantry."

"That's because you thought the boy had stolen a knife from the old chest." Rachel decided to tell another lie. "That's what the witness said he heard you shouting." She looked at her book again. "I believe the words used were—*you'll swing, you dirty little thief.*"

"Would the boy not swing for murder, Mrs Belton?" Eli said.

"You see, the sword couldn't have been in the old chest. It's far too long. Your testimony to me was false, Mrs Belton." Rachel looked the woman keenly in the eye. "In a moment, an expert will come to look at the bloodstains." She recalled the ramblings of the chemist who frequented the pawnbroker shop, something about science being the means to understanding the world. "A Frenchman made a recent discovery, a chemical that can be used to identify the presence of blood." All working folk feared the French.

Being attuned to her thoughts, Eli said, "Our expert will prove Scrivens didn't carry the sword to the pantry, but that you picked it up, Mrs Belton, and threw it on the floor before locking the door."

"Me!" Mrs Belton jumped back in shock.

"You picked it up because the boy didn't murder his stepfather." Eli's stern voice conveyed his anger. "A re-enactment of the crime proved Scrivens was too weak to wield the sword." He scanned the woman's sturdy frame. "You could wield a sword, Mrs Belton."

"Me!" She clutched her hand to her chest.

Mr Belton saw an opportunity to escape punishment. He turned to Eli. "The woman lost her mind, sir. One minute she's behind the counter. The next, she's charging at the burly fellow. Stabbed him straight through the heart she did." He lunged and grabbed Eli's arm. "I've been in fear of my life ever since, sir."

"Me! Me!" Mrs Belton's face turned beetroot red. "Liar!"

"See, sir, do see how angry she gets?"

"You said the brute was a thief, said you'd teach him a lesson." In a fit of temper, Mrs Belton grabbed hold of Rachel and shook her. "He snatched the sword from under the counter. He's been hiding it there since them crooks from Holborn stole a rare porcelain figurine."

Eli shoved Mr Belton to the floor and glared at the man's wife. "Release my colleague, madam. Release her else I shall whip up the devil's own fury."

"You can't come in 'ere makin' threats." Mrs Belton locked her fat arm around Rachel's throat. "Happen, you're the only ones what's heard the confession. Happen, we'll run you both through."

Eli gave a confident grin. "Don't say I didn't warn you."

It wasn't the first time Rachel had been choked, but Mrs Belton lacked Jacob Hanaway's determination. Rachel thrust her hand into her pelisse pocket and reached for her knife. She drew the blade, then sank her teeth into the woman's arm and stamped on her toe.

Howling, Mrs Belton released her.

"Fetch the constable, Mr Hunter." Rachel pointed the tip of the blade to Mrs Belton's throat. It took effort not to imagine she was Jacob Hanaway, not to thrust the blade and get rid of the villain for good.

Eli refused to leave but whistled for Mr Bower and Mr D'Angelo, who came charging into the shop. The latter kept hold of Mr Belton while Eli tied the shopkeeper's hands with rope. Mr Bower ran to fetch a constable, and soon men eager to take the Beltons into custody flooded the emporium.

Having agreed to use his carriage to ferry the Beltons to the Hatton Garden office—though both villains continued blaming each other—Eli left with three constables and Mr D'Angelo in tow.

"I'll take you home in Mr D'Angelo's carriage, Miss Gambit." Mr Bower escorted her out into Surrey Street so the remaining constable could secure the shop. "Mr Hunter insisted I wait at Blackstone until his return."

"Thank you, Mr Bower, though I don't need a chaperone."

"I gave my word, miss. Mr Hunter's not a man to cross." Mr Bower opened the door to Mr D'Angelo's elegant equipage. "You must be relieved, miss. Relieved you've solved one case as it brings you closer to finding the traitor."

"Indeed." Rachel failed to rouse a smile as she climbed inside.

Relief was not the overriding emotion.

For the first time since finding the strength to leave Lady Hanaway's home—though after her godmother's death, she'd had little choice in the matter—uncertainty and fear had a grip on her heart.

She was one step closer to catching a deceiver.

One step closer to leaving Eli Hunter for good.

# CHAPTER 18

ELI SAT on the sofa in the Hart Street drawing room, observing Lord Meyer's arrogant bearing as he lounged in the chair opposite. Having sent news to Blackstone of this sudden development, they were awaiting Rachel's arrival.

Lucius Daventry poured the lord a glass of brandy. He crossed the room and thrust it at the gentleman. "My agent should be here shortly, though I'm surprised Peel didn't summon us to his office."

"I'll not have every Whig in Westminster spying on my business."

"Your business will soon be common knowledge," Eli countered. "No doubt Rowlandson will make an amusing sketch of the courtroom drama."

Lord Meyer tossed back his brandy. "There won't be a trial."

"You sound so confident. Have you come to confess?"

The ring of the doorbell proved a welcome distraction.

Rachel appeared looking flustered, yet utterly adorable. "I'm so sorry for the delay. I came as quickly as I could." She stopped abruptly upon seeing the golden-haired peer sitting in the chair.

Eli and Meyer stood.

"Allow me to introduce Lord Meyer." Daventry gestured to Rachel. "Miss Gambit is one of my best enquiry agents and has been assigned to Mary Harcourt's case."

"Agents? You hired a woman to do a man's work?" Lord Meyer mocked. "You've had a damn woman prying into my personal affairs?"

Eli was about to deliver a harsh reprimand, but Daventry seized the opportunity. "Change your tone, Meyer. I don't care who you are. You'll pay my agents the respect they deserve, or you'll get the hell out of my house."

Forced to clear his throat to disguise his embarrassment, Lord Meyer said, "You're as unconventional as they say, Daventry. I suppose I've no choice but to comply."

"If it's unconventional to employ someone on merit, then yes." Daventry motioned for Rachel to sit. "Lord Meyer is about to tell us why he summoned Peel to meet him in Hyde Park this morning."

Meyer jerked his head. "How the devil do you know I rode in Hyde Park?"

"We've had a man watching you for days," Eli informed him.

The lord muttered a curse. "Who paid you to represent Mary?"

"Someone who believes she's innocent," Rachel added.

"I suspect she is innocent," Meyer snapped. "I only discovered the extent of my wife's involvement last night. My groom Briggs came to me, concerned for his position and his life. He gave me a calling card, mentioned an official letter, which led me to consult Peel. Peel suggested I come here."

With a choice of numerous chairs around the room, Rachel sat next to Eli. "So, until yesterday, you believed Mary stole your wife's jewels?"

All the men resumed their seats.

"Indeed. Having spoken to my housekeeper and offered

certain assurances, she informed me she suspects my wife hid the jewels beneath the boards in Mary's room."

"And why would your wife do that, my lord?"

"Because she wanted rid of Mary." When threatened by Daventry to explain his relationship with the maid, the lord blurted, "Yes, yes, I paid Mary to have my child and agreed to let her keep her position. She's a sweet little thing, and it was no hardship."

Eli gritted his teeth lest he grab the pompous cad by his starched cravat and slam his fist down his throat. "And Mary agreed to this arrangement?"

Meyer took exception to the comment. "I didn't force the girl. But I needed an heir before my damn cousin finds a means to do away with me."

"An heir? So, you intended to pass the child off as your wife's," Rachel stated. "You had Lady Meyer fool everyone into believing she is carrying a child and assumed Mary would support the story."

Meyer frowned. "That may have been the original plan, but thankfully my wife is with child. By God's good grace, it happened only a month after Mary confirmed her condition. Consequently, I purchased a cottage for Mary out near Mile End, agreed to pay for the boy's education and provide an allowance. That was before I learnt of Mary's scheme to steal my wife's jewels, steal my son away from me and run off with the footman."

Eli sat back and considered the information.

"And you learnt all that from your wife?" Rachel asked.

"Yes, she found the couple in a clinch. The footman confessed. That's when we discovered the jewels beneath the boards in Mary's room."

"And now?" Eli prompted.

"Now I'm told my wife invented the tale to get rid of Mary and the child." Meyer drained his glass of brandy. "I've told Peel the theft was a mistake. Jealousy made my wife believe Mary was scheming against her. Peel said he wished to hear your evidence before referring the matter. I shall pay Mary for the inconvenience, and she can still have the cottage. For some bizarre reason, you need to agree, Daventry."

"Pay Mary for the inconvenience of almost having her neck snapped?" Eli mocked. "I doubt the Lord would forgive such a sin."

Meyer shrugged. "Mary understands my wife can be quite volatile. There's no harm done."

Astounded at the lord's arrogance, no one replied.

After a prolonged silence, Rachel asked, "Did your wife confess to lying about Mary?"

"No, we've not spoken, but I'm aware Tinsley and his mother are at the cottage looking after the babe. My wife agreed we could send the child to live at my country estate after the trial. Indeed, tomorrow she is retiring there for the last few weeks of her confinement." He gave a nonchalant wave. "I say trial, but that was when I believed in Mary's guilt."

Lady Meyer's plan formed in Eli's head. She would leave London, pretend to have her child early at a coaching inn, perhaps. Then she would visit Mile End and steal Mary's babe to pass off as her own.

What about Tinsley and his mother?

Maybe Lady Meyer would set fire to the cottage so everyone would presume Mary's babe had died in the blaze. She would hide out somewhere for a few months, pretend she'd been unwell after the birth, so that when she presented Mary's child, no one questioned why it wasn't a newborn. Who could tell the difference between a four and five-month-old babe?

Rachel must have arrived at a similar conclusion. "We have evidence to suggest your wife is not with child. We have a sworn statement from her physician in Brighton confirming she is barren and that she asked him to lie about examining her."

"We believe she wanted rid of Mary because she intends to fool you into thinking the boy is her child." Eli relayed his suspicions, and what he suspected was Lady Meyer's plan. "Can you confirm your wife is with child? Can you swear you have seen the physical evidence for yourself?"

Lord Meyer's arrogance abandoned him. "We have separate chambers. After struggling to conceive, she refuses to take risks."

"You mean you've not seen your wife's naked body for some time."

"No. Fear has her bathing herself, dressing herself. She lives in a state of anxiety and cries constantly."

Surely the servants had noticed something was amiss.

Surely those responsible for the laundry knew of the deception.

"Have you been intimate with Mary since learning of your wife's condition?" Eli asked, attempting to establish a motive for Lady Meyer's shocking behaviour. "Have you been intimate with Mary in the months before her arrest?"

Meyer huffed. "I'll not answer that."

"You will," Daventry insisted.

"I won't."

"Then this meeting is over. Tell Peel we refuse to accept your version of events."

Meyer gave a frustrated growl. "Curse the saints! What do you want me to say? That Mary is like a breath of fresh air? That she doesn't burden a man or constantly hold him to account?"

Amid the awkward silence, amid Rachel's mutter of disgust, Daventry turned to Eli. "Having found no association between Belton and our members, we must assume Lady Meyer is the person connected to our traitor."

"Traitor!" Lord Meyer shot out of his chair. "I can assure you, my wife is not involved in a treason plot!"

"Not treason against king and country," Daventry corrected before demanding the lord return to his seat. "While it's our intention to have Mary released, we cannot agree to your terms until we discover if your wife has other secrets."

Rachel reached for her satchel. "As to that, sir, I have managed to decipher the code. Mr Truscott sent books to Blackstone. I've spent the last two hours identifying the symbols." She removed a sheaf of paper. "If you will, I can read the message."

Daventry waved for her to continue. "By all means."

Rachel cleared her throat and read:

*Meet noon Monday Greenwich.*
*Soon you'll see your son.*
*He'll have your mesmerising eyes, your loyal heart.*
*He'll thank you for giving us this chance.*
*He'll thank fate for bringing us together.*
*Love Venus*

"Venus!" Lord Meyer snapped. "Venus! My wife often refers to herself as such."

"This letter was found a month ago, my lord, dropped by a man we're keen to identify. It's written in symbols." Rachel rummaged around in her satchel and removed the original document. She crossed the room and presented it to Meyer. "Do you recognise any of them?"

Meyer studied the letter before handing it back. "Are you implying I'm a cuckold, madam?"

A cuckold? The lord was ignorant to his own hypocrisy.

"We believe your wife manipulated this man because he knew information about Mary Harcourt's case." Rachel returned to her seat. "Rest assured, Peel will hear of your cooperation. Be certain, we will catch this man and then the depth of your wife's duplicity will be known to all."

A small doubt entered Eli's mind. How had Lady Meyer discovered the identity of a council member? No one knew the names of the men who solved problems behind the scenes.

Meyer hung his head while considering his dilemma. He'd been so sure they'd agree to his demands, so confident he had the upper hand.

"Well, Lord Meyer?" Daventry prompted. "Answer Miss Gambit's question. Are any of those symbols familiar to you?"

Meyer raised his head. "My wife has similar letters at home from a childhood friend. They shared a love of the stars, and she often walks the grounds outside the Greenwich Observatory."

"I see." Daventry crossed the room, locked the door and slipped the key into his coat pocket. "I'm afraid I can't let you leave, not until we've established the recipient's identity."

"What the devil?" This time, Meyer lacked the will to stand.

"You've two choices, my lord," Rachel said. "You can assist us by laying a trap for your wife. Then you will discover the truth for yourself. Or we shall send for Peel and see what he has to say on the matter."

The lord sat silently contemplating his fate before studying them with grim curiosity. "You confirm your intention is to free Mary?"

Daventry nodded.

"Very well. What do you intend to do?"

●

The Observatory sat on high ground in a royal park with impressive views over the Thames. Built on the ruined

Greenwich Castle site, one could see their enemies approaching from all directions.

"According to my almanack, the sun is due to set at six o'clock." Rachel squinted to read the page in her tiny book while hiding behind a tree that offered a clear view of the impressive building. "It must be five o'clock now. Let's hope Lady Meyer and her mystery lover are on time, else we might lose them in the dark."

Eli watched the couples and families strolling about the grounds, wondering if the traitor might wear a disguise. "The sun will set in half an hour. One only need consider its position and note the sky's golden hue."

Rachel glanced heavenward. "You're right. These books are often a little vague." She slipped the almanack back into her reticule. "Do you think Lady Meyer will come?"

"Let's hope the letters you crafted will make her and her lover panic."

Under pressure to hurry, Rachel had written five letters in the secret code. One to Lady Meyer—a quick message to meet at five o'clock in Greenwich, a matter of some urgency. She played to Lady Meyer's vanity and mentioned it might be their last rendezvous. Letters were sent to Truscott, Cantrell, Swanson and Young, who were all staying at their London abodes. Indeed, Eli had summoned Young and Swanson to the Hatton Garden office to hear Mr Belton's confession.

"Can we trust Lord Meyer not to charge out of his hiding place?"

"Daventry has him on a tight leash."

The men stood near the boundary wall, watching the winding path leading from the park below up to the entrance. Miss Dutton and Miss Wild sat on a wooden bench, the Observatory behind them, pretending to admire the views across London. Bower and D'Angelo had a miniature of Lady Meyer and were tasked with waiting in the park and following the lady should she make the steep climb.

"My heart is racing." Rachel touched Eli's upper arm. "What if the penny boy failed to deliver the letters and ran off with his bounty?"

"You can trust Daventry to ensure the plan is implemented with the utmost precision." They were moments away from catching a traitor—moments away from concluding the case, from Daventry tearing them apart and giving Rachel another assignment. The need to speak from the heart proved too powerful to ignore. "This might not be the right time to make a confession, but there's something I must say."

"A confession?" Her eyes flashed with intrigue.

"A declaration."

Her features softened. "Whatever it is, it sounds quite serious."

"I've never been more serious about anything." He reached for her gloved hand and pressed a lingering kiss to her palm. "Has anyone ever told you how remarkable you are?"

She smiled. "Only you."

"Has anyone ever told you they'd rather die than spend a night without you?" He knew the answer. "Told you they'll love no one but you their whole life?"

"Never," she whispered.

"I'm in love with you, Rachel. I know it's not the right time to reveal the true depth of my feelings, but at home our passions overwhelm us, and whatever happens here will result in me leaving to deal with the Council."

She glanced behind before cupping his face and kissing him on the mouth. "I'm in love with you, Eli. I'm so in love with you I can barely raise a rational thought." She kissed him again. "And you're right. Had you told me at home, we'd have invariably ended up in bed."

A rush of euphoria left him grinning. He was gathering

the courage to ask her to marry him when she tapped him on the chest.

"Don't turn around. Mr Swanson is trudging up the path. He's alone but seems to be looking for someone."

"Swanson?" he whispered. "Are you certain?"

"Positive."

"Swanson is Lady Meyer's mystery lover?"

"Maybe they share a love of astronomy," Rachel said. "Like us, maybe they share a love for adventure."

Strange. He was convinced Swanson preferred men. And despite all evidence to the contrary, he'd seemed committed to Themis. Still, he had failed in his task to prove David Scrivens innocent. Done a rather shoddy job, truth be told. But how had he accessed the Sanctum with only one key?

"What is Swanson doing now?"

Rachel peered over Eli's shoulder. "He's waiting outside the Observatory. He's pulled his watch from his pocket and is checking the time. Should we approach him?"

Every instinct said no. "We wait for Daventry's signal."

It didn't come.

Five minutes passed. Ten minutes.

"Mr Daventry must be waiting for Lady Meyer to arrive," Rachel whispered. "If we stand still any longer, I'll be plagued by cramp."

Eli brushed the backs of his fingers across her cheek. "Tonight, when we're in bed, I shall massage your toes, your ankles, your knees and thighs. I'll relax you so you'll never suffer from the affliction again."

"Is it possible to get cramp in intimate places, do you suppose?" Her teasing smile faded. "Good Lord, Mr Swanson is leaving. Should we go after him?"

Again, Eli looked towards Lucius Daventry, but the man remained steadfast in his purpose. His patience reaped results. A woman wearing a wool cloak, the fur-trimmed hood raised, came trudging up the steep path, her breathing laboured. She scanned the grounds, then straightened and marched towards the entrance.

She waited for five or more minutes until a gentleman appeared.

Eli turned away sharply. "Damnation."

"Is that Mr Young?"

"Indeed. No doubt he's meeting Lady Meyer." Eli gritted his teeth. He should have known. Young had an impeccable record for saving the innocent. Had foiled a plot to murder the king. Yet, everything about his recent actions cried amateur.

"Yes, he's walked up to her. She's lowered her hood. He's captured her hand and kissed her palm. Oh, she's opened her cloak, and he's touching her swollen stomach."

"Harlot!" came Lord Meyer's cry.

Ladies strolling around the grounds gasped.

Lady Meyer's head whipped in her husband's direction.

"We move now." Eli placed a guiding hand at Rachel's back.

Everyone left their positions and advanced on Young and Lady Meyer. Daventry looked ready to string Young up from the nearest tree. Eli's mood turned solemn. It was never a nice feeling to see a good man reduced to the rank of scoundrel.

"Meyer," the lady croaked. "Must you use such an obscenity in public?"

"Harlot!" the lord shouted again. "Most people meet their lovers in dark, secluded places."

"Or they simply take a trip to the attic."

Daventry cut a menacing figure as he stepped forward. "I'll hear your explanation now, Young. I'll hear it in front of witnesses."

"Explanation?" Young's shocked stare turned into an angry glare. "You're the one who's broken cover. Are we not attempting to prove Mary Harcourt is innocent?"

"You're tasked with saving David Scrivens," Eli reminded him. "And you dropped the coded letter while fleeing Trēowith, else you wouldn't be standing here."

"The coded letter implies Lady Meyer is carrying your child," Rachel added, "which proves you have had relations with her within the last eight months. Why else would you stroke her stomach with such fondness?"

"We're childhood friends," Young countered.

Eli snorted. "You made no mention of that during our meetings. You should have declared the connection, yet you said nothing."

Daventry's mocking laugh could chill a man to the bone. "If Lady Meyer is such a good friend, why did she lie to you? Why let you believe she is with child when she's barren?"

"Barren!" Lady Meyer parted her cloak. "Does it look like I'm barren?" She turned to her husband. "What nonsense is this?"

In a tone filled with indignation, Lord Meyer repeated everything they'd discussed in Hart Street. "You're not leaving London. You'll sleep in my bedchamber. You'll be confined to bed until you give birth or until you prove to be a liar and a fraud. In which case, I shall make an appeal for a divorce. I have proof of your infidelity."

Panic flittered across her face. "I—I am not coming home. I'm running away with Mr Young. We've been lovers for two years. You can tell the magistrate I did hide the jewels beneath the boards. I did make up a story to get rid of Mary."

In planning to run away, the lady was admitting she was barren. Regardless who fathered the imagined child, Lord Meyer had right of ownership.

"Why the devil would you hurt the woman who agreed to help us?" Meyer said, ignoring her admission of infidelity. "Why the hell didn't you just go along with the plan?"

"Because you continued to visit her night after night. I'm

not deaf and blind. And I refused to condone it a moment longer. Mary had to learn her place is in the scullery."

With his brow furrowed in confusion, Young cleared his throat. "Mary had your husband's child so you could pass it off as your own?" He seemed disgusted by the notion. "You were willing so see Mary hang for a crime she didn't commit because you were jealous?" He stepped away.

"Wait!" Lady Meyer reached for him. "Mary taunted me day and night with their affair. She made me quite ill. I might have lost your child. I couldn't let it continue. You must see that."

"His child!" Lord Meyer snapped.

"Sadly, Lady Meyer is carrying no one's child." Rachel approached Lady Meyer and captured her hands. "My lady," she began, her voice brimming with compassion, "you must be exhausted. You've kept up the pretence for too long. It's taken a toll on the health of your mind and your body. Speak the truth now and release yourself from this burden." She glanced at Eli. "The truth is the best argument, the best defence."

A tear trickled down Lady Meyer's cheek.

"My lady, we live in a world where bearing children is considered a woman's only use. I'm proof times are changing. I take risks, love the thrill of adventure, choose my own fate. If I marry, it will be for love, and to a man who understands my needs and desires."

"A barren woman is considered a disgrace," Lady Meyer whispered.

"A man who truly loved you wouldn't think so."

"I need a damn heir," Lord Meyer countered. "It's all that matters."

Rachel ignored the arrogant oaf. "You see, Lord Meyer loves his fortune and his title more than he loves you. He's not worth the lies and deceit. What you've done to Mary is unforgivable, and you must make amends."

Young cleared his throat. "I've loved you all my life, Alice. But you chose wealth and title. Now you've done something unspeakable. Day by day, you seem to lose sight of who you are."

"Young must love you dearly," Daventry said with an air of regret. "He sacrificed everything his ancestors worked for. He's destroyed his reputation to help you."

Young had made the ultimate sacrifice.

Lady Meyer looked at Young. "I made a mistake. Had I Miss Gambit's confidence, I would have married you. But you're too good for me, Guy. You always were." She inhaled deeply. "I've lied, lied to everyone in a desperate bid to prove my worth."

Young shook his head. "I lied to my closest friends. I lied to you, too, Alice." Young looked at Lucius Daventry. "She thinks I'm a land agent. She didn't ask me to steal the files, but when I heard her name, I had to help her." He sighed. "I believed the maid must be guilty. Love blinded me to the truth."

Daventry firmed his jaw. "You should have come to me and told me of your connection. We would have approached the case from a different angle. Things would never have got this far."

Young bowed his head in shame.

"You're relieved of your position. I'll have yours and Swanson's keys delivered to Hart Street tonight. I demand the return of the sacred seal and the files you stole. And you owe Swanson an apology for stealing his key, for sending him a note to meet you here so you could be sure it wasn't a trap." He turned to Lady Meyer. "You'll accompany me to visit Peel, where you'll confess to lying about Mary Harcourt."

Lady Meyer gave a solemn nod. "What will happen to me?"

"Nothing." Those guilty of perjury were sentenced to the pillory or transported. Eli knew excuses would be made for her actions. At worst, she'd be banished to the country and forced to make a substantial donation to the Lying-In Hospital.

"But Mary will be released." Rachel stepped back. "That's what matters most."

"I could have my wife committed to Bedlam." Lord Meyer seemed keen on the idea. "Everyone here can vouch for her mental instability."

"Do that, and I'll shoot you where you stand," Young cried.

A shot rang out. The ear-piercing crack had visitors ducking, walkers fleeing, had everyone looking for the source of the sound.

In a panic, Lord Meyer clasped his chest. He checked his palm, seemed shocked it wasn't plastered with blood. Was even more shocked to see Young hadn't whipped a pistol from his greatcoat pocket and fired.

An icy chill encased Eli's heart moments before Rachel dropped to her knees, and the light in her eyes died.

# CHAPTER 19

Blood seeped through Rachel's blue pelisse, leaving an ever-growing stain on the sleeve. Expecting another imminent attack, Eli dropped to his knees beside her unconscious form, shielding her with his body as fear chilled him to the bone.

"R-Rachel." He choked on the word, his throat closing amid the battle to suppress painful emotions. Such a man proved useless in desperate situations. "Rachel." Gently, he touched the ragged hole in her sleeve, had to suppress another wave of panic upon seeing his fingers glistening red, wet with her blood.

Daventry knelt beside him. "Quickly. Get her inside the Observatory. You need to inspect the wound, remove the lead ball and any fragments. Do you hear me? You know what to do. Hurry."

Eli heard him, but his world had come crashing down. Yes, he knew what to do, but he had never been in love with the person he hoped to save.

"Hunter!" Daventry grabbed his arm and shook him. "I'll take Meyer and find the shooter. Young will help carry Miss Gambit into the Observatory." He turned to Miss Dutton. "Help Hunter. Miss Wild, you're tasked with guarding Lady

Meyer. As she's not with child, use force if she attempts to escape."

Anger surfaced. Eli might have blamed Young for this sorry mess, but logic intervened. Saving Rachel was his only objective.

Eli scooped her up into his arms and turned to Young and Miss Dutton. "Mr Pond is Astronomer Royal at Greenwich. Race inside and find him or his assistant, find somewhere we can lay her down and work on the wound."

"I'll go with them. I'm good at asserting my authority." Lady Meyer seemed desperate to begin her penance, and so followed Young.

Miss Wild was hot on their trail.

Given an ultimatum, Lord Meyer had no option but to help Lucius Daventry question the bystanders for information about the shooter.

Trying to ignore the harrowing sight of Rachel's pale lips and limp body, Eli carried her into the grounds of the Observatory. Numerous buildings lined the courtyard. Miss Wild stood waiting outside a door on the left.

Young and Lady Meyer appeared, accompanied by an older man dressed in black. "Hunter! You can attend to Miss Gambit in here."

Eli hurried into the room containing astronomical equipment. A large desk flanked the fireplace. A giant sextant stood near the open window.

"Clear the desk," Eli cried, and the assistant hurried to gather papers and place them into a pile on the floor. "I need warm water and linen, brandy and tweezers, needle and thread. And light the lamps. It will be dark soon."

Miss Wild and Lady Meyer went with the assistant.

Eli placed Rachel gently down on the desk and unbuttoned her pelisse. Miss Dutton appeared at his side. Looking calm, considering the gravity of the situation, she helped Eli pull Rachel's arm free of the blood-soaked sleeve.

"Rachel has nine lives, Mr Hunter. There's nothing to fear."

"Find her knife, Miss Dutton. It's in her reticule. You know the one."

"I believe it's in her pocket, sir." Miss Dutton slipped her hand into the pocket, removed the small blade, and handed it to Eli.

"Hold her sleeve while I cut the material." The blade was surprisingly sharp and sliced through the fabric with ease. The sight of inflamed skin, of blood oozing from the wound, had nausea rolling in his stomach. "Hurry with the damn brandy!" he shouted over his shoulder.

Miss Dutton removed an ornate looking glass from her pocket, leant closer and examined the wound. "The ball just nicked the surface. I can see the lead is intact. I doubt there's any lasting damage."

"When did you become an expert on gunshot wounds?"

"My father was shot on four separate occasions before he died."

"Shot?"

"When one owes money to villains, it's an inevitable consequence."

Lady Meyer and Miss Wild came hurrying into the room, carrying some of the requested items. The assistant followed behind, hugging a decanter of brandy.

"Miss Dutton, use brandy to clean the needle, knife and tweezers. The rest of you come closer. You must hold her still while I remove the lead ball."

Miss Dutton proved an efficient assistant.

Miss Wild and Lady Meyer held Rachel's legs while Young secured her uninjured arm.

"Who would do such a thing?" Lady Meyer sounded shocked. "I pray it's not one of Mary's devout followers with a gripe against me."

Mary did have a host of people willing to support her claim.

"I know who shot her," Eli said darkly.

Jacob Hanaway was unstable. A cruel man obsessed with inflicting pain. Rachel was right. Eli should never have given the bastard his address. He'd expected the man to come under cover of darkness, not mingle with the crowd and fire in front of witnesses.

There was no time to wallow in guilt.

Eli beckoned the assistant forward. "Pour brandy over the wound while we hold her." He pressed his lips to her brow. Hell, her skin was so cold and damp. "In the name of God, be quick about it."

The man's hands shook as he followed Eli's command.

As soon as the potent liquid touched the damaged tissue, Rachel jerked awake. She writhed like a woman possessed, cursed as if the devil had taken command of her tongue.

"Hold her still! Miss Dutton, talk to her. Keep her calm."

Miss Dutton stroked Rachel's hair from her brow. "Honestly, Rachel, you'll do anything to gain Mr Hunter's attention. Can't you see the man is in love with you?"

Love was too mild a word. Eli's heart burned for her. "This will hurt, but I'll be as quick as I can. Hold her hand, Miss Dutton. Grip it tightly."

With tweezers, Eli dug into ragged flesh.

"Agh! S-stop!" Pain distorted Rachel's pretty features as she tried to wriggle free. "No! Stop!"

"Give her brandy. Pin her down."

The assistant darted away, found a mug and came racing back. He pressed the vessel to Rachel's lips and made her drink.

Eli stroked her face. "Love, I'll be quick. But if we're to have any life together, I must remove the lead."

"Then hurry, Eli." Tears trickled down her cheeks. She gritted her teeth.

As long as he lived, he hoped never to see her suffering like this again.

He set to work and managed to remove the ball intact. "Thankfully, it missed the bone. I need a needle and thread."

When prompted, the assistant cleaned the wound and threaded the needle.

"The good news is you've solved the case," Miss Dutton said, distracting Rachel while Eli pulled thread through the inflamed skin, keeping the stitches neat. "And now, Mr Daventry will give you another task."

The comment filled Eli with dread.

How did he tell a woman who thrived on adventure, working for the Order was a mistake? How could he suggest she marry him and settle into a comfortable life when he'd heard her impassioned speech to Lady Meyer?

He looked at Young, wondering what Daventry planned to do with the traitor. "Find an opium tincture to numb her pain. It's best she sleeps for the next few hours."

"Rachel carries one in her etui," Miss Wild said, "made for her by a chemist. It's quite strong, so I suggest one drop in watered-down brandy."

"Then make the concoction, Miss Wild."

While Daventry's female agent rooted around in the reticule, Eli took hold of Rachel's hand. "You'll be fine, love. Miss Wild will give you something to ease the pain, and then you can rest."

Her eyes fluttered open. "Did they catch him ... catch the shooter?"

"I'm awaiting Daventry's return. Sleep now. When you wake, I'll have news for you." He stroked her hand until Miss Wild appeared with the tincture. Even then, he struggled to let go. He whispered comforting words while she closed her eyes and let the potent liquid take effect, then he covered her with a blanket.

All was quiet until a breathless Bower came bursting

through the open door. "Mr Daventry is on his way, sir. He got waylaid with an incident in the park." He noticed Miss Gambit sleeping on the desk. "The lady's all right, isn't she, sir?"

"She'll be fine, Bower. Did Daventry catch the shooter?"

"The fellow went tumbling down a steep bank and broke his neck, but Mr Daventry will tell you more." Bower glanced at Lady Meyer and Young, who were huddled together near the open window, conversing in irate whispers. "I'm to take Mr Daventry to Westminster once you're done here."

Daventry came striding into the room with a dishevelled Lord Meyer in tow. He tapped Bower on the arm. "I've left D'Angelo dealing with the constable, but it will be an hour until someone returns with the magistrate. Wait with him."

Bower nodded and left the room.

Daventry frowned at Young before giving Eli his full attention. "How is Miss Gambit? With the pistol fired from such a distance, I doubt there'll be lasting damage."

"She'll survive but will have a permanent scar."

"We must watch for a fever."

Eli had no intention of letting her out of his sight. "You caught the shooter. Was it Jacob Hanaway?"

Daventry nodded. "The man appeared deranged. We caught him dancing about and muttering gibberish. He threatened a family with the pistol when he saw us approaching, but hadn't reloaded the damn thing. Meyer wrestled him to the ground, and the fellow tumbled down the bank."

"Bower said he broke his neck in the fall." Eli couldn't hide his relief.

"Yes, by all accounts. He was dead when I reached him."

Something about Daventry's expression said he'd given Hanaway a helping hand. "You're sure his neck is broken?"

"Quite sure." He looked at Young. "The whole thing is a damn mess. Will you take Miss Gambit to Howland Street? I want her to rest there. Miss Trimble is capable of caring for her, and I would rather have her somewhere safe. Peter Hanaway has your direction."

Eli thought to argue, thought to tell Daventry to go to the devil, but he was right. There was no telling what Peter Hanaway would do when he discovered his brother was dead. Protecting Rachel was all that mattered.

"What will you do with Young?"

"His only crime is falling in love with the wrong woman. As long as he keeps his oath and swears to reveal nothing of what he knows about Themis, he's free to leave."

"And Lady Meyer?"

Daventry sighed. "We both know the outcome. They'll have no choice but to set Mary free. They will feed the broadsheets a story to appease the people, and Lady Meyer will donate a ridiculous sum to charity."

They spoke about Mr Belton's confession, about Miss Gambit's ability as an enquiry agent, and when she would be fit to resume her duties. Eli considered telling Daventry that he hoped to marry Rachel but decided to wait.

"And what if Peter Hanaway proves to be a problem?" Eli hoped the man came to Blackstone tonight, for he would be waiting in the shadows. "Might he accidentally suffer a broken neck, too?"

A slow smile tugged at Daventry's lips. "Undoubtedly."

●

The room was dark, the blankets so heavy they might be made of lead. A film of brandy coated Rachel's lips, though the spirit's potency had done little to numb the throbbing ache in her arm. She inhaled deeply, longing for the masculine scent that stirred her senses. Instead, the smell of rosemary and some other herb wafted from an open pot on the nightstand.

"Eli," she called out to him. "Eli!"

Silence.

Despite the searing pain from the gunshot wound, she sat up in bed.

She wasn't sure what distressed her most. The fact she suddenly remembered she had been shot. The fact she had no notion if Eli had caught the villain or that she was alone in her bedchamber in Howland Street.

*Howland Street!*

Panic ensued.

Had she spoken to Eli after he'd pressed his lips to her brow and dug tweezers into her wound? No. She'd not seen him since. Had he raced away to find the shooter? Had he failed to return?

"Eli!" She pulled back the blankets and dragged herself out of bed.

The quick pounding of footsteps on the landing brought Miss Trimble, the thirty-year-old manager of the Order's house. She raced into the room, still knotting the belt of her wrapper.

"Rachel! You should be in bed."

"Where is Mr Hunter? Why I am here and not at Blackstone? Is he hurt?" The next words choked her before they left her mouth. "My God, is he dead?" She clasped her hand to her eyes as she burst into a sob.

"No, no, goodness no. Mr Hunter is alive and well." Miss Trimble drew her into an embrace and stroked her hair. "There's no need to cry. Mr Daventry insisted you return to Howland Street to rest and recuperate."

Relief settled over her like a warm blanket.

"Don't you remember Mr Hunter carrying you to bed?" Miss Trimble said. "He stayed for an hour. You asked him who shot you."

It was Jacob Hanaway. She remembered now.

"Tell me again. Tell me Jacob Hanaway is dead."

"I know what it's like to live in fear." Tears welled in Miss

Trimble's eyes. "Rest assured. The man fell and broke his neck."

Rachel released a long sigh. It was like she could finally breathe again after all these years. She stepped back and dashed tears from her face. "It's imperative I speak to Mr Hunter. I must visit him before Mr Daventry sends him to St Albans."

He might be gone for days sorting out problems with the Council. What if Mr Daventry kept him there permanently, fearing repercussions from Mr Young?

"St Albans? Rachel, you've been shot. It's imperative you rest."

Rachel pressed her fingers to her upper arm and winced.

Hell, it hurt like the devil.

"I must go." Rachel grabbed Miss Trimble's hand. "I'm in love with Mr Hunter. He loves me, too. I must see him tonight." Indeed, she was possessed by love's delirium. "I'm not asking permission."

Being her usual cautious self, Miss Trimble shook her head. "Men can be disingenuous when they feel a physical attraction to a woman. Words do not often reflect their true intentions. Best wait—"

"*Facta, non verba*. It's Mr Hunter's motto." Rachel cast a confident smile. "I know you understand Latin. I have every reason to mistrust men, but I trust Mr Hunter. Now the case is solved, I must discover what he means to do about our relationship."

"You seem determined."

"Most determined."

Miss Trimble sighed. "Mr Daventry will probably dismiss me when he discovers I've let you leave. Lord knows how he expects me to deal with such strong-minded women."

"Does that mean you'll not wrestle me to the floor in protest?" Miss Trimble carried herself with the utmost grace and would never do anything so uncouth.

"It means I'm accompanying you to ensure you arrive there safely."

"I shall come, too," Eliza said from the doorway. "Someone must help Miss Trimble hunt for a hackney."

They woke Honora, who agreed she should remain in Howland Street in case of an emergency. They dressed quickly and hurried towards Fitzroy Square, armed with numerous weapons, shivering to their bones.

"There's always a hackney in the vicinity of the square at midnight." Eliza's teeth chattered, and her lips were tinged blue. "If not, we'll hurry to Regent's Circus."

Miss Trimble glanced heavenward. "There's a chance of snow."

It was so cold they'd be forced to turn back if they didn't find a hackney.

Music drifted through Fitzroy Square, an enchanting melody to rouse passion in the coldest heart. They moved past the row of carriages, hoping to locate a cab. Instead, they crashed into an elegantly dressed gentleman busy fussing with his cuffs.

"Will you mind where you're going, sir," Miss Trimble cried.

The handsome gentleman straightened, a slow smile playing on his lips when he realised they were acquainted. "Miss Trimble. Miss Gambit." His dark gaze slipped over Eliza. "And the delightful Miss Dutton. It seems you can't keep away from me, my dear."

"Trust me, Lord Roxburgh, had I known you were lingering in the square, I'd have taken a different route." Eliza gestured to the mansion house, the home of much gaiety. "Though I should have known to find you at a party for drunken debauchers."

Lord Roxburgh clutched his chest as if mortally wounded. "On my oath, I've not touched a drop of brandy all evening." He looked at the cane she carried. "Perhaps you should dispense with the walking stick and take a strong man's arm. I trust you're heading inside."

Eliza gave a mocking snort. "If I knew a strong man, I might. Besides, it's a swordstick, and I'm a woman of sensible pursuits. I find these affairs quite tedious."

"Then what do you do for pleasure, Miss Dutton?"

Miss Trimble stiffened. "Lord Roxburgh. We're in somewhat of a hurry."

The lord appeared captivated by Eliza's bow-shaped lips. "Tell me where you're going, and I'll have my coachman deliver you there promptly."

"Never mind. We'll take a hackney."

Desperate to reach Blackstone quickly, Rachel said sheepishly, for she knew how Eliza felt about the arrogant lord, "It's so cold tonight. Perhaps we might accept Lord Roxburgh's kind offer."

Eliza's eyes widened, and she shook her head vehemently.

Lord Roxburgh laughed. He raised his hands in surrender. "I'll not accompany you if that's your fear. Take command of my carriage and when you've commenced your business, have my coachman return here."

"What if we plan to use it in a highway robbery?" Eliza teased.

"Then you should know there's a brace of pistols beneath the seat."

"I'd be afraid to look in case I found a lady's discarded undergarments."

"Should you look and find me lacking, feel free to leave your own."

Miss Trimble gasped.

After some deliberation—where Rachel argued in the name of necessity—they agreed to the lord's offer and thanked him for his generosity. They gave the coachman their direction and settled into the fine conveyance, but Lord Roxburgh held the door open.

"Don't forget you owe me a boon, Miss Dutton."

"Expect me to ignore the debt."

"Expect me to persuade you to pay."

Eliza was still grumbling about Lord Roxburgh long after he'd closed the door and watched them ride away, long after they'd passed the Oxford Street turnpike.

Upon seeing Blackstone, Rachel thumped the roof and called for the coachman to stop. "Mr Hunter lives here."

"Shall we wait for you?" Miss Trimble asked while shivering beneath Lord Roxburgh's fur throw. "Will you be long?"

Eliza chuckled. "I expect she's staying the night."

"Wait until the butler welcomes me inside before leaving. Rest assured, I shall return to Howland Street tomorrow."

Rachel bid them farewell and approached Eli's abode.

To the unknowing eye, the house still looked like a sad, lonely place. But there was nothing cold and lifeless beyond the walls. Never had she met a more passionate man.

It took Jacobs five minutes to open the door. He didn't ask what she wanted, didn't insist on summoning the master, who, he informed her, had already retired to his bed.

She entered the house, dark but for one lit candle lamp. Jacobs took receipt of her outdoor apparel before locking the door and ambling away towards the servants' quarters.

Her arm throbbed, but it was the delicious shiver of anticipation that left her panting as she climbed the stairs. Love was the antidote to pain.

Eli's chamber door was unlocked. She slipped inside and closed the door as she'd done the night of Vauxhall. Amber flames danced in the hearth, casting shadows about the room. The bed hangings were open, but Eli was not lounging in Lucifer's bed. The intoxicating scent of his cologne hung in the air. He wasn't far away.

"Miss Gambit, what a pleasant surprise." The words drifted from the darkness. "You seem to make a habit of catching a man unawares."

"Were you not expecting me, Mr Hunter? I thought a hunter possessed keen eyes and sharp perception." She noticed the rumpled bedsheets. "I see you favour black in all things, sir."

"I'm of a mind to change to red."

"Red for danger?"

"Red for lust. Red for love."

Lord, her body ached, and she'd not laid eyes on him yet. "I heard you wish to hire a woman. I came to tell you I'm the woman you need."

He appeared from the shadows and stalked towards her wearing nothing but his loose-fitting trousers. "What makes you qualified?"

Rachel stepped back against the door, desperately wanting to be this man's prey. "You need a woman who has courage abound, who can make swift decisions. Despite being shot today, I left my bed and ventured across town at night to see you."

He came closer, braced his muscular arms above her head. "What else?"

It was hard to rouse a coherent thought when his mouth was an inch from hers, when his warm breath breezed across her lips. "I can bring you pleasure with the mere brush of my hand." She touched his chest, trailed her fingers down to stroke the hard length in his trousers.

Eli hissed a breath. "What else?"

"No other woman loves you like I do."

He bent his head. She expected him to kiss her, but he moved past her mouth to graze her ear. "Do you want another test?"

"Yes."

He looked at her, pinned her to the door with his hungry gaze. "Persuade me, Rachel. Show me why we're meant to spend the rest of our lives together. Show me why I'm so desperate to make you my wife."

She'd been thinking about kissing him, not anymore. "Your wife?"

"I'm in love with you." He claimed her mouth in a wildly passionate kiss that left her breathless. "Marry me. Be my wife. Let us spend our days seeking adventures, our nights a hot tangle of limbs."

The words she'd uttered to Lady Meyer flitted into her mind. "Are you willing to take a wife who's considered unconventional? I can't change who I am, Eli."

"I don't want you to change. I want you, exactly as you are."

"You're willing to accept I work for a living?"

He smiled. "You've no need to work for a living, but you can work for the pleasure."

Love filled her heart. Marrying him was a dream beyond her expectations.

"I'd like to work for the pleasure now." She slipped her left hand over his shoulder. "Have you ever been seduced by a one-armed woman?"

"Minx! You've not accepted my proposal."

She laughed. How could he not know the answer?

"Eli, I love you. I'm counting the minutes until you make me your wife." She captured his mouth in a ravenous kiss, a kiss that conveyed lust and longing and a love soul-deep.

"You've achieved things few women do?" he said.

"Because I persuaded a cold-hearted bachelor to marry?" How could she have ever thought him cold?

"No, my love. You've challenged convention and snared a hunter."

CHAPTER 20

*Three weeks later*

THEY MARRIED in the new St Pancras Church, a Greek-inspired building of some majesty, those who worked for the Order being the only guests. As one of Mr Daventry's agents, and a man who knew how to host a wild celebration, Mr Sloane insisted on holding a wedding banquet at his estate in Little Chelsea.

Now, mere days later, they'd been summoned to Trēowith while Mr Daventry contemplated whether the men on the Council might keep their positions.

"I don't see how he can dismiss you." Rachel looked across the carriage at her husband. She'd never tire of staring at his handsome face. "You're the one who solved the cases and caught the traitor."

His smile turned her insides molten. "No, you solved the cases and caught the traitor. I merely rode alongside, watching in awe. In truth, I don't care if Daventry does dismiss me."

And yet, he'd told her his work gave him a purpose.

"Of course you care. What will you do with your time?"

An image burst into her mind. Him waiting in bed when she returned home after a hectic day. Him drawing her bath and massaging every aching muscle.

"I'll assist you when Daventry gives you a new case."

Ah, now she understood his motive.

"You can't be my shadow, Eli. I can protect myself."

His gaze dipped to her right arm. "Had Jacob Hanaway been a few feet closer, you might have lost your arm."

His words made her shudder. "If we all lived fearing what could happen, no one would dare venture from the house. Besides, more people die falling down the stairs than being shot in Greenwich."

Still, it brought to mind the fact Peter Hanaway was still breathing. He was by no means as cruel as his brother, but men consumed by vengeance were often irrational.

"And when one considers the many times we've made love these last three days, it won't be long before I'm with child."

Eli exhaled a contented sigh. "You begged to have all of me."

"I'm not complaining, merely stating that my time on the battlefield is limited." She wouldn't stop working for the Order but would ask Mr Daventry if she might scrutinise witness statements, look for clerical errors and decipher codes.

"I never expected to father a child." His tone carried a hint of gratitude and a pensiveness that reflected those years he'd spent alone. "I never expected to fall in love, fall in love so deeply."

"I never expected to find you. I love you so much it hurts."

"Were we not five minutes away from Trēowith, I would demonstrate the depth of my devotion." A sensual smile touched his lips. "Thankfully, we're staying the night. I want to make love to you in the place where we shared our first kiss."

Rachel jerked her head. "We kissed in Mr Daventry's bedchamber."

He laughed. "Perhaps not the same place. Daventry may share my philosophy, but he'll share nothing else."

Rachel laughed, too. She never thought she could be so happy.

It drew her mind to Lady Meyer and Mr Young. While an ecclesiastical court had ruled the Meyers could legally separate, Lord Meyer needed a legitimate heir and so had applied to Parliament to have the marriage dissolved. While the proceedings might take years, Lady Meyer and Mr Young had stolen away in the night and were last seen boarding a ship to Boston.

Upon her release, Mary Harcourt had taken ownership of the cottage near Mile End, and Lord Meyer had proved to be a frequent visitor.

Mr Truscott came hurrying to their carriage as the vehicle rumbled to a halt in Trēowith's courtyard. "I hear congratulations are in order." Their feet had barely touched the gravel when the gentleman shook Eli's hand and bowed to Rachel. "Who would have thought a man as affable as Young could rob the Sanctum? I'm only glad I could be of some help."

Rachel forced a smile. "Thank you, Mr Truscott. I pray no one need question your loyalty again. Has Mr Daventry arrived?"

"Indeed. He asked you meet him in the Sanctum." He gestured for them to follow him inside. "Mrs Gale will have a footman collect your luggage."

Mrs Gale was waiting in the hall. She gave a strained smile upon greeting them and asked if she might speak privately with Rachel.

Rachel followed the housekeeper to the dining room.

"Forgive me, Mrs Hunter, but I feel I must explain my actions the last time you were here."

"You mean when you entered my bedchamber to snoop?"

A blush stained Mrs Gale's cheeks. "A master of Themis once saved my life, ma'am, and I swore to repay the debt. I needed to be sure you weren't up to no good, that's all."

"I understand." Rachel touched the woman's arm. "After the theft, you wished to protect what you have here and couldn't be sure I spoke in earnest."

Mrs Gale nodded. "Mr Daventry explained everything. He's in the Sanctum. Best not keep him waiting."

The thought of entering the tunnels filled Rachel with dread.

Eli escorted her to the rear courtyard, to the open iron door giving access to the narrow passageways. "Do you wish to hold on to me?"

She scanned the breadth of his shoulders. "I'd snatch any opportunity to touch you, but I suppose I must conquer my fears." Every muscle in her body stiffened as she teetered on the top step.

"I'm right behind you. Never forget it."

She could feel the power of his presence, protecting her like an impenetrable shield. It gave her the courage to descend the worn stone steps and shuffle through the dim corridors.

Mr Crocker greeted them from his position outside the Sanctum.

They found Mr Daventry sitting in the master's chair at the circular oak table, studying an old leather tome in the candlelight. He looked up, asked about their journey, then gestured for them to sit.

"I received word before leaving Bronygarth." Mr Daventry pushed the tome aside and drew the open letter closer. "The Beltons are to hang for murder. Although Mr Belton confessed, Mrs Belton is considered an accessory."

"She lied and was prepared to see an innocent boy die," Eli said.

"Now David Scrivens' release is secured, I've arranged for

him to receive private tuition. Should he prove himself, he will be given an apprenticeship as a clerk at the offices of Hellman, Jones and Reed."

Rachel blinked in astonishment. "That's wonderful news." She felt proud to have helped prove the boy's innocence.

"I've also done what you asked, Mrs Hunter, and met with Peter Hanaway. We came to an agreement a few days before your wedding, but I saw no reason to ruin the celebrations."

She felt the weight of Eli's stare, saw a flash of disappointment in his eyes when she faced him, for she had not mentioned her need to put an end to her quarrel with Peter Hanaway.

"I asked Mr Daventry to discover what Peter Hanaway thought was a fair inheritance. I don't want to spend our married life worrying when he might seek revenge."

"I would have visited the devil."

"And you might have killed him. I can't lose you, Eli."

He breathed a weary sigh but admitted, "At the very least, I'd have broken his jaw."

"Hanaway suggests ten thousand pounds is fair," Mr Daventry continued. "If you agree to him contesting the will, agree Lady Hanaway was over-generous, his solicitor feels you might come to an agreement."

"Very well."

"We don't need the money," Eli said. "Why not let him contest the will and keep it all? I can't help but think Lady Hanaway hid a mean streak. She must have known what would happen when she left you such a large sum. Perhaps she liked the thought of you fighting for your rights."

Rachel fell silent.

While living at Henfield Park, she'd kept the extent of Jacob Hanaway's cruelty to herself. Yet Lady Hanaway had a habit of reminding Rachel how much she needed her, how she should fight for a better life. It was always after a harrowing experience. Perhaps it wasn't a coincidence.

Perhaps Lady Hanaway had used her to teach her sons a lesson.

"But without my inheritance, I bring nothing to this marriage."

Eli's gaze softened. "You bring yourself. I want nothing more."

She would have kissed him had they been alone. She reached for his hand and squeezed it tightly before addressing Mr Daventry. "Very well. I want nothing from the Hanaways. Will you make the arrangements, sir?"

Mr Daventry nodded. "Of course. And to put your minds at ease, Hanaway was overjoyed upon hearing the news of his brother's death. He's set to inherit the house in Salisbury Square, which pleased him no end."

Rachel bowed her head and sighed with relief.

Mr Daventry stood. "We should send for the other members, to discuss the upcoming changes. There are new cases to hear, and time is of the essence."

Rachel pushed to her feet. "I shall wait in the drawing room." Truth be told, she was rather glad she didn't have to gulp three goblets of wine.

"You'll stay, Mrs Hunter. I have a proposition for you." Mr Daventry gripped Eli's shoulder. "Your husband will struggle to sleep if I send you out onto London's streets alone. The world is changing. It's time we had a woman sit on the Council, and Hunter needs a partner who can match him in courage and intellect."

It took a moment for her to understand his intention.

"You want me to take Mr Young's place?" Rachel clasped her hands to her chest. "But Mr Truscott will never agree."

"All members have already agreed."

"All members?" She shot Eli a curious glance.

He raised his hands. "I knew but didn't want to spoil the surprise."

"Well, will you accept the seat, Mrs Hunter? Will you

pave the way for women to follow your example? Might your daughter see you as a woman who sought to change her fate?"

To say she was honoured was an understatement.

She could hardly find the right words to thank him. "I—I will gladly accept the seat. And know I possess my husband's temerity when it comes to seeking the truth."

"Then it's settled."

Mr Crocker alerted the members, and soon the meeting was underway. They heard of a kidnapping case, and Mr Cantrell revealed his suspicions about the identity of the spy passing secrets to the French. A heated discussion between Mr Swanson and Mr Truscott resulted in Mr Crocker ringing the bell and them all repeating the pledge and downing the wine.

With the objectives set, the meeting ended.

Rachel waited for everyone except for Eli and Mr Daventry to leave before attempting to stand. Consuming too much wine had made her a little dizzy.

"I'm afraid I'll need an hour to recuperate. Must you drink the wine so quickly?"

Mr Daventry smiled. "Hunter will take you to your room. I'll speak to the members about you having half a goblet in future."

Thankfully, Mr Daventry remained in the Sanctum and didn't witness her stumble in the subterranean passageways or almost trip up the grand staircase leading to the first-floor landing.

Eli's private chamber was almost as dark as his room at Blackstone. The walls were slate grey, the tester bed carved oak, the coverlet the deepest blue.

Rachel flopped onto the sofa near the window.

Eli locked the door and turned to face her. Perhaps it was the wine that caused heat to pool in her sex. Perhaps it was the fact they were alone at last or the hungry gaze in his eyes that said he wanted to strip her bare and ravish her senseless.

"I expected to find you waltzing about the room."

"For some reason, I don't feel in the mood to dance." She wanted to make love to him before the wine took complete command of her faculties.

He stalked towards her, his strides purposeful, sleek. "And yet the last time we danced at Trēowith, you were perched on the drinks table and I was seconds away from gathering your skirts and plunging home."

Only he could make dancing sound so divine.

"Well, if you put it like that, I'm definitely in the mood for one dance."

"Only one?" Eli captured her hand and drew her to her feet. "Usually, you're insatiable." His arm swept around her waist, and he pulled her against his hard chest. "Move with me."

They danced the waltz like nothing seen in the lavish ballrooms in London. Their bodies melded together as they moved, the slow, sensual grinding a prelude to something far more erotic.

He cupped her buttocks and held her against his erection. "The last time we danced, we both made confessions. Mine was to say you had passed the test at Vauxhall. Though I never told you the whole truth."

"You said you'd liked me from the moment we met."

"I felt you entering my heart before you arrived. The same way your scent enters a room seconds before you do. Like the piquant smell of orange blossom, you remained with me long after I left Vauxhall."

The beauty of his words brought a tear to her eye. "I failed to convey the depth of my feelings, too. It wasn't a need to prove a point that had me racing across town, but an inner knowing, a desperate need to discover more about you."

He bent his head and kissed her. "Perhaps we should thank Daventry for playing matchmaker. He's the one who suggested we meet."

"He must have known we were made for each other."

He cupped her cheek. "He must have known we would fall in love."

They had fallen so deeply, their meeting had to be fated.

Yes, theirs was a soulful love. A truthful love. A love to last a lifetime.

# THANK YOU!

I hope you enjoyed reading **More than a Masquerade.**

When a murder in Lord Roxburgh's garden leaves his sister's reputation in tatters, the gentleman seeks the help of an enquiry agent.
With an utter dislike for the handsome rake, will Miss Eliza Dutton accept her first assignment?

Find out in ...

*Mine at Midnight*
*Ladies of the Order - Book 3*

## More titles by Adele Clee

### Lost Ladies of London

The Mysterious Miss Flint

The Deceptive Lady Darby

The Scandalous Lady Sandford

The Daring Miss Darcy

### Avenging Lords

At Last the Rogue Returns

A Wicked Wager

Valentine's Vow

A Gentleman's Curse

### Scandalous Sons

And the Widow Wore Scarlet

The Mark of a Rogue

When Scandal Came to Town

The Mystery of Mr Daventry

### Gentlemen of the Order

Dauntless

Raven

Valiant

Dark Angel

### Ladies of the Order

The Devereaux Affair

More than a Masquerade

Mine at Midnight

Made in the USA
Coppell, TX
27 September 2021